Calling Out

by

Scott Sutton

Dedicated to my amazing family,
especially my wife,
who has supported and encouraged me
all along the way

Chapter 1

Dreams

They can't be counted. The waves. Long before our first ancestors set foot on these shores, the waves were crashing, rolling, pushing, pulling. They brought us here. They sustain us. They are at the foreground of every sunrise and every sunset. They are mentioned in all of our stories. They fill our ears with the persistent, echoing reminder of their presence. They are as much a part of who we are as the tales of the people who have gone before us.

And they can't be counted.

Sometimes I come out to the shore just to watch them, wondering what lies beyond the horizon and if someone over there is watching the waves crash upon their shore, too. Sometimes I wade out into them until I'm mostly submerged, dig my feet into the sand, bow out my chest, determined to hold my ground against their lifting and swaying. Sometimes I wait for the tide to go all the way out and begin its climb back up the beach. I pick a spot near the top of where the tide will peak and build a mountain of sand. Then I dig trenches - deep trenches - all around the mountain. Finally, I build a wall around the trenches. Two, if I have time. I want the walls to be high enough, the trenches deep enough, the mountain strong enough to withstand the force of the sea. But as the tide rolls in, the walls are inevitably overcome. The trenches fill with water and sand melts into them so they become level. Finally I watch as the mountain crumbles, crumbles, crumbles, until all that's left is a lump of sand.

It never fails.

I think to myself, *if only I could make the mountain stronger, or the walls taller, or the trenches deeper, maybe I could build something that holds back the tide, that endures time, that inspires someone else to want to be strong, too*. But the tide always prevails. The waves roll up the beach, toward the dunes, and eventually back down the shore, leaving the sand as smooth as the sky.

I watch them, amazed at their power, their rhythm, their resolve, wondering how many people before me have sat in this very spot, watching the waves dance this very dance. Crash...crash...crash...

Losing count of them...

Losing track of their thoughts...

Losing their sense of time...

"Uri!" The sound of my name jolts me forward, nearly planting my face in the sand. "You wandered off! I thought you left me! Time to go! Time to go!"

I shake off the trance of the waves. Slowly rise to my feet. There's no rush to be anywhere, but today I'm gathering berries with Mehan. And when you're with Mehan, you're always rushing somewhere. I tend to get distracted when I pick, but Mehan has an intensity and focus unlike any other that I know. As he picks a berry, his eyes have already spotted the next three that he will pick. And even as he picks, he's usually pointing you toward the berries that he wants you to pick. It can be annoying, but it makes the work quick and easy, leaving plenty of time to enjoy the rest of the day.

Mehan sets his basket of berries next to mine, claps his hands at me, plants them on his hips, and looks at me expectantly while he catches his breath and I slowly pull myself upright. Glancing down at our baskets, I notice that while mine is reasonably full of berries, Mehan's is nearly overflowing. I frown. *Full* seemed like enough, but next to Mehan's basket, it now seems lacking. I cup my hands together and transfer a couple of big scoops from his basket to mine. "Please. Allow me to lighten your load." I smile with all of my teeth. Mehan is good to gather with; he isn't very good to joke with. He narrows his eyes and glares at me for a moment before picking up his basket and turning around to begin the journey home. As he turns, I notice the slightest smirk on his face.

From this point on the island, we should be home shortly after the sun is at its peak in the sky. This point is the furthest from our village on our island, but it's also our favorite place to gather. None of the other gatherers venture this far, so the berries are big, juicy, sweet. A lot of work, but a lot of reward. For Mehan, the work itself is the reward. He loves walking the longest route, climbing the most challenging path, finding ways to reach the ones that are just beyond reach. For me, it's neither the work nor the berries, but the journey from our village to this place that's the reward – a journey that takes us all the way across the center of our island.

Beginning from our village, we trace the coast until the beach narrows, giving way to rocks that become larger and more numerous the further down shore you go. The ocean on our side of the island is calm. On some days, it's so calm that I feel like I could step out onto it and walk all the way past the horizon. Perhaps to another island. Perhaps back to the land from which our ancestors came. Or perhaps on a never-ending journey across a never-ending expanse of sea.

At a certain large rock, we turn inland and

cut through a thin band of trees toward the center of the island. On the sea side of the trees, the ocean commands your attention, especially at sunrise. But as soon as you emerge through the inland side of the trees, the majesty of the island seizes your attention and you forget about the ocean. A forested mountain to the left. A forested mountain to the right. And a valley of grassy plain down the center, as vast as the sea itself, rising up to a ridge that connects the mountains to one another. Every time this panorama comes into view, I stop and catch my breath. Every time. When I'm with anyone else, they stop with me. When I'm with Mehan - and I'm with Mehan most of the time - he nudges me to move on.

Walking across the lush green grasses of the valley, you suddenly feel overcome by the urge to run. Stretch out your arms. Feel the wind against your skin. And run. And run. And run. As fast as you can. Until you fall down. But a gathering trip is pretty exhausting on its own, so we don't run. We walk. Admiring the mountains on either side of us with each step.

The mountain to our left is the more imposing of the two – taller, skinnier, more rugged, looking as though it was shaped long ago by the pinch of a giant hand. It is the less traveled of the two mountains, partly because of its ruggedness, partly because it is the further of the two from our village, partly because it doesn't contain anything we need for daily survival. But the views from the top are more spectacular, the trees are more ancient, the challenge of the climb more fulfilling. And it is one of the few places on our small island where a person can go to be alone.

The mountain to our right is shorter, smoother, more rounded at the top. Though you can't tell it from the valley view, the top of that mountain is actually a giant bowl that collects the rain. Every day, a group from our village climbs the mountain to draw water from the bowl for everyone to drink. At times I'm envious of their job. Envious that they get to climb the mountain every day and witness the lake shimmering in the sunlight, the ocean stretching out in every direction, the view of the island from the sky. It's all spectacular. But the views we get from the grassy valley are pretty spectacular as well.

The island didn't always look like this. They say that when our ancestors arrived here, the mountains were bald and the valley was a dense forest. But through the generations, the interior mountain slopes have become forested, while the forest in the valley has receded to the point that it's now nearly gone. I try to imagine the island the way it once was. Bald mountains, forested valley. But I can't hold onto the image for long. It's too foreign to me. The way the island looks now is the way it has looked my entire life. And to imagine the island without forested mountain slopes is to imagine our tribe without its identity. The mountainside forests are a part of who we are. Every tree distinct from every other tree. Towering. Strong. Proud. They tell the story of our tribe, each tree proclaiming its own distinct legacy, and the sum of all the trees together is a legacy unto itself. The forest on the mountain to our left is named the Old Grove. The forest on the mountain to our right is named the New Grove. Collectively, they're named the Grove of Ancestors. Every generation, the Grove of Ancestors grows and, with it, our identity as a tribe grows as well. It's as central to our tribe as the sound of ocean waves in our ears.

My earliest memories are of hikes through the Grove of Ancestors with a group of children my age and a teacher, stopping at various trees to learn about the specific legacy each one proclaims and the story behind that legacy. In fact, the Grove of Ancestors is the setting of most of my childhood memories. Climbing, playing, exploring, learning. The legacies of the trees inspiring us to be bold and to leave legacies of our own, to leave a permanent mark upon the face of the island and the face of our tribe. Traversing the valley, the Grove of Ancestors looming on either side, I can't help but feel a sense of pride, gratitude, purpose.

Anytime I crest the ridge of the grassy

valley, I love to close my eyes and take the deepest breath I can. My head fills with the convergent scents of the ocean, the Grove of Ancestors, the tall grasses, and, on days where the wind shifts, the faint aroma of the fires burning down at our village. This is home. I don't have words to describe the wonderful history of our people. I don't have words to describe the beauty of our island. But I have this smell. And I have this place. And when I run out of words, I come here to remember.

From the ridge of the grassy plain, it's a quick downhill trip to the far side of the island where Mehan and I like to gather berries. On the far side of the island, it's a little easier to imagine what the island might have been like to our ancestors. No village. Lots of trees along the shore. Seldom another person to be seen.

We gather quickly, always taking a quick break to fill our bellies with berries before heading home. Once we return to our village, whatever we pick is to be shared evenly among the village. But as long as we are out gathering, we enjoy as much as we want. It's what makes gathering the best job on the island - at least that's what Mehan and I tell ourselves. There are water carriers, fishers, wood cutters, builders, weavers, rock cutters, caretakers, and gatherers. Then there are young children, people watch over the young children during the day, and elders who teach our children about the history and legacy of our tribe. Everyone has a role to play. And, somehow, in the end, no one has need.

By the time Mehan and I arrive back at the village, the fishers have already brought in several hauls of fish. During the day, people eat sporadically, whenever they have a break or after they finish their daily work. But after the sun sets, we share an evening meal together around fires that are spread throughout the village. Clusters of huts circle each fire. Mehan's family and my family share a fire with several other families. The berries we gather will feed our entire cluster as well as any others that have need. And the satisfaction we get from seeing them enjoy the work of our hands never gets old.

We set our baskets by our fire. Grab a couple of fish. Throw them on the fire. Take our seats among the few neighbors who are already eating. Across from me, Choko carefully picks the meat off the bones of his fish. Upon noticing me, he smiles with a full mouth. He points at my basket, motioning for me to give him some berries. I grab a handful, reach across the fire, and drop them into his hand.

"Thanks," Choko sputters through the corner of his mouth as he swallows his fish. He looks down at the berries in his hand admiring their shape and color, turning them over in his hand, studying them carefully as he rubs his thumb over their skins. This is how he eats. This is how he does everything. He's a stone cutter. Stone cutters have a special eye for the intricate beauty in all things, as their job involves transforming lumps of rock into useful and beautiful things. The rock on our island is delicate. In order to cut and carve it, you must patiently respect this delicate quality. Stone cutters who have been working with this rock for years learn to approach everything in life with this patient respect. When Choko takes the extra moment to admire the berries we pick (and he almost always does), I'm filled with this sense of accomplishment, as though I had something to do with their beauty. It's another reason why I go with Mehan to the other side of the island to gather the ripest berries our island has to offer.

"Good berries," Choko says as he pops the last one in his mouth, wipes his hands, and rises to return to his work.

Mehan flips our fish from the fire to the rocks around the fire to cool. The fish hit the rocks with their familiar sizzle as I hear a voice from behind us. A voice I know well. My favorite voice. "Hey, friends."

Brisa.

"Hey Brisa!" I reply a little too eagerly for Mehan, who rolls his eyes. He knows. He knows how I feel every time Brisa comes by. He notices how I stand a little taller and puff out my chest when she's around. He notices how my voice sounds different for her than it sounds for anyone else. I'm not bothered by him knowing. I'm not even bothered by him rolling his eyes. While I'm not public about my feelings for Brisa, I'm not embarrassed by them either. "Would you like some fish?" I offer her. Mehan narrows his eyes at my offer, quickly sliding his fish closer to himself and hovering over it as he picks its meat.

"Sure!" She jumps down to the ground beside me. I slide my fish across the rocks to her.

"Are you finished with your work?" I ask.

"Almost. I started late. I just have one more net to mend." Brisa makes rope. We use rope for fishing nets, boats, huts, hauling, and so many other aspects of life in our village. Making and repairing rope isn't difficult work, but it's constant and tedious.

"Come meet me in the New Grove when you're finished?" I intend for that to be a statement; instead, it comes out like a question. Brisa nods and grins, the wind blowing melodies through her hair. Before this moment, I hadn't even noticed a wind in the air. She makes me notice. I rise to my feet and give her a small wave good-bye. She returns the wave. I turn to Mehan and nod. He nods as he stands, pats his stomach with both hands, stretches his back, and looks around for a few moments before deciding to head toward the shore.

Aside from the time we spend completing our duties for the day and sharing our evening meal together, our time is our own. Mehan spends most of his spare time helping other people do their duties. Or he swims, runs, climbs, exercises. He can't sit idly. I appreciate this about him, but I don't understand it. I like to spend my time idly - watching the ocean, walking around the island, napping. Or with Brisa.

I depart from the fire toward the New Grove rising directly above our village. A distinct line of trees carves across the mountain about a third of the way up, marking the edge of the New Grove against the grassy plain where native trees once grew. At a certain place along this line of trees is a rock whose size and shape and slope make it perfect for reclining. It's high enough up the mountainside that I can see above the village, out across the bay, to the place where the ocean and the sky blur together. This is where I come to sit idly or nap on days that Brisa and I have plans to meet.

Out beyond the bay, I notice several fishing boats at work. From here, the boats appear motionless. But on the decks of the boats, there is a flurry of activity working nets, dropping lines, cleaning catches, adjusting sails, shifting positions. To sit upon the deck of one of these boats watching the fishers execute their impossibly choreographed maneuvers is simply astounding. Brisa's dad, a fisherman, takes me out on fishing excursions from time to time. The boats themselves are simple vessels - a platform and a sail floating on two hulls, similar to the boats upon which our ancestors sailed to this island. They have become much smaller and simpler down through the generations, since they are only used for short fishing trips these days, not for epic journeys across the untamable sea. I love watching the fishing crews bring the boats to life. Five or six of them who have fished together every day for years. You can tell when a crew has been together for a while. They don't even need to speak while they work. They navigate the sails, nets, ropes, lines, rudders, oars, and other equipment in perfect tandem. It's a fluid dance, orchestrated by the wind and the surf.

From my spot on this hillside, I focus on one of the boats, envisioning the crew dancing its dance. The rest of the world slowly becomes fuzzy as I feel myself becoming lighter, lighter, lighter until it feels as though there's no longer a rock or ground beneath me. No downward pull of the island. No forward pull of time. There is only this moment, suspended in eternity. Suddenly, a foreboding curtain of cloud rushes across the sky, shutting out the sun. The ocean surges and swells. I look to the boat to see giant waves rock and toss and crash against it. As the waves grow, the sea level rises, engulfing the village, engulfing the trees above the village. Meanwhile, the fishing boat drifts closer and closer to me until, with a thunderous clap, it tears in half. The platform and one of the hulls are swallowed by the angry sea. Stunned with fear, I look back to the other hull, still afloat. Only it has changed. It's larger. A lot larger. Larger than any boat I have ever seen. The crew, rather than sinking to the same fate as the other hull, strains and maneuvers against the storm from atop their single floating hull. I notice that the crew itself has grown in number as well. Perhaps thirty of them - all of them working in tandem as though they were still the crew of six atop the small double-hulled fishing boat on calm waters. I watch this strange single-hulled boat in amazement, wondering how it fares so well in the storm while carrying so many people aboard.

"Wake up, Uri." A voice overpowers the sounds of the storm as the storm itself becomes silent. The chaos of the wind and the waves and the boat and the crew becomes slow. The voice echoes again, "Uri." Brisa?

Intense light floods my vision as I squint into the daylight. A glowing silhouette above me. I can't make out its face. But I recognize the wind in its hair. "Brisa," I say aloud.

"You sleep like that rock you lay on," she says playfully.

As my vision returns to me, I slide up the rock to a sitting position. Painful tightness in my neck. "You finished your ropes?" I ask, surprised that I had been asleep for that long. She nods. I must have been out. I pull myself to my feet, rubbing the soreness out of my neck. Looking out across the sea, most of the fishing boats have returned to the shore, finished for the day. How strange. Would a boat like the single-hulled boat in my dream actually float? Or was it like most dreams, where the rules that govern this world are pleasantly absent? No matter. It was clearly a dream. But Brisa is real. And she is here now.

" Are you okay?" She asks.

"I think I was dreaming just now."

"Tell me," she enquires. Brisa always loves hearing about my dreams, though she rarely shares hers.

"It was nothing, really," I say, preoccupied by the image of that single-hulled boat and the soreness in my neck. "Just a boat caught in a violent storm. It was so violent that it tore the boat apart, but one of the hulls somehow grew into a boat of its own. A huge boat. Like, almost as tall as the most ancient trees of the Grove of Ancestors. And there must have been thirty people sailing it."

"Strange," she furrows as she turns her attention to the spot on the sea where I had been staring. "It's been a long time since we've had a storm like that. Do you think your dream means that a storm is coming?"

"You never know with dreams, right? Maybe it was nothing at all. Just a dream. Like the time I dreamed that you and I were fish."

A laugh escapes her. She looks back out toward the sea. After dwelling on the sea for a few moments, she lifts her focus to the New Grove. "Let's climb to the top today." Brisa doesn't like climbing to the top of the mountain, but she knows that I do.

"Are you sure?" I ask skeptically. "Why so adventurous today?"

"Why not?" She quips back flippantly as she flirtatiously skips past me, brushing my arm. Just like the wind.

I run past her, nudging her with my shoulder as I do. She staggers a few steps before catching herself and sprinting after me. So we run. Into the New Grove. Up the mountainside. Until we have to stop and let our wheezing return to normal breathing, where we find ourselves completely immersed in the middle of the New Grove, captivated by the majesty of all the trees all around us. Every tree unique. Every tree a story. Every tree a legacy. This is why we come to the Grove of Ancestors. To learn. To remember. To be inspired. And, on days like today, to be alone together.

We stop at the base of one of the trees, peering straight up its towering trunk. Branches don't extend from this tree until quite a distance up its trunk. But when they do, they are massive, spreading prolifically in every direction. And for every branch that grows from the trunk, its twin grows from the opposite side of the trunk. An exact twin – length for length, twig for twig, leaf for leaf. Perfect symmetry and balance in every direction.

I look down to the ground at the foot of the tree. A thin, square rock post stands about knee-height out of the ground. Embedded in the top of the post is a circular stone – a legacy stone. Legacy stones tell the history of our island. No single stone contains the entire history; yet all of the stones together sing a chorus. More than describing what we've done, they describe who we are.

I rub my fingers over the top of the legacy stone. A number at one edge of the stone. *Twenty seven.* The twenty seventh generation. Beneath the number, a name. *Adal.* And beneath the name, a phrase. *Justice like the sun.* It's a phrase commonly associated with the judges of our tribe. Just as the sun is impartial, accessible to everyone, and unchanging, so is justice. Judges promise to uphold justice like the sun. They guard and administer justice, ensuring it doesn't become obscured by the clouds of corruption, bias, or falsehood.

"She was a judge," I say, returning my gaze

back up the trunk of the tree to the branches hanging in perfect balance, capturing the sun.

Our tribe's identity is in these trees. A few generations after our ancestors landed on this island, they discovered something they couldn't explain. Something they had never seen before. Something that defied belief. They found that when a person died and their body was returned to the earth, a tree grew in the exact place where they were buried. And each tree somehow seemed to capture the essence of the person whom it replaced. Like this tree, beautifully depicting the justice that Adal sought to impart during her life. Now this tree stands as a silent witness. A reminder to us of Justice. And her legacy stone points to her time and place in our tribe's history.

These trees are monuments to who we are, guideposts to who we strive to be. Elders in our tribe bring groups of children to the Grove of Ancestors every day to teach and to instill awe in them. And as the children stand amazed at the giants before them, they are inspired to attain such heights for themselves, to leave a legacy that others might someday gaze upon as well.

I look to Brisa by my side, her head cocked slightly as she admires the symmetry of Adal's tree. There are thousands of trees like this cascading down the inner slopes of the two mountains on our tiny island. Mountains that were once bald, now adorned with countless memorials to the unseen forces that have shaped us over the course of forty generations.

Brisa shuffles her feet and looks over to me. Our eyes meet. We resume our hike, walking in silence for a while before her voice pierces the void. "How do you measure someone's legacy?" She asks with a dreamy curiosity.

"Measure it?" I ask, confused by her question.

"How do you decide what someone's legacy is? Like Adal. All that we know about her is justice. That's her legacy. But she wasn't only a judge. She might have been a mother, lover, friend, neighbor. Maybe she was charitable, maybe she was creative. Or maybe she was short-tempered, or lazy, or abrasive. But, looking at her tree, all you know about her was that she was just. Why that and nothing else?"

I've never considered this before. It has always seemed so obvious to me. Until now. "I don't know. Maybe the legacy you leave behind is the one that you most desire it to be."

"But if that were true, couldn't someone spend their entire life stealing while leaving a legacy of charity just because they desired it to be? Even if their life had nothing to do with charity?"

"Maybe it's how others perceive you to be, then."

"But did all people perceive Adal as just? What about people who received an unfavorable judgment from her? They may have perceived her as harsh."

"But if Adal's judgments were truly fair, then it doesn't matter how people felt about them. They were just or they weren't."

"Exactly. So if a person's legacy isn't measured by them or by the perceptions of other people, then how?"

I think through this for a while before conceding, "I guess I don't know. If it's not how you desire to be remembered, or how others remember you…" I trail off, not sure how to finish that thought.

We walk in thoughtful silence for a while before Brisa says, as though picking up from where my thought left off, "It's like the world is full of things that we can't see. And our lives give people glimpses into those unseen things. For Adal, it was Justice. Through Adal, people could understand it the same way they could understand the seen things. And even though she is gone, her tree is still with us, continuing to give us a glimpse into something bigger, enduring, unseen. Maybe legacies reveal themselves; and it has less to do with how we see ourselves or how others see us, but more to do with how we connect to those unseen things."

I nearly stumble backward under the

power of her words. She does this. Out of nowhere, she utters these musings that are as insightful as anything I've ever heard even from the mouths of our tribal elders. Feeling compelled to provide some sort of response, I simply say, "I think I understand." I don't though.

I glance up the trunk of the nearest tree, watching it slowly sway in the wind. "Uri," she eventually asks, "What do you think my legacy will be?"

"The wind," I reply before she even finishes the question. Like a reflex. As soon as the words leave my mouth, I wish they hadn't.

She laughs loudly. "That isn't a legacy!"

I chuckle, pretending to laugh at my own joke, but mostly just out of embarrassment.

"Have I had you fooled all this time, Uri?" She asks as she motions for me to lean in close to her. I lean in. She starts to say something, stops herself, and motions for me to lean in even closer. I lean in closer as she whispers, "Don't tell anyone else this, but I don't actually make the wind!" The loveliest whisper, veiling laughter.

"No, but you make the wind beautiful," I whisper back. Again, wishing I could retract the words as soon as they leave my mouth.

This time, her smile becomes smaller with my remark. Smaller, but sweeter. She tucks a lock of hair behind her ear and slowly pulls away from me. I realize that if I continue this conversation, I'm likely to end up saying something that will get me in trouble...or may get my heart broken. I look uphill. We've almost reached the clearing just below the rock face that climbs to the crest of the mountain. I run ahead and stand triumphantly in the clearing. Brisa runs to catch up.

We stand in that place, watching the sun begin to drop in the sky, sending the mountain's shadow across our village. The peak of the other mountain is the only thing closer to the clouds than us, draped with the ancient glory of the Old Grove. Ocean spilling over every horizon all around us. We stand for a while, in awe of the endless blue. In awe of the lake of water resting in the mountaintop bowl. In awe of the view of the world from this great height. I rarely wish to escape from this tribe or this island, but when I do, it's to be alone with Brisa forever, without the unspoken beckoning of our village, demanding that we end our time together and return home.

Somehow, without so much as a word, we both know when it's time to head back. Afraid I've confessed too much today, I resolve not to say anything further unless she says something first. She doesn't. So we walk the entire distance back to the village in silence. I don't know what to make of the silence. It isn't uncomfortable; but, then again, it isn't comfortable either. As we cross the trees into the village, I look to Brisa and wave. She looks to me, pauses, smiles, waves back, and turns to her house.

Dinner soon. And then a Council meeting tonight.

Chapter 2
Council

"Uri, you were with Brisa today." My mom emphatically points her finger at me as she speaks.

"Yes," I reply warily.

She raises her eyebrows suggestively. "All day?"

I know where she's going with this. I won't let her. "I went gathering with Mehan this morning."

"You left with him *early* so you could spend more time with her after!" She proclaims delightedly, as though it were the solution to a perplexing riddle that she just pieced together. Then she cackles. A loud, obnoxious cackle. The other ladies sitting with her join in her cackling.

Being at an age where most of my peers are starting to wrap their lives around one another and begin families of their own, there is a certain expectation when two people begin spending a lot of time together. Watching my mom wipe tears of laughter from her eyes, I wonder if Brisa thinks about this, too. Surely she must. If there was ever any doubt in her mind about my feelings for her, my outbursts today should have confirmed it for her. She became quiet afterward. Why did she become quiet? Does she love me the way I love her? Or does she see me simply as a childhood friend with whom she enjoys spending her time?

My train of thought is broken as a few other families join us around the fire and begin preparing their dinner. The volume of conversation grows as more and more people gather. Around the fire every evening, we share stories from our day, we watch the younger kids run crazy until their parents coerce them into sitting and eating, we chatter about so-and-so and such-and-such. Lately, I've gotten the sense that there has been quite a bit of chattering about me and Brisa. A group of ladies will lean in close to my mom and a few moments later, every head will turn in my direction with an inquisitive expression. They probably wonder what we're waiting for. I wonder that too sometimes.

Throughout the village this very scene is occurring around twenty four fires. People usually start gathering as the top of the sun drops below the ridgeline in the middle of the island. We sit together until long after the sunlight has faded and night rules the sky. As our bellies fill and the conversation wanes, people wander from fire to fire, visiting with other friends and family members throughout the village. Most evenings, this carries on until the fires die out; then we all go back to our homes and sleep until morning. But on full moon nights like tonight, the Council meets. And on nights when the Council meets, the Council members - two people from each fire cluster - excuse themselves once the last bit of daylight completely fades from the sky. Shortly after they excuse themselves, a few random people my age and younger look for the opportune moment to slip away from our respective fires without being noticed.

I find Mehan's eyes across the fire and shoot him a knowing look. He returns it. Our moment presents itself when one of the ladies says something that sends another lady tumbling backward off of her seat in laughter. This enraptures the entire group with raucous laughter as a couple of people rush to her side to help her up. With everyone's attention on the spectacle, Mehan and I roll off to the side and into the cover of darkness. That was easy. Usually we have to be more discrete.

Those of us who carry on this covert tradition are too young to be members of the Council. But a curious fascination compels us to hide in the brush outside of the Forum where the Council meets so we can eavesdrop on the Council meeting. These meetings are supposed to be private. Everyone in the village respects this expectation of privacy. Except the dozen or so of us who conceal ourselves within earshot of the Forum every full moon.

The Forum is the largest building in our village. Tall, thick posts sticking out of the ground, each post flush against its neighbor. No roof. Inside the Forum, three rows of seats are arranged in a half circle, focusing on the spot where the chief sits. The seats are carved out of rock, with the blocks of each row a head's height higher than the row in front of it. The Council meets here every full moon to discuss the affairs of the village and any issues demanding attention. Some meetings are interesting. Others are boring. But what began as a dare between Mehan and I to see who could get closest to the Forum during a Council meeting without being caught has become a fascination of ours ever since. We were surprised to discover that we weren't alone in this fascination.

"Good evening," the Chief's voice emanates from inside the Forum. "Let's get started quickly tonight. I want to have plenty of time to discuss what we need to discuss." The murmuring from inside the Forum fades. "A few days ago, our tree cutters were cutting down a tree on the far side of the island. When the tree fell, they noticed something: they had reached the other shore. Between that tree and the ocean was nothing but rocks." The Chief pauses to allow the realization to settle in with the group before stating it himself, "We're running out of trees."

The pause lingers.

"While we haven't completely run out of trees yet, there aren't enough remaining on this island to sustain us beyond this generation. We're using them much faster than they can grow. As you are well aware, our tribe can't survive apart from its dependence on trees."

"Can't we find ways to use less?" A woman asks.

"How can we?" The Chief replies. "The trees of the valley have become our boats, houses, ropes, fires, tools, and baskets. Not a splinter of wood is wasted and we use only what we need for survival…and yet, it appears that our use of them has become the greatest threat to our survival…"

The woman's voice again, "So what then? What can be done?"

The Chief breathes deeply and exhales with a sigh. So loud, that we can hear it from outside. "I've been wrestling with that very question since the day I received news of the wood cutters' discovery. There are no good options. Only bad ones. Only painful ones. Only ones that involve loss and sacrifice. And as I've wrestled with that question for many anxious days and sleepless nights, the option that seems most promising is also the one that involves the most uncertainty." A heavy pause. "An exodus. We leave the island. We find a new home."

Stunned silence, followed abruptly by frantic muttering. One of the Council members asks in audible exasperation, "This is our best option? Where would we go?"

"I don't know. Like you, I've never left this island. Our ancestors arrived on this island from some other place forty generations ago. So we know that there are other lands beyond the horizons."

Another voice interjects, "But Chief, this is our home. How could we leave it?"

"Believe me, I don't take this lightly. I have the same doubts and fears. If we wish to overcome them, we must be bold and determined. Like our ancestors were when they left their land to cross the ocean to this island."

Another voice interjects. "Excuse me, Chief." A voice I recognize. Keras. "But I disagree." Silence again. I imagine all eyes in the room, wide and fixed on Keras. "The best option isn't for us to leave; the best option is for us to stay."

"How do you figure, Keras? We will starve if we stay. We can't reduce our use of trees or increase the growth of new trees fast enough to stay here and survive."

"You're right, Chief. I don't dispute either of those assertions. What I dispute is your claim that we have run out of trees. We have plenty of trees. Look at the hillsides, dense with trees.

Enough to sustain us for several generations, until we are able to naturally reduce our tribe to a size that achieves harmony between our use of trees and the island's provision of trees."

"The hillsides are the Grove of Ancestors, Keras. Are you suggesting that we sacrifice the enduring legacies of generations past while simultaneously sacrificing the posterity of current and future generations, all on a daring wager that we might hopefully be able to achieve balance between the size of our tribe and the size of our island?"

"Yes," Keras replies resolutely.

"But these trees are our tribe's legacy."

"No, this island is our tribe's legacy."

"These *trees* are our tribe's legacy, Keras," the Chief sharpens his tone and commands his voice. "When our ancestors arrived on this island, they were at war with one another. They were brutal, self-interested, and hostile in everything they did. But from the moment the first tree grew upon these hillsides in the precise spot where their beloved had died, they became captivated. Enchanted. They began to change. They began to understand that there are unseen forces at work all around us. Things like Honor, Love, Beauty, Hope. Their lives became preoccupied by the pursuit of those things as they abandoned the petty, passing things that had brought them only division and strife. Each and every tree on the hillsides represents a step in that journey from where we were forty generations ago to where we are today. And you would have them cut down, like they were common, accidental, and meaningless. What if, even after all of that, your plan hasn't panned out as you envisioned it, Keras? We would simply have become a desperate and destitute people, absent the legacies that made us great, having missed our one opportunity to alter our fate. This is no plan at all."

Keras has nothing to say to this. The Forum is silent. Then, cutting through the silence, a voice as prominent as the Chief's. "Keras is right, Chief." Another voice I recognize, though I can't quite match a face to it. "Your plan is too risky. What if we launch from this island, only to never find another land? Our entire tribe, adrift in an endless ocean until the last of us dies an agonizing death. What, then, will our legacy be? What, then, will it have mattered that we preserved a few trees on the hillsides of a tiny island? If our tribe perishes upon the waters, then it will have all been in vain. Keras is correct, Chief: This *island* is our legacy. Absent the Grove of Ancestors, our tribe can persist. Absent the island, our tribe could disappear in an instant without anything to show for the last forty generations."

The Chief responds, "You speak confidently, Abis." Upon hearing Abis name, I instantly match the voice to his face. Mehan and I grew up playing with his son, Degi. The Chief continues, "But I fear what we will have become several generations from now, having regarded the Grove of Ancestors as little more than a stockpile of wood. To regard it in that way would be to regard the deeper things that they reveal as disposable and irrelevant as well. On the other hand, if we leave the island with the trees intact, we will have honored their significance, their place in our history, and their role in our future."

"It's only a tradition, Chief. We can create new traditions to honor the values that our tribe holds in highest regard."

"It's more than a tradition, Abis. It comes from something greater than any of us or the island itself; something greater, even, than the legacies that the trees proclaim. It comes from whatever set the island, and our lives, and the unseen forces of this world in motion."

"There is no greater thing. There is only this island and the lives that it sustains. These trees aren't actually our ancestors, Chief. You know it. Everyone seated here knows it. The entire tribe knows it. The trees are a wonderful tradition. As our ancestors learned how to live peacefully, they established virtues that helped them maintain and build upon that peace. And it makes sense that they would start to see those virtues represented in the world around them –

even in the trees that grow on this island. But it isn't the trees that teach us lessons about things like peace and justice and equality. We learn those things for ourselves and we create traditions that help us remember them. Traditions such as the trees."

"This kind of talk has never come from you before, Abis. It surprises me. It disappoints me."

"Disappoints you? It disappoints me to listen as you coerce the Council into making such a rash and ill-advised decision tonight. You would have the leaders of our tribe risk its welfare over a mere tradition."

"It's more than a tradition, Abis! These trees are the signposts of our culture and identity. A person dies. We bury them. Within months, in the exact spot where the person was buried, a tree grows, embodying the very traits that defined them."

Abis incredulously retorts, "Trees grow! This is nothing new. When you bury someone, you loosen and condition the soil. Of course something will grow in that spot. And, being surrounded by forest, why should anyone be amazed that the thing that grows in that spot happens to be yet another tree? We let ourselves believe that the tree bears characteristics of the person because it's hard for us to accept that they're gone. As a child, I once buried a fish in the forest to see what would happen. Do you know what happened? Nothing. To this day it's still a patch of grass at the edge of the New Grove. Why should we assume that it's any different for us? And why should we risk our tribe's future on such an assumption?"

Another silence. It's common for the Chief to be challenged at Council meetings. It's common for the Council to debate one another's reasoning. But it's uncommon for anyone to cross over from engaging in rigorous debate to standing in staunch defiance. Keras bordered on it. Abis completely crossed over. And, having never heard anyone so publicly and condescendingly challenge something as central to our tribe's identity as the Grove of Ancestors, I can only imagine the tension in the room as the Council awaits the Chief's response.

"Abis," the Chief begins, his voice collected yet firm, "it is one thing to question my proposal. But it is quite another thing to so flippantly unravel the delicate fabric of our society, especially at a time as critical as this. Our tribe's legacies aren't arbitrary matters. We have built our lives and our entire way of life around them. Over the course of this Council, you and Keras have proposed sacrificing both our past and our future in the name of subsistence. Generations from now, when our mountains are bare and our tribe has dwindled, we would be unrecognizable. A limping shadow of the tribe we once were. Nothing to root us down. Nothing to guide us forward. No regard for the things that have been revealed to us over the course of forty generations. While I have always taken pride in the openness of these Council discussions, I must impose my decision here and close this topic from any further discussion."

After a brief pause, violent shuffling can be heard from inside. Abis bursts through the threshold of the Forum. Mehan and I shrink back into the brush. He paces furiously through heavy breaths. Keras emerges as well, along with several others. Together, they stomp through the forest back toward the village.

As their crashing footsteps fade into the darkness, the Chief clears his throat. "Thank you for being unified with me in this decision. We will need unity to forge ahead through this crisis. Our tribe hasn't seen days as desperate or uncertain as these since our very earliest generations on this island. This is the most critical and difficult crisis this Council has ever faced or will ever face. We will be tested in every possible way. Without unity, we will fail. With unity, we will have the opportunity to leave a legacy that will carry through every generation to come after us." The Chief pauses for effect before asking, "Before we adjourn, are there any other pressing matters that require our attention tonight?" Nothing. Everything seems mundane in comparison to what just took place. The Chief waits for a response. When none comes, he concludes, "At our next meeting, we will discuss the plan for departure. Bring your best ideas. And remember my plea for unity. Good night."

A slow, gradual rustling from inside the Forum as the Council rises with heavy hearts and minds. This is the cue for me and Mehan to make our quick dash back to our homes so we aren't noticed. I'm not sure if either of us fully comprehends what just took place.

Leave this island?

Take a chance on the ocean?

Resettle in a new land?

My stomach rises up to my chest as I consider it. Fear. Doubt. Anger. Is the Chief really making the right decision? Are Keras and Abis seeing the matter more clearly? But their plan doesn't sit well with me either. I could no more imagine this island without the Grove of Ancestors than I could imagine our tribe without the Grove of Ancestors.

The village with its smoldering fires comes into view as I'm still trying to digest everything that just took place. As we reach the spot where Mehan and I typically part ways, I whisper, "Good night." Nothing from him. He is as preoccupied by this as I am.

Slipping into my house, I feel my way through the darkness and lay down. I try to sleep. I don't sleep. The night is long, filled with intermittent nightmares. Of the ocean. Of a dying tribe. Of Brisa, slipping away.

Chapter 3

Smoke

Morning. It rescues me from the night. Rescues me from wrestling in the darkness with gnashing fear. I lift my head. Soreness grips my shoulders, through my forehead. I lay back down. This will take a while.

I recount the previous day. Gathering with Mehan. The dream of the boat in the storm. Walking with Brisa. The Council. Could the entire day have been a dream? Will I walk outside this morning to gather with Mehan, walk with Brisa, and listen to a typical Council meeting where they talk about the typical issues of tribal administration? No mention of trees or leaving or defiance?

The mere possibility that it was all a dream is enough to lift me to my feet. I step outside, grab a handful of berries from a basket by the fire pit, pour the rest of the berries into another nearly empty basket, and take the empty basket with me to meet Mehan.

As I approach our typical meeting place at the edge of the village, no sign of Mehan. Maybe he went on without me. Maybe he's late. I decide to wait a little while. I look out across the bay. A boat is embarking on its first fishing trip of the day. The sight reminds me of my dream. If yesterday had simply been the bad dream that I'm desperately hoping it was, should I still make anything of the vision of the boat in the storm? I close my eyes and recall every detail from it that I am able to, searching for clues.

I'm lost in memory of the vision when a sharp gust of wind grabs my attention. I look around. Mehan is rarely this late. Maybe he isn't coming. Or he's already moved on. Either way, I'd better get going. I follow the shore until I reach that certain rock, cut inland through the thin line of trees, and climb the grassy hill to the center of the island. When I reach the ridge, I take in the view around me. Wooded mountainsides to my left and to my right, stretching for the sky. Ocean before me. Ocean behind. Wind weaving through it all. I stretch out my arms and close my eyes like I always do when I cross this spot.

Home.

My home.

Our home.

I can't imagine leaving it. But I can't imagine staying here and losing it either. Is it true what Abis said? That the trees are only a tradition? I think of Adal's tree. Perfectly symmetrical. A legacy of Justice. Similar only to a handful of other trees on the island, which also represent the legacies of judges from our history that proclaim Justice. Gazing upon them helps me understand Justice more clearly. Yet, if it weren't for the legacy stone planted at its roots informing me about Adal, would I have looked at the tree and immediately thought of Justice on my own? I could have thought, instead, of Love – each side complementing the other in perfect respect, adoration, and service. Do I see Justice because the tree actually proclaims Justice, or because I am expecting to see Justice when I look at it? Maybe the trees are only a tradition. And, yet, both Justice and Love are legacies that are bigger than life itself. Even if they are a tradition, they point us toward things that are more than tradition. Where do those things come from, if not from us?

I inhale deeply. Exhale deeply. Lower my arms. Open my eyes.

Something new. A thin pillar of smoke rising into the sky from the far side of the island where Mehan and I typically gather berries. Mehan? I run down the hill along the edge of the Old Grove. Through the trees. A small fire, like the ones we cook around, comes into view. Intentional and contained. But why would there be a fire here, so far from the village?

"Uri," a harsh whisper from my left. I peer through the trees, unable to see anything. "Hey!" I look again for its source. This time I see Mehan's hand waving at me from a crouched position behind a tree. I crouch down and waddle over to it as quickly and quietly as I can.

"What's going on?" I ask Mehan.

"I don't know," he replies. "Where were you this morning?"

I must have lost track of time while wishing yesterday away. "I couldn't sleep."

"Me neither," Mehan says somberly. "I've never heard a Council meeting like that before."

So it wasn't a dream. And with the cloud of denial removed, I suddenly understand exactly who set this fire and why it's here. "You didn't set this fire?" I ask Mehan, already knowing the answer.

"No."

"You!" Another voice darts at us from a few trees away. We freeze. I squint to make out the figure of a boy approximately our age. I don't immediately recognize the voice, but as the figure creeps closer to us, I recognize the face. Degi. Abis' son. Holding a fishing spear.

Degi doesn't fish.

"Degi," I call to him, "what are you doing here? Did you make that fire? Why do you have that spear?" Again, asking questions to which I already know answers.

"I'm keeping out people who don't belong here." I can tell by the way he says those words that they aren't his. They were given to him when he was given the fishing spear but wasn't asked to go fishing.

"Are you telling us we don't belong here?" Mehan challenges.

"You tell me," Degi snaps back. "Do you belong here?"

Mehan won't have any of it. "Why wouldn't we?"

"Well that depends. Who is your chief?"

"Our tribe only has one chief, Degi. Chief Sangra."

Mehan feigns pity, "Then you don't belong here."

At this, Mehan straightens himself upright, clenching his jaw. Degi lowers his spear and points it at Mehan. Mehan, unwavering, declares, "Uri and I gather berries here. We have for a very long time. If anyone belongs here, it's us."

Degi doesn't respond. He doesn't say anything. He doesn't move. He just stares into Mehan's eyes, undeterred.

In the stillness of the moment, I look into Degi's face and remember him when he was young. When we would play together. When he would climb a tree and wait for someone to walk nearby. Once a passerby walked within range, Degi would throw something near their feet - a rock, a stick, whatever he could find. The passerby would invariably startle and nervously search the area around their feet.

Then Degi would throw an even larger object a short distance away from them and they would jump and search frantically in the direction of the noise. By this time, those of us who were watching the whole episode take place from a hidden location would start laughing hysterically. The subject of Degi's taunting would usually assume it was us who had been throwing things and chase after us in embarrassed frustration. It never stopped being funny. Even now, the simple memory nearly brings me to laughter before the tension of the moment sobers me back into focus.

Neither of them flinch. Angry. Afraid. Steadfast. I've never seen Mehan like this before. And, yet, I'm not surprised to see it either. He treats his work with the same kind of relentless intensity. But work never fights back. Degi is fighting back. So he gets to see a side of Mehan that no one else has ever seen before, including Mehan himself.

As I watch these two childhood friends converted to adversaries overnight, I feel a nervous emotion rise up my throat. I've seen people fight before. I've seen strong wills collide. But this is something different. This isn't a disagreement or misunderstanding. This is something more catastrophic. More permanent. More primal. The emotion rises, rises, rises, until it becomes words pouring out of my mouth. "Look at yourself, Degi! Pointing a spear at your friends. Do you even know why you are doing this?"

No response.

"I didn't think you did," I sneer. And with that, I turn and walk away. I expect to hear Mehan's footsteps behind me. Nothing. I keep walking. Nothing. Any moment he'll be in step with me. Nothing. Finally, I turn. They haven't moved.

"Mehan!" I call out to encourage him to follow. Instead, his first motion is a step in the direction of the berries, past Degi. Degi shuffles to the side to block Mehan. Mehan keeps stepping. Degi thrusts his spear. In one motion, Mehan knocks the tip of the spear to the ground and stomps in its middle, snapping it in half. Mehan swoops down, picks up the pointed end of the broken spear, spins upright, spear point extended, abruptly stopping within a hand's width of Degi's throat. Degi looks stunned. Afraid. He doesn't move, holding the broken stick out in front of him as though it were still the spear he had approached us with. They hold that pose for a few moments. Glaring into one another's eyes. Masking fear with rage. Mehan nonchalantly walks over to his basket, keeping his head and newly acquired spear pointed at Degi. He picks up his basket and slowly steps backward toward me, never breaking his glare with Degi. Degi doesn't move.

As Mehan approaches me, he turns completely away from Degi, toward me, and walks past me. I try to keep stride with Mehan, occasionally glancing over my shoulder to see if Degi's next move will be to come after us. Instead, he drops his broken stick and sprints back toward the little fire on the far side of the island.

I turn to Mehan, amazed at what I just witnessed from him. I'm impressed, proud, bewildered. Mehan doesn't look at me. He maintains his brisk stride and coldly asks, "Why did you walk away?"

"What?" I didn't expect this question from him and don't have an answer for it.

"You walked away from Degi. Why?"

"Mehan, I'm sorry if –"

"Don't be sorry. Imagine what would have happened if we had both walked away from Degi. What message would that have sent him? That he's stronger. That his chief is the true chief. That we don't belong on his side of the island. That you will always walk away from him when he challenges you."

"It tells him that I won't play into his game," I contest. "That I won't acknowledge his fake tribe."

"By walking away!?" Mehan practically laughs the words out of his mouth. "Do you honestly think that's what he believes when you walk away from him? No way. He doesn't care what you will or won't acknowledge. This isn't a petty quarrel between friends. In fact, this has nothing to do with you, me, or Degi."

"Then why stay and fight?" I try to come to my own defense.

"Because it sends a message to their entire tribe – or, whatever they are. You walk away, they feel entitled to the entire island; you stand your ground, they learn that they must respect you and tread cautiously."

The weight of his words. I've never thought about other people in this way. I'm shocked to hear Mehan speak about it so casually. I feel foolish. Naïve. "What does that solve? Say I stand my ground against Degi. Say I stand my ground against him and prevail. What happens when Abis comes after me? What happens when I stand my ground against Abis and he prevails? What message does that send?"

Mehan scrunches his face, "Don't you understand? It isn't about prevailing. It's about standing. Degi. Abis. Win. Lose. It doesn't matter. Stand." He inhales like he's about to say something else. Cuts himself short. Looks at me. Shakes his head and picks up his pace.

The day swirls in my head. I set out this morning to gather some berries, hoping to shake the memory of a horrible yesterday. Instead, by midday, I've helplessly watched a tribe that has lived in harmony for nearly forty generations fall to pieces. Childhood friends threaten each other's lives. My quiet, diligent gathering partner instruct me on the arts of combat and politics. It scares me how comfortable he is with it. It scares me how uncomfortable I am with it.

By the time we return to our village, there is widespread commotion. Ten huts were found empty this morning. A stolen boat. Stolen baskets. Stolen rope. Stolen food. Chief Sangra has been holed up with the most senior Council members all day.

Worry. Anger. Fear.

Smoke billows ominously from the far side of the mountain, staining a once perfect view of a once perfect sunset.

Chapter 4

Emergency Council

Given the events of the day, I had feared another restless night. Instead, I slept. I slept soundly. I slept well into the morning.

And I dreamed.

Another storm. Another boat breaking apart under the storm's fury. Another hull, growing into a giant boat unto itself. But something new. In this dream, the mast of the new single-hulled boat is short, no taller than the mast of the fishing boat from which it had broken apart. With a gust of wind and a crash of lightning, the mast snaps in half. All hope appears lost. Suddenly, a tree grows in its place. A towering tree. Like the trees that grow in the Grove of Ancestors. Branches fan out from either side of the tree, dense with leaves that catch the wind. Like a sail. The storm finally settles. The single-hulled boat with a giant tree for a mast coasts gracefully across the ocean surface.

It's been with me all morning. I turn the image over in my mind as I sit by the morning bed of coals of the fire just outside my house, wondering why my unconscious self has been especially obsessed with boats lately.

Empty baskets by both of my feet. We came home without berries yesterday after our confrontation with Degi. Today will be a long day of gathering to refill the four empty baskets that circle our fire. Two days' worth of work into one.

Wait, four baskets? I had assumed that, since I slept in, Mehan would have just grabbed two of the baskets and gone on without me, scouting out a new spot for us to gather. But if all four baskets are by the fire, then he hasn't left to gather yet. Is he still sleeping, too?

I grab a basket and set out down the coastline. Instead of turning inland to cut across the island at the certain rock, I follow the shore beyond the rock. The sandy shore gives way to more and more rocks. Small and round at first, but eventually transitioning to rugged, jagged rocks. Rocks that jump straight out of the ocean at you. Navigating the rocks makes gathering on this edge of the island go slowly. But until things get worked out between our villages, it's where I plan to do my gathering.

As I exit our village, I'm startled by the sight of someone's back. Just standing there in perfect stillness. Spear in hand. The figure appears to be a boy roughly my age. Degi? I drop my basket and try to scamper behind the cover of a tree. He hears my shuffling behind him and half-turns his torso in my direction.

Sees me. Waves. "Hey Uri!"

Upon seeing his profile and hearing his voice, I recognize who it is. But it's his distinct wave that gives him away. Penja. An old friend who was just beginning his training toward becoming a fisherman in the days when Brisa's dad took me out on the boats to gauge my interest in fishing. "Penja, what are you doing?" I ask.

"Watching."

"Watching for what?"

"For danger."

Danger? There isn't danger on this island. There is danger in the sea. There is danger in the sky. But not on the island itself. If Penja is watching for danger, it can only mean that he's watching for Abis' group. "Are we in danger?" I ask warily.

"Uhhh." Penja looks around, slightly embarrassed, as though he feels the need to justify himself. But when nothing comes to him, he answers with a simple, "No. Not really. Not yet, at least."

I nod, not surprised, but relieved. "Has Mehan come by this way?" I ask.

"Nah, he's right over there." Penja points his spear inland. I see the outlines of two figures standing just as Penja was when I came upon him, spears in hand. One of the figures is an earshot's distance away from us. But it doesn't look like Mehan. The other figure is about an earshot further; too far to discern if it's Mehan, but it's the only other person Penja could have been pointing to.

"Is he watching, too?" I ask.

"Yep. Chief Sangra called a group of us together late yesterday and told us that our job from now until we leave the island is to protect our village by watching for danger. He sent us out to form a perimeter just outside our village in such a way that we can always hear the next watcher and see the next two watchers." I turn and look to our left, where the line of watchers should continue. Nothing but sand that gives way to ocean. Penja looks to me and shrugs, "No danger that way. The fish are on our side."

I smile, pat Penja on the shoulder, and walk toward Mehan. His assured pose strikes me. As long as I've known him, he's carried himself with confidence. But this is something different. Looking at him right now, you could almost mistake him for the Chief himself. Composed. Determined. In control of everything around him. And yet, the moment he recognizes me approaching, his posture relaxes and he becomes my gathering partner once again. He rests his weight on his spear. A slight, proud smirk. I look down at the basket in my hand, which looks so childish compared to the spear in Mehan's.

"I thought you had gone gathering without me again," I exclaim as I draw near to him.

Mehan shakes his head. "No more gathering for me anymore. Now, I watch."

"You just…watch?" I ask, doubtful that Mehan is capable of spending a moment, much less an entire day, without moving.

"Watch. Protect. Keep danger away from the village." Mehan says defensively.

That word again: Danger. Do we really think Abis is dangerous? I scrunch my nose and look across the island to the thin pillar of smoke. What have we become in the span of just a couple of days? It seems such a waste to have Mehan standing still all day, when he gets so much done while he's moving. Some of the strongest people from our village, standing around waiting for some of the other tribe's strongest people, who are themselves standing around waiting for ours. Why not have these people out fishing, gathering, cutting, building?

"Did you hear about the emergency Council meeting tonight?" Mehan asks.

"No. You and Penja are the first people I've spoken to today. Do you want to try to sneak out and listen?"

"We don't need to listen anymore, Uri. They want us to come be a part of their meeting."

"Who?" I ask skeptically.

"The Chief summoned me after we got back from our gathering trip yesterday. He summoned a group of us, actually. Asked us to form the Watch Crew. He also said that he wanted me and all of my other spy friends to join the Council meeting tonight rather than spying on it from the bushes."

"Spying?"

"I guess our eavesdropping hasn't been such a secret after all. The Chief said that if we're interested enough in the Council to endure it from the bushes, we might as well endure it from inside the Forum."

This sounds strange to me. The process for nominating new members to the Council is fairly formal, requiring lengthy debate at a Council meeting. They debate your character, the soundness of your decision-making, your ability to compromise, your ability to stand firm, and your ability to know the difference between situations that require compromise and situations that require firmness. After the nomination is approved by the Council, the nominee is presented to the fire group that they will represent for a vote. So for them to add us without a nomination process or vote seems odd. That is, until Mehan interrupts my thoughts with, "They found fourteen more empty huts this morning, Uri."

"Fourteen?" My stomach rises. Mehan nods, mirroring my concerned expression. That makes twenty four. Twenty four empty huts in a village of (according to the count announced at the last Council meeting) one hundred forty huts. Twenty four tears in the fabric of our tribe. Twenty four doubts in the minds of those who remain. Twenty four reasons to ask roughly a dozen or so boys and girls who are on the brink of adulthood to help play their part in unifying the tribe by joining the Council so it doesn't become twenty four more.

"So you're coming?" Mehan asks, mildly annoyed at having to pull me out of my inner frenzy once again.

"Sure." I look across at the other watchers, standing proudly in their positions, spears in hand. I'm reminded of the basket in my own hand. "We're out of berries. Is it okay for me to leave so I can gather? You're only keeping people out, right? You aren't keeping people in?"

"No," Mehan studies me. "But-" he catches himself. An anxious look flashes across his face, which he quickly forces into a grimace. He's worried about me. Because I walked away from Degi yesterday. He's worried that I can't protect myself. I break eye contact and brush past him.

I spend the rest of the day gathering. Gathering is no good. It's clear that Abis' tribe has been gathering here too. It takes an entire day just to fill the four baskets. With every trip to and from the village, I avoid Mehan. I don't stop to rest, or think, or enjoy the beautiful day. By the time I finish, I'm exhausted. I decide against going to the emergency Council meeting. I'm too tired. And, after my encounter with Mehan earlier today, I question if I even belong there.

I limp into my hut and lay down, exhausted. The late afternoon shade has crept across the village, but the sky is still bright. Ambient sunlight peers at me through the spaces in the thatch wall. Ambient sounds from outside float past my ears. The churning of the ocean. The crackle of the fire. The voices of people returning from their day's work. The sounds and the lights and the smells weave together and drape across me. Heaviness overcomes my eyes as my mind detaches from the present moment.

Suddenly, I awaken to screaming. I scramble to my feet and burst through the door to my hut. When my foot hits the ground, it splashes into water. Water covering my ankles where there is supposed to be dry land. Water invading the entire village. The ocean is rising. Climbing up my shins. People scramble toward the fishing boats. Though we only have a few boats in the entire village, somehow I see dozens out on the water. Maybe over a hundred. People toss their children and belongings onto the boats, straining to pull themselves up as well. I'm paralyzed with shock. The water rises. Rises. Rises. To my chest. Over my shoulders. As it creeps up the sides of my face to claim me, I'm violently jerked out of the water and lifted high into the sky, to a place just above the mountaintops where I can safely observe the chaos below. The rising water becomes increasingly turbulent, crashing onto the decks of boats as people struggle to stay onboard. Some are swept away. Boats capsize. Boats crash into one another. Boats are flung adrift.

The raging sea continues to climb up the sides of the mountains, until it swallows the trees. The ancient and mighty trees of the Grove of Ancestors, gone in an instant. How can this happen? How can forty generations be undone in an instant? The ocean overtakes the mountaintops, leaving no trace that the island ever stood. Only ocean. Raging ocean. Raging sky. The boats flail under the storm's ravaging aggression. It's only a matter of time before the ocean claims them and all is lost. I want to cry.

Suddenly, twelve trees from the Grove of Ancestors emerge from the ocean. They forcefully crash up through the water's surface and buoy upon the waves. At the base of each tree is a single-hulled boat, just like the ones I've been seeing in my dreams. The trees stand mightily as the mast of each boat, roots planted firmly in the hull. The struggling fishing boats maneuver toward the single-hulled boat nearest to them. People climb aboard. The ocean continues to rage. But aboard the single-hulled boats, there is a sense of security. Control. Hope.

I feel a sharp poking at my side. I look down to my side. Nothing. The poking becomes sharper and faster. "Uri." I'm Uri. "Uri!"

The scene disappears. I open my eyes. Mehan is standing above me poking my ribs with the blunt end of his spear. I sit up. The darkened room spins. I brace my head in my hands. Still spinning. I look up to Mehan. He looks at me, amused. "I've never seen anyone sleep like you sleep. You're practically dead, you know. One day I'm going to find you asleep and poke you and poke you until I realize that you actually are dead and I've been poking a corpse all that time. Then how foolish will I feel?" I'm not in the mood to joke with him right now. "Let's go! Don't want to be late for the Council meeting," he urges me.

Don't want to be late. I release my head from my hands, nod slowly, and spit on the ground next to me. I guess I'm going to the emergency Council meeting, after all.

• • •

The Forum is quiet, somber. Some murmuring. Some whispering. Mostly anxious staring. I feel uncomfortable sitting in the room rather than outside in a bush. Like I don't belong here. Like someone might realize that I don't belong here and ask me to leave.

The room is dimmer than I imagined it. And, despite seeming so spacious when it's empty, it seems so crowded as people trickle in. Mehan is by my side. I catch him in the corner of my eye, gazing around the room in childlike wonder. He's been ready to sit in this room for a long time. I might have been fine staying in the bush for the rest of my life. What am I doing here? I'm about to ask this very question to Mehan when Chief Sangra walks into the room. He looks calm. Composed. Noticing us newest Council members, all sitting in a row, he acknowledges each of us with a nod. I nod back. Maybe he doesn't see through me. Maybe he doesn't see that I'm still a boy. Maybe he believes, as Mehan believes, that I actually do belong in this room.

"Thank you for being here," he addresses the Council. "What a tumultuous few days it has been. We're missing some faces. We're joined by some new faces. We'll need each of us and all of us to prevail through this crisis. And we will.

"As for the faces that are not with us, and for all who have abandoned our village, let's remember this day and every day forward that they are above all, our brothers and sisters. We must never lose sight of that, no matter how great the divide between us may appear. With that said, Abis' path is the path of fear, the path of denial, the path of surrender. We can't allow those things to creep into our own hearts. The moment we do, we will have all but guaranteed ourselves failure.

"So, what now?" Chief Sangra asks. "How do we leave this island?"

Uncertain expressions on everyone's faces. Uncertain if the question is rhetorical. Uncertain if there's an answer for it.

Chief Sangra prods us. "I'm looking for your ideas. This is a problem that will require the input of the entire Council if it's to be solved."

Finally, one of the Council members asks, "How did our ancestors sail here?"

"They sailed here on boats similar to the ones we have today," Sangra replies. "Though their boats were far more sophisticated than ours are today, built to withstand long journeys across the open sea. Regardless, you must remember that our circumstances are different than theirs. Only a few dozen ancestors sailed to this island. Now, we are a group of several hundred trying to leave it."

"So we build more boats," another Council member says matter-of-factly.

"That's the option I keep coming back to, myself," Chief Sangra agrees, "but there are a couple of problems with that course. The first is the sheer number of boats that would be required to carry everyone. How do we manage a fleet of nearly a hundred boats? I don't even know where to begin with that. Secondly, our fishing boats are designed for short trips in familiar waters, not long journeys rife with unforeseen perils."

"Could we build bigger boats?" Another Council member suggests.

"What do you think, Chuan?" The Chief looks over to Chuan, a member of the Council who is also the primary boat builder for our tribe. Though his job title is boat builder, he mostly spends his days cleaning, inspecting, and repairing boats. Boat builders don't actually build that many boats. And they never design new boats.

Chuan is surprised by the mention of his name and the abrupt attention of every eye in the room. He searches for words, at a loss. Meanwhile the mention of the phrase "bigger boats" has stirred something in the back of my mind. The single-hulled boats. The larger crews. The safe passing through the storm. Are the boats in my dreams the answer? The way we escape this island? Have these dreams been coming to me for a reason? Do I dare mention them? Is it even my place to speak at this Council? I feel so out of place; if I speak, will I only confirm my misplacement in the minds of everyone else? I look over to Mehan, hoping for guidance. He's craning his neck toward Chuan, awaiting a response. The words throw themselves from my mouth, "We can build bigger boats."

The rushing sound of every head in the room pivoting from Chuan toward me. I close my mouth, clenching my lips between my teeth. I wish I hadn't spoken. But I did. And the eyes in the room aren't leaving me.

"And what do you know of boat building?" Chief Sangra asks in a vaguely condescending tone.

"Nothing," I admit.

An awkward pause. "Well, thank you for your encouragement. I know Chuan appreciates it." The Chief looks back over to Chuan.

Some of the other eyes in the room follow the Chief's. Other remain fixed on me, including Mehan's, wider than I've ever seen them. I feel wounded. Upset at the Chief for so easily dismissing me. Upset at myself for being so easy to dismiss. The words well up in my throat again. "Chief." The sound again of heads pivoting, including the Chief's. "While it's true that I know nothing of boat building, I know that we can build bigger boats. And not just bigger boats. Different boats. Unlike any boats we've ever built before. I've seen them. They came to me in a dream. And they are spectacular."

Silence in the room. Mehan hasn't blinked. Am I out of line? Out of my mind? Dreams have merit in our tribe, but we've never had to stake our entire future on one of them.

Chief Sangra peers at me. I can't tell if he's intrigued or resentful. "Tell us more," he enquires. "What are these boats like?"

I take a deep breath and let the words come out, "Imagine a boat with one hull, not two. And the hull is bigger than our hulls. Much bigger. Big enough that you could fit several huts on top of it if you wanted to. Big enough to fit maybe twenty or thirty people on top of it. Instead of having a deck resting across the hull, the top of the hull *is* the deck. It has giant masts. And giant sails." Should I mention the trees of the Grove of Ancestors as masts? It might cause a stir. And I don't know if it even means anything. I decide against it, leaving my description as it is.

Chief Sangra is visibly impressed, his curiosity stoked. "Interesting. Tell me more about your dream, Uri. How did these boats come to you in your dream?"

I take another deep breath, "In my dream there was a storm, so crushing that our fishing boats couldn't withstand it. They split apart. And one of the broken boats became one of these giant, single-hulled boats. After it transformed, the boat was able to withstand the very storm that engulfed the island and broke apart our fishing boats."

Chief Sangra ponders my words. "Split

apart," he mumbles distantly, as though it's the middle of a thought. The Council sits in stillness, awaiting his reaction. After a few moments, he gathers himself, looks to Chuan, and asks, "Would such a boat sail?"

"It's possible," Chuan says reluctantly. "The hulls on our fishing boats can float on their own. The challenge is finding a way to build them to the scale that Uri describes. A large free-floating hull will behave very differently from a small hull that floats in tandem with another."

"Can you build one by our next Council meeting?" Chief Sangra asks.

Chuan swallows in disbelief. "A month? Not possible."

"Why not?" The Chief presses him.

"There are only two of us boat builders. Even if we worked all day every day, there's simply not enough time."

"What if you had twenty people? Thirty people? Forty people?"

Chuan hesitates. "We don't have enough wood cut and prepared."

"What if I could guarantee you that you would? You would have all of the carpenters, cutters, weavers, and builders you require."

Chuan looks around nervously, stripped of his excuses. "But you are asking us to design and build a boat that none of us have ever seen before."

"You can have Uri. He's seen them. He can describe them to you."

"In a dream, Chief," Chuan sharply, abruptly challenges. Chief Sangra seems taken aback. Chuan continues, "He saw this boat in a dream. Knowing what a boat looks like from the outside is completely different from understanding how it is built on the inside. Especially when you've only seen it in a dream."

"But it wasn't just one dream," I interject, "It was three dreams. And they were somehow different from normal dreams. I can't explain it. Reality has a certain time and motion to it. Dreams have yet another. But these dreams had a time and place and motion all their own. Somewhere in between."

A heavy silence hangs in the room. Chief Sangra looks to Chuan expectantly. Chuan finally breaks the silence by conceding, "We can try, Chief. We can try. But I will need every person and resource you can give me."

"I don't enter this lightly," Chief Sangra says bluntly. "The future of our tribe is at stake here. There's something about Uri's dreams that I can't ignore. I feel like we at least need to try. If we fail in trying, then we will have lost a month. But there is possibly so much more to be gained. Thank you for your willingness, Chuan. Does the Council favor this proposal?"

Most of the hands in the room go up in

support.

Chief Sangra confirms, "Very well. Work begins tomorrow morning. Chuan, let us know of anything that you need. We will make sure you get it quickly." Then he turns to me and warmly says, "Looks like your gathering days are over, Uri."

Mehan still hasn't taken his astonished eyes off of me. I'm trying not to let him see the fear in mine.

Chapter 5

One Month

It's amazing how quickly a month passes. When it's filled with lazy days – afternoon naps, tree climbing, berry gathering, leisurely walks through the Grove of Ancestors – a month seems to last forever. When it's filled with sunrise-to-sunset working, thinking, moving, lifting, cutting, yelling, a month is gone as quickly as it begins.

People are born, people die. The tide rises, the tide falls. The moon wanes and waxes again. We eat, we sleep. We celebrate, we mourn. In the course of a month, nothing changes; and yet, everything is changing.

I rise early every morning, grab some food, walk down to the shore – a walk that leads me past Brisa's hut. I long for Brisa. If these were normal days, I would be pursuing her. I would make my love known to her. I would ask her to wrap her life around mine. I would build a house for us. We would begin a family. And our love would never stop growing. But these aren't normal days. And with each passing day, my love for her feels more like a fantasy than reality.

When I reach the shore most mornings, I find Chuan already there, laboring over some nuance of the boat that only he can perceive. He asks me to describe the boats to him. He asks me to remember as much about them as I can. Every little detail. Shapes. Proportions. Placements. No detail is insignificant. I close my eyes, imagine the boats, and describe them as best as I can. Then he spends the day trying to match whatever phase of the boat we are building with my description of the boats in my dreams. Sometimes it matches. Sometimes it doesn't.

We work all day. Building. Tweaking. Testing. Starting over. We are constantly asking for more rope, more wood, more workers. True to Chief Sangra's words, every request is granted. We laugh together. We argue. We remind each other to press on.

The boat building crew has become a mini-tribe unto itself. People from every job on the island arrive at the boat every day. And I've started to recognize the unique personalities inherent to each one. Carpenters, with their creative, methodical approach to everything. Rope makers, always exasperated at how quickly their rope gets used. Builders, constantly trying to impress one another and slightly crass. Fishers, rowdy and loud, seeking new thrills and reliving old ones. Water carriers, quiet and studious. Gatherers, patient and inquisitive. And many more.

I'm amazed. I never realized how much went into building a boat. Of course, we've never built a boat to this scale before. We work until the last shades of light have faded from the sky. Squinting, holding up torches, whatever we can do to make each day last a little longer. Then we go home exhausted, eat, try to sleep while are minds are racing.

On the shore all day, it becomes easy to forget about life inland. Easy to forget about the mundane details that mark each passing day and hour. Easy to forget about the people and places that were once so familiar. I haven't spoken with Mehan since the night of the emergency Council meeting. Our paths simply haven't crossed. He spends his days watching. I spend mine building. But every once in a while, the image of his face crosses my mind. And I miss him. Not like I miss Brisa. A different kind of longing. A longing for his companionship. We used to see each other every day. Now I don't see him at all. And I miss him. I picture him standing guard. I wonder if he longs for my companionship too.

Every morning, women from the village bring their young children down to the still waters of the bay. From the day we enter the world, our mothers make a point to bring us down to the bay every day and dip us in its refreshing waters. To acquaint us with the sea.

To plant within us a love for it. To connect us with the mysterious expanse that stretches from our shores to the horizon. From time to time, I stop and watch them, recalling days when my own mother would bring me and my sisters down to the waters. Mehan's mother would do the same with him and his siblings. Those days seem so far gone now.

Even as it becomes easy to forget about life inland, it also becomes easy to forget about the strife that has gripped every facet of life since smoke first rose from the far side of the island. Occasionally, someone coming down to visit us on the shore brings anxious reports of village life. How the other tribe accidentally crashed the boat that they stole from us into the giant rocks that stagger the shoreline of the far side of the island. The waves, the currents, the wind, they simply made the rocks too difficult to navigate. And now the boat is on the craggy ocean floor. Without a boat to fish, they tried catching fish by wading into the water and casting nets. But the same rugged conditions that sank the boat also make net fishing very risky and unsuccessful. Someone nearly drowned trying. They tried staging an invasion of our village to steal another boat, but our watchers saw them as soon as they crested the ridge of the grassy valley and drove them back to their corner of the island.

Without fish, Abis' village began to starve.

One morning, everyone in his village fanned out across the island and picked every berry they could find. When our own gatherers came back that day with meager baskets, Chief Sangra immediately sent some Council members to confront Abis. In the end, they arranged a deal where their village would gather berries while our tribe fished. Each day, members from each of our tribes meet and exchange fish for berries. Apparently, it isn't only berries that Abis' village has been stockpiling. Wood, water, even spears. Abis refuses to explain why and refuses to surrender them. Now our tribes are conjoined by this tense, awkward, unnatural need for one another.

Other reports from the island are comparatively dull. A few new empty huts. A few people who had initially followed Abis changing their minds once the hunger set in and returning to our village.

On the shore, where our lives revolve around the boat, time isn't marked by the routines that mark the rest of the island. It's marked by progress on the boat. It's marked by solving problems. It's marked by failures and fixes. It's marked by breakthroughs that propel us forward and reinvigorate us. It's marked by the moon, measuring out days, drawing out worries, spurring us ahead when we feel like giving up, lighting our way home after the sun has set. And as the moon grows, dueling emotions of anxiety and relief overcome us. Anxiety that the month is almost over; relief that the month is almost over.

Tomorrow night, the moon will be full. The entire tribe will gather on the shore shortly before the midday high tide to witness the launching of this strange new boat. Will it sail? Will it carry us? Will it save our tribe? I wade out into the water to the place where the boat has been staged in anticipation of tomorrow's high tide that will lift it to its first and fateful voyage. It looks so much like the boats in my dreams. Except one glaring detail. The masts. The largest native tree on the island was cut down to become the mast for this boat. It's more than twice as tall as the masts on our fishing boats; yet, it looks half as tall in comparison to the boat itself. Chuan knows it doesn't look right. He questions its dependability. But it's our only option.

I place my hand on the bow. Sturdy. Footsteps in the water behind me. Another hand places itself on the bow. Chuan. He admires the boat for a moment. Then gives it a few firm pats. "It's a beautiful boat, Uri." He glances at me and then back to the boat. "Absolutely beautiful. You must feel so proud."

I nod. A lump forms in my throat. This month has been the most intense of my life. The exhausting days. The risk of failure. The absence of Brisa. The rift in our tribe. And now, the satisfaction of seeing the finished boat coupled with Chuan's words, *so proud*. I can't describe the emotion that's crawling up my throat. But pride is definitely part of it. "You too," is all I can muster without the lump in my throat making its way to the surface.

Chuan pats my shoulder. "I am proud of it," he agrees. Then, his voice shifting to a grave tone, "The only thing that worries me is that mast. After scouring the entire island, that's the biggest tree we could find. Except in–" he cuts himself off. But I know what the rest of that sentence would have been: *except in the Grove of Ancestors*. I still haven't mentioned that part of the dream to anyone. Up to this point, I had been afraid of what the consequences would have been if I had shared it. Now I'm afraid of the consequences of having not shared it. "Except in the Grove of Ancestors," he hesitantly completes his thought.

I nod. He notices my nodding and, surprised, asks me, "Did you know about this?"

"My dreams," I blurt out. "In my second dream, the mast of the single-hulled boat snapped in half and a tree from the Grove of Ancestors grew in its place. Then in my third dream, the ocean rose higher than the mountains. And as it covered the mountains, twelve boats emerged from the ocean. Each of the boats had a tree from the Grove of

Ancestors as its mast. I didn't know what it meant at the time, so I didn't mention it. But now it seems clear. And I wish I had."

Chuan rolls his eyes and places his fist on his forehead in frustration. "Details like that matter, Uri! Does the Chief know about those parts of your dreams?"

I shake my head. "He only knows what I described at that Council meeting."

"He won't like this," Chuan breathes in and out sharply, "but he needs to know."

"I know," I agree. The distant chatter of the tribe settling down for the evening meal can be heard through the trees. Tomorrow, everyone will know.

We remain at the boat for a while, not saying another word. Anticipating tomorrow. Staring at the moonlight. Waiting for the noise from the village to die down so we can slip in without having to speak with anyone else. When all goes quiet, we wish each other goodnight, return to our homes, and don't sleep.

• • •

I stagger out of my hut as first light breaks on the morning of the full moon. Exhausted, but wide awake. Chuan is already on the shore, admiring the silhouette of the boat against the sun rise. I join him. No work to be done. Just the demonstration of the boat. And confessing my dreams to Chief Sangra. The very thought of it makes me nauseous. I sway slightly. Without averting his gaze, Chuan calmly advises, "Go eat something, Uri."

"I can't," I mutter through heavy breaths.

"We've done everything we can. No one could have imagined that we would build such a magnificent vessel in one month's time. If it doesn't work we will find a way to do whatever is right for the tribe. Even if it means launching a hundred fishing boats into the great unknown. So why be nervous?"

As he says those last words, I lurch forward and vomit. Surprisingly, I feel much more at ease afterward. I'm amazed at Chuan's poise. He has worked harder and longer over the past month than anyone else, insisting on perfection all along the way. When a problem seemed unsolvable, it was usually Chuan who would find a way to solve it. He never flinched. He has the most invested in this boat of anyone on this island, including me. And now, he's standing here completely at peace, confident and satisfied with his work. I try to be at peace alongside him. But my mind is too busy.

The sun has crested the horizon. Our shadows are still long, but it's full morning. People are stirring. And it will only be a short time before they make their way to the shore. I stand with Chuan for a while before walking back to the village to placate my stomach with berries. On the way back to my hut, I pass by Brisa's. Her father is outside fixing something. He looks over his shoulder. Upon noticing me, he squares his body in my direction and smiles. "This is a big day for you, Uri. The boat is amazing. You must be proud."

I nod. "Yes, proud. Mostly nervous, though."

He laughs knowingly. "Be nervous. But don't forget to be proud, too, son." Son. He's the only person on the island who calls me that. My father died when I was young. Men throughout the village stepped into my life to be a father to me after he died, including Brisa's father. I have memories of exploring this island with him and his children. Memories of him teaching us how to swim. Memories of him patiently teaching us his endless knowledge of various knots, gained from a generation's worth of time as a fisherman. *This one is good for nets. This one is good for holding things in place. This one is secure but you can undo it quickly just by pulling here*. Most of the knots I've forgotten, but the memories are still vivid. It was through the time that I spent with him and his family that I first met Brisa.

He continues, "I was going to start teaching you how to be a fisherman. Like me. Like your father. But instead, you went and learned how to build boats." He lets out a small laugh as he looks down toward the shore. “Everyone’s excited to see your boat sail today, Uri. You’ve done a good thing.”

“Thank you,” I say meekly. Though his words come as an encouragement, they also send the nerves that Chuan helped calm racing through me once again. Knotting my stomach. Crawling up my neck. At the moment they nearly overtake me, Brisa’s head emerges from the door and they scatter. Suddenly, she’s all there is, and everything else fades away.

Her smile. “This is a big day for you,” she says encouragingly, echoing her father, causing me to wonder if I’m a topic of conversation around their household. And if I am, how those conversations go.

“It is,” I say, distracted by how she has managed to become even more beautiful in the month since I last saw her, “because it’s the first day in a month that I’ve gotten to see you.”

She blushes as she tucks a lock of hair behind her ears. Then, becoming conscious of her father standing beside her, she takes on a more serious demeanor. “No, because we get to see your boat. It’s a big day for you. It’s a big day for the entire tribe.”

“Only if it works.”

“It has to work,” she says with conviction. “It came to you in a dream.”

“I hope you’re right,” I say unconvincingly, wishing her dad would leave so I could be alone with her. He must sense this, because after an awkward amount of silence, he kisses the side of Brisa's head and retreats to the hut, giving me a warm smile as he turns. I smile back at him.

When he's inside, I look to Brisa and confess, "I've missed you so much. Every day that I was on that shore, I was thinking about you, Brisa. I couldn't wait to see you again, to talk with you, to get lost on long walks with you."

Brisa walks over to me and takes my hand. "Me too."

"So let's do it. Tomorrow. First thing. We'll go out to the New Grove and stay there until the sun is gone."

"You will need to be back on the shore tomorrow building boats, right?"

"The boat is built already."

"Yes, but after it sails today, they will want to build a whole fleet of those boats as fast as they can. They will want to get started on the next one tomorrow. You will be needed for building and I will be needed for making ropes."

"When will we have time for each other, then?" I ask more harshly than I intend to.

"We'll find time, Uri. I want to be with you as much as you want to be with me. It just isn't up to us anymore. Not as long as we're working to leave this island. We'll have to take whatever time we can find and be content with that. Our tribe needs us right now."

She's right. But the part of me that acknowledges her rightness is overpowered by the part of me that wants to have her all to myself forever. That part of me drops her hand, turns my back toward her, and walks away. *Go back! Go back!* My mind screams. But my mind clearly isn't in control right now, reeling in the wake of a rampant and injured heart.

By the time I reach the fire pit by my hut, I'm breathing furiously through my nostrils. Pacing. Frantic. I want to scream. I want to run away. I want to tell Brisa I'm sorry. I want to go back to the days when work was easy, when we had time to do nothing together, when the future was clear.

Caught up in my swirling anger, I nearly collide with Chief Sangra. I look up at him. He looks at me and with genuine concern asks, "Something bothering you, Uri?"

Yes. "No."

"Are you worried about today?"

"Chuan says we're ready," I reply, trying to deflect the conversation.

"I just saw him. He says he's ready. But his eyes say he's fearful. I came here hoping you could help me understand why."

The masts. Chuan must be worried about the masts and my revelation to him about my dreams. Should I tell the Chief, too? I look at him. He peers into me. Reads me. Surely he sees the fear in my eyes, too. "Chief, there's something I didn't share during the last Council meeting."

"What is it?" He asks sharply, as though I just confessed to stealing from him.

"I didn't even share it with Chuan until this morning."

"Tell me, Uri." His voice even sharper.

I search for words that might soften the impact. When they don't come, I give up and concede everything. I tell him about the mast snapping in my second dream and being replaced by a tree from the Grove of Ancestors. I tell him about the trees from the Grove of Ancestors serving as the masts of the boats in my third dream. I tell him about how the mast of the boat that we've been working on for the past month doesn't look quite right. By the time I'm finished, he's dumbfounded.

"Uri, why wouldn't you tell us this?"

"I didn't understand what it meant until this morning. I wasn't being deceitful, Chief. I just didn't realize that it was an important detail until this morning."

"Every detail is important, Uri. Every detail is important!" He pauses and puts his hand over his mouth to collect himself. "I've torn our tribe in two. I made such a spectacle out of refusing to sacrifice the Grove of Ancestors. I can't go back on that now. Do you understand?"

I nod, on the verge of tears.

"Have you told anyone else aside from Chuan?" He asks.

"No."

"Let's just see how today goes," he says with a contrived nonchalance. "Maybe the mast is fine the way it is. Maybe your dreams mean something other than what they seem."

But what else could they mean? It didn't make sense at the time, but it seems pretty clear to me now. Still, recalling the fierce debate that Chief Sangra had with Abis and Keras, I understand his reticence. I simply respond with another nod.

"Good." Chief Sangra resolves, placing his hand on my shoulder. He starts to walk away, but catches himself, as though his hand has somehow become attached to my shoulder. He locks eyes with me and slowly asks, "It's been a hard month, hasn't it, Uri?" My eyes mist almost immediately as he continues, "A month ago you were gathering. And now…all this. You aren't a boat builder. You aren't a councilman. Yet, overnight, you were forced to give up what you were and become those things. It's a lot to figure out all at once. I've had to become things that I'm not as well, Uri. I've had to become Peacekeeper with a hostile tribe, Commissioner of a fleet of new boats, Trader of fish and berries."

I chuckle at the last one. He laughs with me before continuing, "It's hard to make those kinds of changes overnight. Probably even more for you - you're also transitioning from boyhood to manhood. I would never have wished this on you. Or me. But our tribe needs us, Uri." Those last words are eerily reminiscent of Brisa's. I feel the same discomfort when the Chief says them as I felt when she did. I shift my weight anxiously. But the Chief tightens his grip on my shoulder to bring me back into focus. "This is your legacy, Uri. The tallest, strongest, thickest trees in the Grove of Ancestors are the ones who endured the greatest hardships for their legacies to be made known. Every legacy matters; some just cast a larger shadow than others. Already, your legacy stands a little taller and a little bolder. The entire tribe, for every generation that's yet to come, is the direct beneficiary of your legacy. Remember that, Uri. No matter how painful the struggle, you are struggling for something far greater than yourself." Chief Sangra beams proudly at me, moved by his own words. Then he releases his hand from my shoulder and walks away.

I'm moved by his words, too. Emboldened, I forget to eat and head back down to the shore in a daze. Chuan is standing ankle-deep in the ocean with a group of sailors surrounding him. Probably explaining the differences between this boat and the fishing boats they are accustomed to. They will sail the boat out to the cusp of the bay, turn around, and head back to the shore. A simple, unimpressive maneuver that has everything to do with the future of our tribe. People stream down to the shore as the tide rises. Before long, the sand is covered with bodies. Attentive, expectant bodies.

The high tide reaches its peak. Chief Sangra descends to the ocean's edge. Not a whisper from the shore. He quickly commences, "Chuan and Uri and everyone who has worked tirelessly over the past month, you've built a magnificent boat. Thank you all for giving our tribe this great gift. Without further delay, let's see how it sails!"

The sailors climb into the boat. Those of us who built it wade into the water and find our spots around the hull. When everyone is set, we begin pushing. We push and strain until the boat is free. It drifts for a few moments before the crew opens the sail. The sound of the sail opening and the wind catching it evokes a collective gasp from the shore.

We're enamored. Enchanted. It's unlike anything we've ever seen. Our hopes carried upon its deck. Our imaginations captured in its sails unfurled against the deep blue sky. Our future set free in its bow, pointed proudly toward the horizon.

The hull cuts through the waves with ease.

Our small, simple fishing boats tend to bob and bounce on the waves. This boat doesn't. It doesn't waver. It sails smoothly, steadily, in command of the sea. Just like my dreams, but even more impressive because it's real.

And then.

Creaking.

All boats creak, but the creaking that's shooting through our ears now is somehow different. Straining, not rubbing. Sharp, not dull. I glance toward Chuan, whose head is cocked to the side with one ear seabound, His face is motionless, perplexed, trying to understand the creaking. The creaking strains. Sharpens. Builds. Chuan's eyes, which had been fixed on some nondescript point on the ground, suddenly dart up to mine. They widen.

Creaking gives way to popping…popping gives way to cracking…cracking gives way to snapping…until…

Crash! Like a fierce clap of thunder.

Chuan and I break our gaze with one another and frantically look toward the boat. From the shore, everything looks fine. Instinctively, the sailors drop the sail. Fishers board the fishing boats and sail out to our boat, which sits helplessly at the edge of the bay where it had been poised to begin its turn.

Everyone on the shore is stunned. It's visible in their faces. It's audible in their silence. Chuan and I return to one another, mouths gaping. What just happened? What does this mean? I can't bring myself to look in the Chief's direction, afraid of what I might see.

Out at sea, five fishing boats speed out to the stranded boat. For a few moments after they arrive at the boat, there is indiscernible skirmishing. Ropes are thrown down from our boat to each of the fishing boats. The sailors on our boat then slide down one of the ropes to a tethered fishing boat below, which then backs away and returns to shore. The other fishing boats wait, acting as a sort of anchor to the crippled boat that was designed to replace them.

As the fishing boat with the sailors on board nears the shore, curiosity overcomes me and I bring myself to glance over to the Chief. His arms crossed, his stature unmovable. Sensing my eyes on him, he immediately darts his eyes from the ocean to me. They are piercing. Though he doesn't display anger, I sense anger. He flips the same glare over to Chuan. Then he subtly motions for me and Chuan to approach him. Aware of the hundreds of eyes upon us across the rest of the shore, we approach him as steadily as possible.

Through a clenched jaw, Chief Sangra whispers, "What happened?"

"I don't know," Chuan whispers back with raspy panic. "The hull, the rudder, the shrouds. They're all fine. The mast –" He catches himself, unsure how to complete that thought.

He doesn't need to. Chief Sangra completes it for him. "Uri told me about his dream. And I told him it was out of the question. We'll have to find another way."

The tension between the three of us is interrupted by the sound of whooping and cheering from down shore. We all look toward its source. The fishing boat has beached and, as the sailors jump down from it, they cheer and embrace one another in jubilation. After they've sufficiently celebrated, they turn to the crowd on the shore and are taken aback by the multitude of blank stares. They jog over, find Chuan, gather around him, and eagerly telling him everything they love about the boat. The size. The control. The smoothness.

Chief Sangra inserts himself into the commotion. "What happened?" He asks. "What was that crash we heard?"

One of the sailors replies, "The mast broke. Split right down the middle. We need to build the boats with stronger masts. Everything else," the sailor pauses with a look of euphoria on his face before continuing, "is perfect."

"We can't build the boats with stronger masts," Chief Sangra quickly replies. "That's the tallest, thickest, strongest mast we could find."

The sailor's voice becomes grave as he admonishes, "But Chief, we must. If we're going to sail past the horizon, we need boats like Chuan's. And the only way for Chuan's boat to sail is with a stronger mast. We must find stronger masts."

The Chief looks uneasy. This complicates things. He glances up the mountainside at the Grove of Ancestors, boasting the cherished legacies of our tribe's past. "We'll discuss this further at the Council meeting this evening," he says, and leaves it at that.

Meanwhile, my mind is swarming. It sailed. The boat actually sailed. And it looked magnificent. The dreams became reality. A month's worth of sleepless nights, tireless work and rework, and the persistent burden of time. All of it culminating into something magnificent upon the waters. But the mast. The only trees on this island sufficient to serve as masts are the very ones that we've vowed never to cut down.

I look across the shore. People are bewildered by the spectacle of it all - the fishing boats coordinating a retrieval of our boat, the jubilation of the sailors, the dilemma of the mast.

Was this a good thing?

Was this a bad thing?

No one knows.

Tonight, we'll know.

Chapter 6

Twelve Moons

The sun falls. All turns dark. Except for the moon. Even at its fullest, the light of the moon can't compete with the light of the sun or the light of a fire. By the light of the sun we work; by the light of the fire we gather; by the light of the moon we mark the passing of time.

I've always regarded the light of the moon with a certain indifference, mostly unaffected by its marking of time; yet, over the past month, the unassuming light of the moon has been more oppressive than either the blinding sun or the burning fire. And tonight, in all its fullness, the light of the moon is chief above all others. I gaze upon it. No longer with indifference, but with trepidation. No longer with wonder, but with dread. No longer with serenity, but with turmoil. It illuminates my path through the trees to the Forum. To the place where this endeavor began. To the place where it may end…or overcome us all.

My foot crosses the threshold of the Forum and instinctively hesitates. I still don't feel like I belong here. Avoiding eye contact with everyone in the room, I quickly shuffle to the same seat as last month and sit with my eyes fixed on the ground. A few moments later, a set of toes slips into view. Mehan's. His toes line up opposite of mine as he stands in front of me, presumably to get my attention. I keep my eyes to the ground. It's been a month since I last saw him. I've longed to see him again. But not here. Not like this. I long to see him like we were a month ago, when our days were spent gathering berries together. Before I dreaded the moon. Before the tribe was torn apart. Before we set a course to leave this island. Before watchers. Before new boats. Before broken masts. Before the shame that weighs on me now.

He wiggles his toes. I want to smile, but I don't have any smiles in me right now. When he realizes he isn't going to get my attention, his feet spin around as he takes his seat beside me. The room may be against me, but not Mehan. He is for me. He always has been.

The chatter of the room grows as more Council members enter. Then it abruptly becomes silent until the only sound is a single set of footsteps making its way to the center of the Forum. Chief Sangra. He inhales loudly. Exhales loudly. Then he begins, "What a day it has been. Perhaps the most important day of the last forty generations on this island. Ironic that its importance marks the beginning of the end of our time on this island..." Chief Sangra trails off, his voice cracking. My eyes lift from the floor. He tries to continue, "…this glorious island…" his voice cracks again as he places his hand over his mouth. Never before have I seen him as overwhelmed by his emotions as he is right now.

He pauses to collect himself, breathes deeply again, and continues, "This past month has seemed hopeless at many times. The thought of leaving. The rift in our tribe. The crisis that brought it all about. But today…today we caught a glimpse of hope, our first glimpse in a while. But this hope hasn't come without its share of disappointment. Uri and Chuan, your boat was built soundly. The mast simply wasn't strong enough. Unfortunately, no tree on this island will be strong enough to carry the boat securely." A cryptic pause. "Except the trees in the Grove of Ancestors."

Quickened murmuring in the room.

"What does that mean?" One of the Council members asks. "Are you suggesting that we–"

"I'm suggesting that this boat is our best chance to leave this island. If we're committed to leaving, we must find a way to make these boats sail. Everything required to build these boats can be harvested from the native trees of this island. Except for the mast. We need twelve boats to carry us all. Twelve boats need twelve masts. Twelve masts would require wood from twelve trees. I'm suggesting that we carefully select twelve trees from the Grove of Ancestors to become the twelve masts."

Silence. I'm learning that as much is said in the silences of the Council meetings as is said in the spoken words themselves. This particular silence is screaming.

Finally, the silence is broken by a Council woman's challenge, "Chief, before coming to this meeting tonight, I felt I understood the difference between Abis' plan and your plan. Now I'm not so sure. How can we switch from being so uncompromising in our regard for the Grove of Ancestors to now being so compromising?"

"I don't know," Chief Sangra concedes. "I've been grappling with that very question all day, ever since that mast snapped. Abis proposed harvesting the entire Grove of Ancestors. By the time his plan played out, our mountains would be nearly bare and, with them, our tribe's identity. What I'm suggesting tonight would allow the Grove of Ancestors to endure."

"But some trees *will* be cut down. It begins a slippery slope."

"Only twelve trees, and each one for a very specific and unique purpose. We will not harvest a thirteenth tree. I stake my position as Chief on that commitment."

Another protest from the room. "Surely

there's another way! Chuan, isn't there another way?"

Chuan considers his response for a few moments before slowly saying, "I'm afraid there isn't. And it appears that we've been destined for this dilemma since the very beginning." He looks directly at me. My dreams. No one in the Council knows about this part of my dreams aside from Chuan and Chief Sangra.

"Since the very beginning? Well then why didn't you tell us about this earlier, Chuan?" A Council member asks with exasperation.

Chuan starts to answer, but before he can utter a word, I interject, "Because he didn't know." All eyes rush toward me, sucking the air out of the room. "In my dreams, the masts of the twelve ships were trees from the Grove of Ancestors."

"Why didn't you mention that at the last Council meeting?" The Council member turns his anger on me.

"I didn't know what it meant at the time," I reply, the shame apparent in my voice.

"All the more reason you should have told us!" The Council member's voice fluctuates in pitch and volume.

"He's just a boy," Chuan declares over the Council member. "Don't forget that he's just a boy. Even if he had told us, would you have known what the dream meant at the time?

Would I? Perhaps he should have told us about it sooner, but I can understand why he wouldn't. And rather than obsessing over the past, we would be better served determining our future."

Silence once again. The anger disarmed, the tension persists.

Someone asks, "How will Abis respond? The moment the first tree hits the ground, he will be furious. You can be certain he will respond."

Chief Sangra nods. "I will speak with him. I don't expect it to ease his fury. But he deserves to know. In the meantime, I would like for Chranit to select twelve trees from the Grove of Ancestors." Chranit perks up in his seat at the sound of his name. His old, wiry frame straightens as he realizes the honor that's just been bestowed upon him. Chief Sangra continues, "By the next full moon, I will have spoken with Abis, Chranit will have selected the twelve trees, and Chuan will have prepared the boat to receive a new mast. As soon as that boat is ready, you are to begin construction on additional boats. You have twelve moons to finish construction of all twelve boats. Whatever you need, whomever you need, it's yours. And on the thirteenth moon we embark into the unknown, just as our ancestors did so many generations ago. Does the Council support this plan?"

Around the room, most hands raise in support. Chief Sangra is wearing a myriad of emotions: relief, sorrow, fatigue. Chuan is solemn. Mehan is looking at me like I have three eyes. I still can't believe any of this is actually happening.

• • •

The morning after the Council meeting, more huts are found empty. At this point, one out of every five huts is empty, their occupants having followed Abis to the other side of the island.

When Chief Sangra visits the other village to announce the plan to cut down twelve trees from the Grove of Ancestors, they seethe at him. Meanwhile he remains resolute, even defiant. It's a side that few of us have ever observed in him before. He typically looks for common ground whenever he's faced with a conflict. But he's never had to face a conflict like this before. None of us have.

Chranit doesn't waste any time with his assignment. He gathers the elders together at sunrise following the Council meeting to walk through the Grove of Ancestors in search of twelve suitable trees. He says he wants to pick twelve trees that tell our story the best. Twelve trees that show how we've changed and grown into the tribe we are today. Twelve trees that will carry us away from the island with the greatest sense for the tribe we must always strive to become.

I'm anxious to see which trees they will choose, recalling countless childhood memories among them. The sights and smells gripping our senses as the elders told stories from generations past, setting our imaginations alive. When the elders stopped at a tree to tell us its story, we would climb up into its branches and hang from limbs, feeling the texture of the bark against the palm of our hands, rubbing the leaves between our fingers, testing the density of the wood under our weight. We'd carefully survey the colors and curves and defining features of each tree, wanting to apprehend the hero of each story through the shape of their legacy. We learned about Strength as we rested upon strong limbs. We learned about Perseverance as we admired branches that never stopped climbing toward the sky. We learned about Kindness as we sat engulfed in a lavish cloud of leaves. And in this collision of our senses, Strength and Perseverance and Kindness and the host of legacies that the trees proclaim became a part of us too.

Selecting only twelve trees out of these thousands will be difficult, but Chranit has taken to it with zeal. I smile every time I see him speaking passionately to a group of elders while making broad, elaborate gestures. If he's overwhelmed by the destination, he certainly isn't letting it hinder his enjoyment of the journey.

I had hoped that after the first month, I would be able to separate myself from boat building. I don't know why I allowed myself to have that expectation. Our village isn't in the business of berry gathering anymore and I don't have any other skills. Chuan bluntly reminded me of those truths when I suggested that maybe I wouldn't be showing up at the shore again.

But boat building is much easier now than it was that first month. Less tense. Less chaotic. Less exhausting. Shorter days. Now that we know how to build these boats, Chuan has been able to organize people into shifts. Quite a few people choose to stay out the entire day and there is always plenty of work for them to do. But Chuan encourages everyone to get plenty of rest. It's the only way we will be able to sustain our work for twelve more months.

I spend as much of my free time as possible with Brisa. We walk. We tell stories. We laugh. But something's different. I'm not exactly sure what it is. It feels like we're having to work so much harder to do something that used to come so naturally. Like rekindling a fire from a bed of coals.

Twelve more months of this.

Then what? We board the boats, sail to a

new land, and everything goes back to the way it was before?

Or will we look back on the people we are today and see strangers?

Chapter 7

The First Moon

The morning of the first moon is especially calm. It's one of those rare mornings where it feels like the world itself is trying to slow down time. Something about the thickness of the air; the stillness of the sea. Everything is heavier. Slower. Quieter.

People are gathering at the edge of the village. Before long, Chranit will lead the entire village up one of the mountains for the first of twelve legacy talks. The legacy talks are Chranit's way of ensuring that the trees we cut down receive the honor they deserve. For the next twelve months, on the morning of the full moon, before any food is eaten or work is done, the entire tribe will meet at the edge of the village at sunrise and follow Chranit to the tree that the elders selected for that month. At the foot of the tree, Chranit will share its story and legacy.

The calmness of this morning coupled with the absence of the sounds of cooking and working that typically fill the village by this time gives it a certain eeriness. Surveying the faces of the crowd at the edge of the village, it seems like every one senses it.

I feel a jab at the back of my knee, causing it to buckle. Turning around, I find myself staring directly into Mehan's toothy grin. I laugh and throw a mock punch at him. He dodges it and gently slaps my ribs. Taking position behind me, he straightens himself and gazes out at the sunrise completely motionless. This amazes me. When I gathered berries with Mehan, he never stood still. He couldn't stand still. He was always busy. Always vibrating with energy. Always doing something, even if it was as subtle as tapping his fingers against his thigh when there was nothing else to do. But here he is, after only a couple of months standing at his watching post, standing as firm and still as the trees themselves.

Chranit strolls past us, joined by a host of elders. Upon reaching the front of the crowd, he turns to acknowledge us before continuing up the hill toward the Old Grove. We mimic both their silence and their footsteps. Hundreds of us. Across the grassy hill. Into the throng of towering trees that proclaims legacies without words.

Chranit stops at a particular tree and motions for us to fill in the spaces uphill from it. I know this tree. It's one of my favorites. It stands out among the hillside even from the grassy valley below. We find our seats, squeezing together so everyone can hear

Chranit clearly, which turns out not to be a problem, as normally soft-spoken Chranit opens his mouth and announces in a loud voice, "When a stone cutter begins her work, she approaches a rough, misshapen lump of rock. Then, through a countless number of taps and scrapes and chips, the sculpture emerges. The identity of the rock is made known. When our ancestors first arrived on this island, they were the formless rock. They were hostile, vindictive, and preoccupied by gratifying each passing selfish need.

"Then the trees began to grow. And our tribe began to change. Slowly, painstakingly, like stone beneath a cutter's chisel, we learned our identity. We began to learn about unseen things that fill the spaces between seen things. Unbound by time, because they reach across all times past, present, and future, connecting moments to moments to moments. Unchanging, even while the world around us is always changing. Permanent, even while the world is passing. When I look at our tribe today compared to who we were forty generations ago, I see a masterful and beautiful sculpture. Yes, we still have our rough edges, our cracks, our unfinished portions; but there is also beauty and shape, growing every day.

"Each of these trees is a tap of the chisel. The tap is made and then it vanishes. But its effect is enduring, just as each of the lives that each of these trees represents has left an enduring etching upon our tribe. And just as the trees have altered the face of this island, they have also altered the face of our tribe. Some have had a more noticeable impact on our tribe than others, but each one has had an impact. And to look at these trees and deny their significance would be to compare a sculpture to an untouched boulder and insist that you can't tell a difference between the two. They call out to us, demanding that we stop, that we take note, that we learn. We don't fully understand what causes these trees grow, but we understand their purpose. And we honor that purpose.

"The elders were challenged to select twelve of these trees. Twelve trees that will become twelve masts. Twelve masts that will carry twelve boats. Twelve boats that will sustain our tribe across the treacherous unknown and give us a future. We selected twelve trees that represent distinct legacies; twelve legacies that are vital to who we are as a tribe. When we leave this island, these are the legacies that we must carry with us always."

Chranit lingers on that thought before turning toward the tree behind him. He admires its resilient beauty for a moment, then turns back to the crowd and continues, "When I look around our village every day, I see countless acts of selflessness. Most of the time, you probably don't even realize what you are doing. You do it without thinking about it. Helping, sharing, working to the best of your ability knowing that everyone benefits from the work you do. While we've always depended on one another for survival, it didn't always look like it does today. This is something that has had to be sculpted into us. And we can't tell the story of how this has been sculpted into us without telling the story of Poshar.

"In the fifteenth generation our village was smaller and less organized. The mountains and valley were changing, but they still more closely resembled the island that our ancestors discovered than the way it looks today. A young fisherman named Poshar awoke one particular morning and began to prepare for the day as though it was just another day. Only it wasn't. Not for him. Not for anyone.

"He kissed his sleeping wife gently so as not to wake her and stepped outside. Threw a few logs on the fire, grabbed a handful of berries, and headed toward the fishing boats on the shore to meet his fellow crewmembers and prepare for the day's excursion. When all was ready, they set sail. The winds were steady, the skies were clear, the ocean currents were light, the surface was calm – a fisherman's perfect day.

"A good distance from shore, they snagged their first catch of the day. A beautiful fish. As they were pulling it in, the boat suddenly lurched. The back of the boat dipped under water and violently bobbed back up again, sending one of the fishermen overboard, near the snagged fish. Only the fish wasn't the only thing they had snagged. It had unwittingly become bait for a shark! Larger than any shark they had ever seen. And it wanted their catch for itself. The fallen fisherman was merely an arm's length away from it all. For a moment, everyone froze. The size of the shark. The rows of teeth. The ferocity in its eyes as it thrashed and thrashed and thrashed.

"Poshar came to his senses, realizing that if the shark gave up on the fish and went for the fallen fisherman, they would be hopeless to save him. So he grabbed a rope, tossed one end to the crew, fastened the other end to a fishing hook…and leapt. Into the water. Into the danger. Into uncertain fate. He swam to his companion, wrapped the hook around both of them, and cinched the hook onto the rope. The crew hauled the two of them in as fast as they could and pulled them aboard. Then the fishing line snapped. The shark was gone with their beautiful catch. And everything became peaceful once again.

"Amidst that peacefulness, a sense of disbelief rose among the crew. Amazement. They gaped at Poshar. Did that really just happen? The shark? The fisherman? Poshar's great rescue? It all happened so quickly. None of them had ever seen anything like it before - neither the shark nor the selfless act of bravery. They sailed back to shore, no one saying a word the entire time. But the moment the hulls touched the sand, the fishers erupted with cheering. They fanned out into the village telling everyone they saw about the amazing attack and the amazing rescue that accompanied it. But the fisherman whom Poshar had rescued stayed behind and simply embraced Poshar. Perhaps he would have survived even if Poshar hadn't jumped in. But it didn't matter in that moment. What moved everyone so deeply was Poshar's selflessness and sacrifice. It was unlike anything any of them had ever witnessed.

"But the extent of Poshar's legacy was yet to be seen.

"That night, the whole tribe gathered together for a celebration around a giant fire. They sang. They danced. They clapped. They ate. They asked Poshar to tell the story over and over again, listening each time as though it were the first. Other fishers chimed in with their own embellishments. The festivities continued until late into the night, when the last few people retreated to their huts and fell asleep.

"Some time later, Poshar was awakened by the sound of deep rumbling and screaming. He rushed outside to see a towering wall of flames spewing from where the center of the village once stood. He woke his wife and told her to head to safe ground before the fire spread to their house. And then, as instinctively as he had leapt into the water earlier that day, he rushed toward the flames. People were crawling out of the smoke, charred and wheezing. They were the lucky ones. Many people were still trapped. You see, at that time, the village had simply been built among the trees that grew along the shore. They didn't clear the trees before building because the trees cut the wind, muffled the sound of the crashing waves, and provided shade throughout the village on sunny days. Unfortunately, those same trees were now providing ample fuel that allowed the fire to spread quickly and devastatingly. It consumed entire huts in moments, jumping from tree to tree to tree with great speed. And it disoriented everyone who was caught alive within its walls.

"Poshar charged into the flames. The smoke immediately began reaching its fingers into his lungs, searing his throat with every breath. He could hardly see, relying primarily on the sounds of screaming to guide him. He stumbled upon three screaming children trapped in a collapsed hut. He pulled them out and carried them to a safe place beyond the edge of the fire. Caught his breath, then ran back into the flames. He stumbled upon a young woman and carried her to the same place as the children. Caught his breath, and he ran back in a third time. Two more children. By this time, the heat had badly charred him, the smoke had invaded his lungs, falling debris had injured him with blisters and burns and open wounds. As he placed the last two children safely outside the fire, he laid himself down next to them.

"He never woke up.

"There was great devastation that night. Parents lost children. Children lost parents. But there were also countless acts of heroism. Several people who had run into the flames to save others later said they had been inspired by Poshar's tale of bravery on the sea from earlier that day. Thus inspired a movement within our tribe, guided by the notion that others are more important than ourselves. Poshar embodied this not only on his last day, but every day of his life leading up to that day. This idea that our lives are best spent serving others rather than the preserving ourselves. It endures among us to this day in big ways and in small ways.

"Choosing only twelve legacies was challenging. It was equally challenging to select which of the twelve legacies to share at our very first legacy talk. But we kept coming back to Poshar's story. He could have chosen the safe path. On the boat. In the fire. No one would have criticized him for doing so. But there was something buried deeply within Poshar that sent him into the mouth of danger to save those who couldn't save themselves. And he inspired his tribe and descendant generations to put their own comfort and ease behind the needs of others. It doesn't always look as dramatic as it did for Poshar. But it is no less brave. We will need brave people to push us forward in the days to come. We will need brave people to leave the only place they've ever known and sail to a strange land so the generations after them can prosper. It would be easy for us to stay on this island in comfort, allowing the next generation to bear the pains wrought by the shortage of trees. But that isn't who you are. You are brave. You are selfless. And your legacies will echo for generations to come."

Chranit stops and turns to admire Poshar's tree. In silence, all of us admire it with him. Its mighty trunk rises from the ground, branchless at first. At roughly the height of a grown man, large branches mightily splay out in every direction, their ends curling upward. As you continue following the trunk skyward, you become lost in dense, vibrant foliage of reds and yellows and oranges that steal glory from the sun. As a child, I loved the colors. And I loved sitting at the base of the trunk, beneath the powerful branches, feeling so safe and secure, as though the whole island could be shaken but you alone would remain unscathed under its fiery canopy.

We stare at it, knowing that this is the last time most of us will see this tree standing. None of us have a recollection of the island without it. Sad to see it go. Afraid of what it means. We remain for a while, not wanting to leave. Knowing that when we leave, they will begin cutting down the tree. Knowing that the moment the first cut is made, everything will change for us forever. A foretaste of how it will feel to gaze upon this island one last time from the stern of a boat that is destined for the horizon.

The elders slowly begin making their way back down the mountain toward the village. The tribe gradually follows behind. I rise and immediately feel a warm hand on my back. Brisa. She doesn't say anything. She just continues her gait. I rush beside her. We keep formation with the rest of the tribe until the grassy valley. But as they merge down toward the village, we break away toward the New Grove.

Her pace, abrupt and determined. We don't say a word or even look at each other until we're safely under the cover of trees. But the moment we're out of sight from the rest of the tribe, Brisa relaxes. Her breathing slows and deepens. Shoulders dropped. Curious gaze. Whimsical stride. And for a moment, if only for a moment, it feels like old days once again.

Afternoons after gathering. Hiding ourselves away in the New Grove where we can be fully ourselves. Together. Losing track of time. Without the distractions or worries of the world outside. It's only a moment. But I cling to it.

"What did you think?" She breaks the silence with an innocent tone. I know this tone. It's the tone she uses when she's pondering a question that doesn't have answers. At least not easy answers. Some of my most favorite and memorable conversations with Brisa have been invoked by this tone.

"Poshar's story?" I ask. She nods. "Amazing. It makes me wonder what I would do if I were faced with those situations - the shark, the fire - would I have that kind of courage or would I have fear?"

Brisa stops and examines me for a moment. Shrivels her nose and concludes, "I think courage." Her words send a rush through my body. Returning to her original tone, she continues, "But so much cruelty…"

"What? Me?" I stutter.

"No, not you. Poshar. Or, not really Poshar, but his story. His legacy. So much cruelty…"

I skim through Poshar's story for hints of Brisa's meaning before admitting, "I don't understand."

"His legacy is bravery. But the story of his bravery is filled with so much suffering, as though the suffering is what produced his legacy. Like berry juice that can only be drawn by crushing the berry. Maybe it would be better if the fire had never happened. I'm sure Poshar would have left some other legacy with a beautiful tree that we would still admire. We are supposed to look at his tree and be reminded of bravery. But instead, I look at his tree and all I can think of is the suffering that crushed the bravery out of him. It seems cruel to me."

This catches me off guard. I had found his story so inspiring. Brisa's perspective hadn't even crossed my mind. "Are you saying that we shouldn't celebrate Poshar's legacy?"

"No," she replies quickly, choosing her next words carefully. "Bravery is a good legacy to celebrate. I want to have the kind of courage that Poshar had. But when we celebrate his legacy, it feels like we're also celebrating suffering. Because we wouldn't have known his bravery apart from the suffering. It just seems cruel to me that the only way for his legacy to be made known was for him and so many others to have to suffer so deeply."

"But isn't that what bravery is? Overcoming suffering or at least the fear of suffering? How can you have bravery without also having suffering or the threat of suffering? It seems like any story that would teach us about courage would have to involve some kind of suffering."

She considers this for a moment. "I would rather have a world without suffering," she concludes. "Without pain or death or the hurtful things people do to each other. I would be fine to live in a world without courage if it meant that we also lived in a world without suffering."

"Me too. But we don't," I say gently. "We live in a world where suffering is real. So we might as well learn and celebrate courage along the way. It's one of the few things that help us cope with the suffering."

"Why?" Her voice, pointed like a spear. "Why is suffering real? Why does it exist?"

I'm at a loss. I don't know why. I just know that it's there. "Maybe we don't understand suffering," I offer, not really comprehending my own words. "But what's the alternative? Never hurting? Never needing or wanting anything? Is that really better?"

"Yes!" Brisa exclaims as though the answer is obvious.

"No!" I exclaim back to her. "Because the things that bring suffering also bring good things - love, happiness, pleasure."

Brisa looks at me, unconvinced.

My life has been fairly free of suffering. Minor physical injuries. Rare occasions where there wasn't enough food for the tribe and we wrestled with hunger pangs through the night. Growing up without a father. My mind flashes with memories of my own limited suffering, the suffering I've witnessed in others, tearful burials of the deceased upon our sacred hills.

"For some reason," I begin slowly, "it seems like we are incomplete. Being incomplete brings us suffering. But it also causes us to reach out. It's what inspires us to love, to create, to look up to the stars and dream. If we didn't hunger, if we didn't need love or companionship, if we never hurt, why would we need each other? We couldn't make ourselves vulnerable to others, because we wouldn't have any vulnerabilities. We'd be isolated. To live without suffering would be to live without connecting to others and without imagination. But doesn't that sound sad?"

Brisa nods, considering my words, before rebutting, "It may sound sad to us, but maybe we'd be perfectly content with being isolated. If we were perfectly content without being connected to others then we'd never know the difference. We'd never feel like we were missing out on anything, right?"

"But I feel like that isn't even possible. Think about it. If we never died, never needed food or water or sleep, never hurt, never felt sadness, never became bored, what would we spend our time doing? We wouldn't strive for anything. We wouldn't create new things or have fun. We wouldn't spend time with each other. We would spend eternity just standing there, nothing to inspire us, but no sense that we need to be inspired. It seems like we are supposed to be incomplete. That being incomplete, while it may bring us suffering, it also brings us even greater fulfillment than we would have had in a world without suffering. So maybe that means that we should be less concerned about why suffering exists and more concerned about how we respond when we see suffering around us. That's really what Poshar's legacy is about. It's about reaching into the suffering of others. Maybe if we all reached into each other's suffering, there would be a lot less suffering in the world. And we'd still know the sweetness that comes with creating and connecting."

I suddenly become aware of how much I've been talking. I glance toward Brisa, who is staring at me, her mouth slightly gaping. Upon noticing me glancing at her, she breaks her gaze and closes her mouth. We walk for a while in measured paces before she responds, "That's beautiful, Uri. But even if everyone did their best to reach into everyone else's suffering, there would still be suffering."

I can tell that those words are coming from somewhere deep inside of her. "I guess there are parts of ourselves that are so incomplete," I gently acknowledge, "even other people can't complete them for us."

We don't talk for the rest of the hike, both

of us lost in thought. But as we cross into the edge of the village, Brisa leans into me and kisses my cheek before parting from me. The kiss never leaves me. For the next month, everywhere I go, every plank I fasten to boats, every meal I eat, I feel the persistence of that kiss. The softness of her lips. The warmth of her breath. The residual excitement radiating through my body.

It takes the wood cutters several days to cut down Poshar's tree. Its ancient trunk stronger than any of the native trees that they had cut before, dulling cutting tools and exhausting muscles. And when it was finally fashioned into a mast, a large group of people had to carry it down the mountain, through the village, to the shore. As it passed through the village, everyone stopped whatever they were doing and solemnly watched it pass them by. This pillar of our tribe's history. This looming legacy.

Gone.

And, yet, with us now in a new kind of way. A more important way. Poshar's courage sustaining our courage. Calling out to us as we embark on a new, perilous path. We will need his kind of courage to succeed. To survive.

By the end of the first month, the test boat has been repaired and Poshar's tree has been set in place as its mast. The old mast had made the entire boat look lopsided. Too short. Too skinny. But now, with Poshar's mast in place, it looks perfect. Powerful. Courageous. Though stripped bare of its branches and leaves, it retains its grandeur.

With the leftover wood from Poshar's tree, the wood cutters found ways to cut usable planks and posts that can also be used for the rudders, shrouds, keels, and cross-beams. Several other boats, already in various stages of construction, line the shore. Chuan's goal is for us to always have a boat ready to receive a mast and to always have plenty of work for everyone to do.

By the end of the month, the second boat is ready for its mast. The second mast. The second tree. The second moon.

Chapter 8
The Second Moon

The morning of the second full moon is marked by the same calm as the first. I step outside my hut and look out over the harbor. Poshar's mast reaches toward the sky - a proud testament to the tribe's effort and diligence over the last three months. We've poured ourselves into work like never before. All of us. With so many people cutting wood, making ropes, and building boats, the others in the village have had to work harder and longer as well just to keep the village functioning.

A collective fatigue veils the faces of those of us gathered at the edge of the village awaiting Chranit's arrival. We all look a little more tired. A little less talkative. A little less excited to be awake so early. This is no way to live. But we endure it, doing our best to keep our spirits lifted, because we know it's temporary and it's for a purpose. This voyage is the legacy we will leave to our children and their children when we've settled in a new land.

Legacy.

The word has assumed a certain intensity lately. From the time we are children, we are taught to think about our legacies. We are taken on hikes through the Grove of Ancestors so we can crane our necks at the imposing legacies on display. We are taught stories and challenged to think about what our story will be. When someone dies, we gather at sunrise - much like we have been doing for these legacy talks - and hike up the hill to the New Grove. We bury the deceased as the people they loved tell stories of the legacy that the person left with them. Then we hike back down in silence and spend the rest of the day remembering the person, remembering their legacy, and pondering the legacy of our own lives.

So the concept of legacy is always on our minds, even in normal times. But in normal times, it's on our minds the same way that the island itself is on our minds - part of our way of life, a constant presence, an inescapable reality. Lately, however, the concept of legacy has become an obsession. We think about it all the time. We talk about it all the time. It carries a weight with it that has begun to feel more like a burden than a reminder. And, for all that we obsess over it, I'm not even sure we fully understand it - elusive and mysterious like the monsters of the sea.

Chranit strolls through the crowd and continues up the hillside toward the Old Grove with the tribe in tow. He leads us past the site of last month's legacy talk, now a yawning cavern in the forest. A gaping hole in the canopy of leaves. Even if I weren't aware that an enormous tree once stood in this place, I would be able to tell that something wasn't quite right. Something isn't as it should be. The grove hasn't adjusted yet. Neither have we. People slow down to admire the broad and mighty stump where Poshar's tree once stood. There's a sense of longing for the tree to be back in its place coupled with this sense of gratitude for what the sacrifice of this tree means for our tribe and for the Grove of Ancestors as a whole.

I'm suddenly more convinced than ever of Chief Sangra's reasons for refusing to cut down the Grove of Ancestors. I envision barren hillsides full of lonely stumps. Fallen legacies. Abandoned histories. Though they would never be intentionally abandoned, they would eventually be forgotten. Even without the blazing foliage of Poshar's tree, we could certainly value courage. But forty generations from now, would we have forgotten what courage looks like? Or would our definition of it have become diluted? Misguided? Reinterpreted to something totally different than it truly is? It's hard to know. And probably not worth the risk to find out.

The tree to which Chranit leads us is another familiar one. By far, it's the best climbing tree on the entire island. I have memories of entire days spent playing up and down the branches of this particular tree. So numerous, you could climb it a hundred times and never climb the same route twice. We would climb as high as we could, until our queasy stomachs told us that we had climbed high enough. And then we would try to climb just a little bit higher anyway. Races. Climbing games. Afternoons perched in its branches, letting time drift by like the clouds above.

Chranit stops at the base of this tree. We fill in the hillside above.

"Throw a rock into water," he begins. "Ripples shoot out in every direction around it. The rock sinks from view. But the ripples keep going. So it is with legacies. Long after the bearer of the legacy is gone, the ripples of their legacy continue through the hearts and minds of every life they impacted. Across the endless surface of time. Even if you never saw the impact of the rock, you can understand much about it just by studying its ripples. You can look at the size of the ring or ripples and understand how long ago it happened. You can look at the height of the waves of that ring and understand how big the rock was. You can find the center of the ring to judge the place where the impact occurred.

"Last full moon, we stood near this very spot to honor the story of Poshar. His legacy of courage. His willingness to confront danger, overcoming his own fears and reservations, in order to obtain some greater thing. Courage is accepting the most negative possible outcome and deciding that the most positive possible outcome outweighs it. It's sacrifice. For Poshar, his courage was evidenced by the sacrifice of his own life to save the lives of others. Twice. He felt that those lives were more important than his own. So he jumped into the water. So he ran into the flames.

"Out of the flames, he pulled six people – five children and a young woman. Their families' lives were lost. Brothers, sisters, parents, the young woman's new husband. And they were badly injured by the flames which would have taken their lives if it weren't for Poshar's courage. Together, these six survivors, buffeted by the ripples of Poshar's legacy, were about to learn a kind of courage of their own.

"The young woman whom Poshar rescued, Raksa, awoke several days after the fire. In pain. Disoriented. Flashes of memory from the fateful night. Flames. A thunderous crash. Her husband, pinned beneath a flaming corner of their hut which had collapsed in on itself. She was too shocked and powerless to do anything about it. Then, blackness.

"Now there was daylight. And pain. Extreme pain. It hurt to move. The simple act of opening her eyes sent pain searing through her. As she cracked them open, adjusting to the bright daylight, she could make out the silhouette of her dearest friend sitting by her side. Crying. Raksa was concerned and confused by her friend's sadness and tried to sit up to console her. But the pain sent her back to the ground, writhing, screaming, sobbing. She passed out and didn't wake up again for several days.

"When she awoke again, the slightest movements still sent shocks of pain throughout her body. She tried speaking, but her face burned when she moved her lips. She tried uttering simple sounds, but the smoke still hadn't left her lungs and nothing came out. Perhaps she would have lost hope if her friend hadn't been by her side comforting her, whispering into her ear that everything would be alright. And that's exactly what her friend did. For an entire moon cycle.

The breadth and depth of Raksa's wounds were substantial. Her body needed healing from the flames. Her mind needed healing from the fear. Her heart needed healing from the loss of her husband, her home, her life as she knew it. The sorrow nearly overtook her at times. She envisioned herself walking into the ocean until she was completely submerged, until the last gasp of air left her lungs, and allow the ocean to forever relieve her of this great suffering. But something inside of her held on.

"After the passing of another moon cycle,

Raksa had healed enough that she was able to move. She was eventually able to sit up. Then, eventually, to stand. Then, eventually, to walk. Painfully, but surely. The first place she walked was to the hut where the five children that Poshar had rescued were healing. Raksa's friend had told her about them and how their entire families - parents, aunts, uncles, grandparents - had perished in the fire. The tribe had been pulling together to care for them, but their long-term prospects were still uncertain.

"They were lost and lonely. Just like her. So she walked to their tent and sat with them. They shared many of the same physical scars as Raksa. Being so young, the children had been healing at a much faster pace than she. But their hidden scars - scars of loneliness, scars of anguish, scars of fear - were still as tender as hers. That first day, they just sat together. They didn't do anything, they didn't say anything. They just sat. But somehow, the simple act of being together was like a balm on their hidden scars.

"Day after day, Raksa returned to their tent. To be together. To help each other heal. To figure out where their lives would go from there. Broken as they were, they felt awkwardly complete when they were all together. Soon, Raksa began sleeping in their tent with them. They shared meals. They shared life. They had all the markings of a family: a messy, hodgepodge family, but the closest thing to a family that any of them had anymore. They were gradually becoming a family unlike any family that the tribe had ever seen before. Five children, some from different parents than others; one very young 'mother', who wasn't actually related to any of them; no father. It was awkwardly natural.

"At first, people were skeptical. Some doubted Raksa's ability. Her stability. Her commitment. But as the years passed and this family only grew stronger, those doubts were stilled. And something else happened. The tribe began to learn a more generous definition of family. They showed it in how they supported Raksa and her family, which spilled over into how they cared for their own families. These children went from having mothers and fathers to having no mothers and fathers to having only a single mother to eventually having more mothers and fathers than they could count. They would spend their entire lives healing, but they would never lack love.

"And this tree is an invitation to all of the children of the island - as it has been for generations - to come to it whether you are sad or lonely or happy, to climb up into its branches, and to remember: you are loved, and you will never be without family."

With the last syllable of Chranit's story, a

high-pitched scream bursts forth from somewhere in the crowd. Every head turns. A young child pulls himself free from his mother's restraint and sprints toward Raksa's tree. Upon reaching the tree, he jumps, grabs one of the lower branches, and after trying unsuccessfully to pull himself up, lets himself dangle freely. There's a moment of hushed surprise before more high-pitched screams burst forth from the crowd, from other children charging headlong toward Raksa's tree. The elders try to dodge out of their way. A few are trampled. They fall to the ground and sit themselves back up with laughter. The children scale the branches, realizing that this is their last chance to climb one of their favorite trees. Several adults join the children. They flop over the branches legs kicking, trying to pull themselves up as the kids do with ease, as they probably once did with ease when they were children. A few fall off the branches and back to the ground. A few give up trying and hang limp, slung over the branch like fabric hung to dry. The children in the trees point and laugh, as do the adults scattered on the hillside.

We've needed this. We've needed something to give us reprieve from the stresses and strenuous routines that have come to fill our days. Something to lift the fatigue from our eyes so we can smile. Laugh. Play. Even for a moment.

We stay for a while before heading back to the village. Our faces and stomachs hurt from laughing so much. One of the best aches I've ever felt.

But for me, that ache is slowly replaced by another ache. Reflecting on Raksa's story, I can't help but reflect upon my own. Of growing up without a father, who died on a fishing excursion long before I could walk or talk or capture memories. For as long as I can remember, I've heard stories about who he was, what he liked to do, what he meant to people. And when my mother speaks of him, she still gets this very particular smile in the corner of her mouth. A smile I only see when she speaks of him. His smile.

My entire life, even after my own father had departed, I was never without some semblance of a father. Men who loved my father took it upon themselves to care for me. To be my dad for me. They would do things with me that other kids' dads did with them – teach me, challenge me, encourage me, take me on adventures, show me how to do the things that they do. Men like Brisa's father, who was on the boat with my dad on the day that he died. I have countless memories with Brisa's father. Walking along the shore. Teaching me how to tie knots. Preparing me to become a fisherman. Chasing across the grassy plain. Play fighting with sticks. Swimming in the bay, racing from one end to the other. As I've grown older, I've spent increasingly more time with Brisa and increasingly less time with Brisa's father. If it bothers him, he doesn't show it. But I still feel guilty from time to time.

Despite the myriad of fathers in my life, each of them has been only a piece of a father to me. And even the sum of all those pieces couldn't replace a whole dad. Today I feel the weight of his absence more than I've felt it in a long time. Walking down the hill to the village, I scan the crowd and find my oldest sister, Annak. I walk to her side. She looks at me warmly.

"Want to walk?" She asks, as though she already knows what's on my mind.

I nod. We cut across the grassy plain toward the New Grove. The day is perfect. The sun. The breeze. The air. Perfect. Clouds race overhead, sending patches of light and shade racing across the plain.

"What's on your mind, Uri?" She eventually asks with sincere concern in her voice.

"Dad." I say plainly, afraid that if I try to say too much I might lose control of the tears that I'm fighting to keep at bay.

"Me too." She confesses somberly. "It's hard to hear a story like that and not think about him." My oldest sister was old enough to remember him well. My other sister is also older than me, but too young to remember much more than passing images of him. But my oldest sister remembers him in completeness. Not just his voice, but his words. Not just his face, but his expressions. Not just his figure, but his actions. She remembers the person he was. The meaningful as well as the mundane. Him.

"Why do I care about him so much?" I ask. "I never even met him."

Annak tilts her head and looks up to the sky. "There's something about a father…" she trails off, lost in thought. Just as I think I might have lost her, she continues, "Moms help you love who you are. Dads help you love who you can be. You are starting to discover who you can be. But you don't have dad with you to help you see it. Maybe that's why he's on your mind. You're longing for someone who can help you love the person you can be."

We trace the edge of the New Grove with slow, thoughtful steps. "Do I remind you of him?" I ask hopefully.

She cracks a smile, like mom's when she thinks of my dad, and without hesitation replies, "Your imagination. He had an amazing imagination. The games we would play. The adventures we would have. What an imagination! You have it too, Uri. Your dreams. The stories you tell. The way you lose yourself in your thoughts. The adventures you would lead your friends on when you were growing up. Your imagination reminds me of his."

I smile at her words, at the thought that I share something that is so personal to me with him. We approach a post with a legacy stone in its top. No tree to accompany it. Carved into the legacy stone is the phrase: *39. Miras. Lights in the Sky.* The thirty-ninth generation; Miras, my father; Lights in the Sky.

Brisa's dad once told me the story of how my father died. They were fishing a far distance from the island. A storm came upon them violently and suddenly, before they could make it back to the shore. Fishers know how to wait out storms. But something happened for which none of them were prepared. A bolt of lightning came screaming from the clouds, striking the mast of the boat. The blast sent them flying overboard. All but two of them were able to pull themselves back onto the boat, injured and badly shaken. The other two were never found. One of them was my dad. Because my dad's body was never found, he was never buried. Because he was never buried, he has no tree to proclaim his legacy. Just a post with a stone to mark his time and place in our tribe.

"So," I ask, "if our dad doesn't have a tree, does that mean that he doesn't have a legacy?"

Annak shifts her focus from his legacy stone to me, with a look on her face like I've just said something outrageous. "It isn't about trees, Uri. You know that, right? The trees help us remember. But there are other things to help us remember, too."

"Like what?"

"Like people who knew him. Like his family. You are his legacy, Uri. I am his legacy. Every life that he touched. Every mouth that the fish he caught fed. This island is full of his legacy."

"What do you think dad's tree would have looked like?" I ask, losing the fight to keep my tears at bay.

The pensive look returns to her face as she slowly recalls, "I remember his big, strong arms. Every time he hugged me, I'd get buried in them. They were the safest place I've ever been. He always took me down to the shore to tell me stories about the ocean. Like the ocean was his closest friend. And he loved fishing. *Loved* fishing. But a tree?" She closes her eyes, trying to imagine it. "Maybe the trunk of his tree would be thick, like his arms. Strong and unmovable like a rock. But, then, the branches would be different. Tender. Like vines drooping down off of the trunk all the way back to the ground. Hundreds of them. Entwined with one another like a fishing net. And when the wind blows, it wraps you in that net. And you feel lost, safe, like you could stay there forever…" She trails off again as tears crest the corners of her eyes.

I wait for her to continue. When it's clear

that she is completely lost in a longing, happy memory, I close my eyes and go to that place with her.

Standing at the foot of a trunk as solid as stone. A thousand green branches hanging down, swaying in the sunlight, obscuring my view. Catching me in their net.

Dad.

Chapter 9

The Third Moon

Annak and I descend from the New Grove to the village as Chief Sangra and several Council members storm past us on their way out of the village. They don't even make eye contact with us. Annak and I exchange a confused expression and continue our walk into the village. Then it hits us. A wall of stench affronts our nostrils. A stench that is reminiscent of the sea, but foul. Rotting fish. Down by the place on the shore where the fishing boats berth, you can faintly detect this smell. But it has never overpowered the entire village like this before. I gag. Annak heaves.

I pinch my nose as I step through the village. People are pulling rotting fish from every imaginable place. Rotting fish in huts. Rotting fish behind trees. Rotting fish hidden around fire pits. Rotting fish everywhere. People pinch their noses with one hand and the tails of rotting fish with the other. They dump them in fire pits to burn them. Some people, overwhelmed by the smell, rush out of the village covering their mouths, in search of fresh air.

It isn't immediately obvious to me how the fish could have found their way into the village, until Mehan comes stumbling out of his hut with his mouth and nose buried in his elbow and a rotting fish corpse in hand. His eyes catch mine and in them I see a rage like I've never seen from him before. In his eyes I see echoes of the expressions I saw on the faces of Chief Sangra and the other Council members as they stormed past us toward Abis' village. And then it becomes obvious to me: Abis' village planted these here while everyone in our village was at the legacy talk.

But why? Why would they do this?

Suddenly, I'm reminded of the Council meeting where the decision was made to cut twelve trees from the Grove of Ancestors. And the warning that Abis would respond with fury. This is his response. A response to everything he resents about us: the cutting of legacy trees, the exchange of berries for fish, the decision to leave the island.

The air, reeking of death and decay, hangs heavy over the village as the fibers that have woven our tribe together for forty generations fray and unravel.

• • •

"This is inexcusable! We can't stand for it!" A Council member shouts across the Forum.

The faint odor of rotting persists in the air, though all of the fish have been burned by now.

“What can we possibly do?” Another Council member shouts in reply, exasperated. “What do they have to lose and what do we have to gain?”

“They can lose their village. Their freedom to roam the island. Instead of placing our watchers outside of our village, why not place the watchers outside of theirs? Contain them to their corner of the island so they can’t threaten us anymore.” A few nods of approval from around the room.

“We would only provoke them,” the second Council member retorts. “They would revolt. If we wanted to be successful with that course of action, we would need to place dozens of additional watchers around their village. And we don’t have dozens of people to spare. We need them building boats.”

“What then?” The first Council member seethes. “We just live in fear of them? Allow them to abuse us however they wish?”

“We have no reason to fear them,” Chief Sangra interrupts. “They won’t harm us. They know there will be consequences for any further aggressions against us. Indeed, there have already been consequences for their actions today.”

“What consequences, Chief?” A Council member asks. Chief Sangra doesn’t respond.

Instead, he simply locks in a stare with the Council member asking the question. A loaded silence.

Chief Sangra slowly, ominously reiterates, "I assure you, they won't be bothering us again. The morning of the next full moon, we will meet at the edge of the village. Chranit will walk us into the Grove of Ancestors to deliver a legacy talk. We will return to our village, undisturbed. Abis and his village won't bother us anymore." Another loaded silence. I become uneasy in my seat. Chief Sangra shakes off the silence, his voice slightly softening, "These legacy trees evoke emotion in us all. Emotion that leads us to desperate actions. I fear what this island is quickly becoming…" Sadness in his tenor. He adjourns the Council meeting and exits the room without speaking to anyone.

What does he mean? What is this island becoming?

• • •

Is it possible for time to accelerate? A day doesn't feel like a day to me anymore. Boats are being built more quickly than I can keep track of. No sooner have we descended the mountain from the second legacy talk than it feels like we're ascending it for the third.

Except for Mehan. He has appointed himself guardian of the village while the rest of the tribe attends legacy talks. Of course, if Chief Sangra knew about it, he would promptly remove Mehan from his self-appointed post, which is why all of this must be done in secret. Mehan is hiding somewhere back in the village. When we're out of sight, he will … well, I don't know exactly what he will do, except that whatever it is will make him feel like he's doing the tribe some great service. I would rather have him at the legacy talk. There is more to be gained on the mountain than there is to be lost in the village.

Two stumps. Poshar's. Now Raksa's. Their absence from the forest conspicuous. The forest hasn't filled their place. It won't fill their place. Not this forest. The native trees in the valley replenish themselves by growing new shoots from cut stumps and by dropping seeds to grow new trees. But the trees in the Grove of Ancestors are different. Each tree is without predecessor and without successor because each tree comes from somewhere other than the forest itself. Though its roots are planted in soil, it rises from somewhere other than the soil. Though its branches stretch toward the sun, its nourishment comes from somewhere other than the sun. Though it's composed of wood, it exists for a much nobler purpose than to simply offer its wood. It exists to point us back to the place from which it came. And when one of them is gone, a window to that place is gone with it. And a piece of us follows.

Once again, every eye takes notice of the bare stumps. Chranit leads us to a tree not too far past them, a tree with which I am unfamiliar. We seat ourselves uphill from it.

"Two months ago," Chranit begins, "we told the story of Poshar and we learned of courage and sacrifice. Last month, we told the story of Raksa, the young woman he pulled from the fire, and we learned of the true nature of family. This month, we tell the story of Gueris, one of the children Poshar pulled from the fire, whom Raksa raised, and we learn about healing.

"Let's go back to that day that Raksa was first able to make the walk from her hut to theirs. When she walked into the hut, she found five badly injured children. Injured bodies, injured minds, injured hearts. When Raksa walked into their hut that very first time, the children winced upon seeing her. The flames had disfigured her, but she hadn't realized exactly how badly until she saw the looks on their faces. Had they allowed their relationship to be defined by that first reaction, they might never have become a family. Instead, they were able to see through each other's scars.

"The littlest of the children, a girl named Gueris, was especially intrigued by Raksa, captivated by this idea that a person's body could change while the person that they are could stay the same. Raksa's injuries caused her to look different from every other person on the island. And yet, inside, she was no different from every other person on the island. For a young girl, this was a striking realization.

"As the children grew, so did their love for Raksa. She helped them feel safe; they helped her feel beautiful. Together, they helped each other feel loved. Sometimes the children would have nightmares of the fire, and Raksa would be by their side comforting them. Sometimes Raksa would start to feel lonely and become quiet, and one of the children – usually Gueris – would sit beside her until she could remember that she was loved. When Raksa's wounds cracked or blistered or itched, Gueris would carefully rub a balm on them and wrap them in soaked leaves. While this helped alleviate some of Raksa's pain, nothing Gueris did could ever completely remove it. Once the balm and leaves were applied and Raksa continued to writhe, Gueris could only sit by her side, whispering encouragements into her ear, crying a little bit, herself.

"Perhaps what Gueris failed to realize was that her mere presence by Raksa's side was an act of healing in itself. It gave Raksa's heart something to cling to when her hands were too weak to cling to anything else. Gueris' compassion and empathy were a balm that soothed Raksa's entire being. And that's what

Gueris' legacy proclaims. Empathy. The simple yet profound act of walking with another person in their joys and in their sorrows; their euphoria and their pain; their abundance and their need. To see beyond appearances and circumstances, into the person themselves. It's in this way that we are able to truly love one another. Gueris reminds us to be a balm to those around us.

"And she continues to be a balm to us to this day, both in the story of her legacy as well as the tree that bears her legacy. The leaves of her tree - like the leaves of others who have followed in her example - can be broken, and a soothing ointment flows from them. It's a reminder of her empathy. That when someone is hurting, we allow ourselves to hurt with them as they heal.

"On this third moon, we complete a succession of legacies. How the bravery of one led to the generous love of another; how that generous love led to the deep empathy of yet another. Poshar surrendered his life pulling six people from the fire; those six people spent the rest of their lives helping one another heal as a family. What we do during our days on this island matters. We impact the lives of the people around us and our legacies impact the lives of generations to come. The elders decided to begin these legacy talks with three stories that powerfully demonstrate this truth. Never underestimate the impact of anything you do. Every action is a ripple. And every ripple can either reinforce or disrupt the legacies that radiate throughout our tribe to shape us into the people we are today. My challenge to you this morning is to be reinforcers, not disruptors. The disruptors are more prominent than ever before. And this comes at a time when our tribe is more in need of reinforcers than ever before. Reinforcers who will live out every moment and action with the legacies behind us and before us in mind."

Chranit says those last words through a giant smile. The crowd stirs. People turn to those sitting around them. Children hop to their feet and chase one another. I stand and stretch. A short distance from me, I see Chuan doing the same. He nods at me and smiles. I walk over to him.

"Back to boat building?" I ask.

Chuan nods as he yawns. "I suppose they won't build themselves."

We walk together down the hill toward the shore. As we exit the Old Grove, Chuan says, "We'll be seeing Gueris again soon. She'll look different. We'll attach her to a boat. She'll sail us to a faraway land. Then, who knows? No one knows. What a strange mission we have undertaken. Do you ever think about that, Uri?"

"Every day," I reply.

"Me too," he confesses, surprised by my candor. "I guess everyone who spends their days building boats spends their days thinking about that, don't they? It's hard to ignore from the shore."

"Probably some more than others. The work is so physical. It's easy to get lost in it and not think about much else. But until recently, I was a gatherer. A gatherer's work is less physical, more mental - looking for berries, figuring out how to get to berries, picking berries. We spend a lot of time thinking while working. A lot of time dreaming. I guess I brought a little of that habit with me to the shore. It's hard for me to force myself to stop thinking about this mission that changed everything for me. I thought it was just a dream. It turned out to be so much more."

"Do you still dream?" Chuan asks.

His question catches me off guard. I try to remember any recent dreams, unable to recall any since the third of the boat dreams. Nothing that stands out or that I can recall with any clarity. "I guess not." Chuan's question and my admission make me suddenly self-conscious about my lack of dreams. "Why?" I ask.

"I assumed you dreamed all the time. It's your legacy, isn't it?"

"Is it?" I ask, noticing an unintentional defensiveness in my tone. "But I don't play any part in creating the dreams. They just happen to me while I'm asleep. Is that a legacy?"

"Well, not when you say it that way. Maybe don't think of it that way. Instead, maybe think of it like you are the person who envisioned the boats that will rescue our tribe. That's a legacy."

While it sounds nobler, I'm still skeptical. Partly because I didn't really envision the boats on my own - they appeared to me randomly in a dream - and partly because I don't know for certain if they will actually rescue the tribe or not. But I don't suggest that to Chuan, since he has invested so much of himself in the idea that they will. Instead I ask try to take the focus off of me by asking him, "What do you think your legacy will be?"

"I hope it's for building boats."

"That's not a legacy," I chuckle, "that's an occupation."

"Well then I hope it's for building *beautiful* boats." He replies, agitated.

"Better. But I still don't think that's quite how it works."

With that, we step onto the shore and our conversation is supplanted by a silent shared awe of the boats lining the water's edge. Two masts are in place. Tall. Commanding. Hopeful. They make me hopeful, too.

I spend the rest of the day working, nagged by Chuan's suggestion that the dreams are my legacy. Or that boat building is his. There has to be more to it than that. Right?

Chapter 10
The Fourth Moon

Sunrise on the dawn of the fourth full moon.

For some reason, I'm awake especially early this morning. Early enough to look from my hut across the darkness to a night sky that is just beginning to glow in preparation for the sun. I lay at my doorstep and watch it grow.

The sunrise. Our beacon of hope each new day. Nine months from now, we will point our boats toward the place where the sun rises and forever leave this island behind. What lies beyond the horizon? Where does the sun come from every morning? If only it could tell us. If only it bore some clues of the place from which it comes. Something to let us know what to expect. To let us know if our fortunes will be better beyond the horizon, or if it would be better for us to stay where we are. If only it could tell us.

Will the journey be long? Will our destination be similar to this place, or will it be entirely different? Is there even a destination for us to find? If we reach land, will there already be another tribe established in that place? What would they be like? How would they receive us?

The glow in the sky catches fire as the top of the sun crests the horizon. And with it, any hope that I might fall back asleep evaporates. I pick myself up from the ground and walk down to the edge of where the village meets the shore. Sit down in the cool sand. And watch the sky fire grow and glow.

As the bottom of the sun clears the horizon, I hear a set of feet shuffling through the sand behind me. The feet come to rest beside me and a body lowers to the sand. Brisa. I recognize her by the warmth that she emanates wherever she goes. I turn to look at her, struck by the beauty of the sunrise across her face. The smoothness of her skin. The breeze gently playing with her hair. This is how I want to see every sunrise. Feeling my gaze, she cracks a smile, keeping her attention fixed upon the sunrise.

"So beautiful." She breaks the silence with wistful words. "Every morning, we get this gift, this amazing gift. And every evening we are given an amazing sunset. Our world is so full of beauty. And yet so much brokenness. Or, what did you call it? Incompleteness. I've been thinking about that conversation a lot over the past few months. Do you remember it?"

"Of course." Every day.

Brisa's hand finds mine. "I love seeing the world through your eyes. You see the incompleteness but look past it to see the beauty. Me, I'm distracted by the incompleteness most of the time. Everything feels incomplete. I love being with you because you help me to see the beauty, too."

I lace my fingers with hers as I reply, "For me, when I see the incompleteness, it helps me to appreciate the beauty all the more. Like the sunrise. The darkness of the fading night makes the colors of the sunrise all the more stark and vibrant."

"But for me, when I see little glimpses of beauty, they only remind me how fleeting they are. The sunrise only reminds me of how much darkness there is in the sky."

"But the sunrise overcomes the darkness."

"Only until sunset, when light fizzles out in glory and darkness reigns once again."

We catch ourselves, both of us noticing the escalating pace and volume of our voices. The crashing waves disperse the tension and draw our eyes back toward the sun.

Brisa calmly continues. "When I cover my face, when I go into my house in midday, there is darkness. This world isn't made in light. It's made in darkness. The light is foreign. You focus on how the light pierces through that darkness; meanwhile, I focus on how, without the light, there is nothing except darkness. And I wish I could see the world the way you do. But I can't."

"Brisa-"

"You have these magnificent dreams, Uri. Dreams of boats like no one has ever seen before. Boats that will rescue our tribe. Boats that will set us free across the horizon. I have dreams too, Uri. I dream that I'm tiptoeing along the highest peak of the highest mountain on the island. And there's a storm coming. I'm trying to keep my balance, but the wind is raging, raging, raging. It gets stronger with every step I take. Until finally I lose my footing and slip. I fall. I go crashing through the trees. Crashing, crashing, crashing. Waiting to hit the ground. But I never do. Instead, the trees eventually give way to open air, and I'm falling forever. Like I'm falling into the sky. Then I wake up. But even when I wake up, I still feel like I'm falling. I always feel like I'm falling."

Tears carve wide paths down Brisa's cheeks. I wrap my arms around her as tightly as I can as she leans into my side. I want to tell her that I'll never let her fall. But even I know that's a promise that no one should ever make. So I just hold her, giving her a safe place to cry, holding back tears of my own. I can always give her a safe place to cry.

For as long as I've known Brisa, I've known her gnawing struggle against this peculiar, ever-present sorrow. It's such a contrast to the whimsical, curious, peaceful demeanor that she typically radiates. She's the embodiment of the wind that journeys from horizon to horizon, gently brushing past everything it encounters along the way. But even the wind doesn't always blow mild. When the clouds darken and the rain pours down, the wind bears a dark oppression of its own. Eventually the storm passes and the wind returns to grace. And it might be days or it might be months before it storms again.

I understand her struggle and I don't. I see the sadness she sees: death, suffering, loss, pain. But to me, they seem like part of the natural cycle of the world. There is good and there is bad. She sees it differently. From her perspective, the bad doesn't belong. It stains the good. And as long as the bad remains, the world is off-balance. And she is nagged by this suspicion that one day it will throw her off-balance, too. From time to time, this suspicion makes its way to the surface and her lofty breezes become tempestuous gales. And until the storm passes, she looks for a safe place. To talk. To cry. To sit in silence. I hope I will always be that safe place for her.

The sunrise blends into daylight. Brisa isn't crying anymore, but she's still leaning into my side. If we could, I would stay in this place with her forever. If I could hold back the sunrise and freeze it at just the right place. If I could wipe the tears from Brisa's eyes. I would stay on this beach holding her for the rest of our lives. Just being close. Never needing anything more.

But the world isn't satisfied to have us sit idly for the rest of time. The sound of stirring from the village as people make their way toward its edge to await Chranit beckons us to leave the beach and join them. I give Brisa a gentle squeeze. She nods, knowingly. We rise and walk in silence toward the group. It's a comfortable silence. The kind of silence that I sometimes see shared between couples who have loved each other for most of their long lives. I imagine what it would be like to be one of those couples with Brisa. On a distant land. Discovering new places. New adventures.

Chranit leads us up to a different part of the Old Grove from our previous legacy talks. Further uphill and more central. When we're settled, he begins, "Over the past three months, we've celebrated three different legacies. And, yet, in some strange way, all of their legacies are the same legacy. Gueris may have never left a legacy of healing if it weren't for Raksa's love. Neither Raksa nor Gueris would have had the chance to offer those legacies if it hadn't been for Poshar's courage. So, in a way, you could say that Gueris' legacy is also Poshar's just as Raksa's is also Gueris'. And so on. Ripples.

"But, as you know, a puddle of water in the middle of the island cannot send ripples out into the ocean. Nor do its ripples travel through other puddles on the island. In order for ripples to travel, water must be gathered together, not separated.

"This is why we live as a village. Gathered together, we impact one another more deeply than we ever could living isolated. Some of that impact is negative. People steal. People gossip. People lie. People anger and begrudge. It happens. But the positive impact we have on each other far outweighs the negative. We share resources. We share time. We laugh. We help each other. We comfort each other. We challenge one another to live out great legacies.

"We haven't always lived together as a tribe. Almost immediately after arriving on this island, we were in conflict with one another. The tribe was split in half. And even within those divisions, there was conflict. For three generations. Divided. Opposed. Conflicted.

"Then, there was peace. It came so abruptly, so unexpectedly, that the tribe struggled to remember what it meant to be a tribe. We suddenly had the opportunity to transition from surviving to thriving, but it's as though people had forgotten how to thrive. We accept our village life today as a given. It comes naturally, almost without effort. But it wasn't given to us. We had to learn it for ourselves. People had to learn how to trust and to serve one another. And before they could learn it, they had to desire it. After three generations of strife, too few people desired it.

"So for the next few generations after peace was established, our tribe was able to maintain some sense of order and stability. But you would hardly consider us a tribe the way we're a tribe today. Families settled and built their homes scattered all over the island. Over the generations, the families grew into small clans. They provided for their own needs. Carried their own water. Gathered their own berries. Caught their own fish. Built and mended their own homes. Tended their own fires. Cut their own wood. They did pretty much everything for themselves, by themselves. A family carved out its existence, while another family not too far away carved out its own. This is how we lived for nearly six generations after peace was established.

"So we continued to merely survive. We gradually looked less like a tribe and more like a group of people who happened to share an island. People occasionally reached out to neighbors, but mostly everyone kept to themselves. You can almost think of peace at that time as little more than an absence of conflict. By that definition, we were living in peace. But the number of people and the number of clans was growing and it was becoming clearer and clearer that we couldn't carry on this way much longer before conflicts over land and resources would ensue once again.

"A new vision was needed. And in the tenth generation, a new vision was born.

"In those days, a lonely hut sat at the end of the bay where our village now stands. In those days, people came down to the bay to fish. Since we didn't have fishing boats, it was necessary to wade into the water and cast nets. The bay, being the only safe place to do that, became a sort of common area where people came to fish or barter with people who fished. Because of the constant fishing traffic, the noise of bartering, and the pungent smells left by people who cleaned their fish on the shore and left the entrails behind, no one lived by the bay, save one lonely hut in which a woman lived with her ailing parents.

"Her name was Gemen. Her parents had been ill for most of her life. She was their only child. They were without siblings or parents of their own. So it was just the three of them in a tiny hut, carving out a meager life. You can imagine how difficult it would be to tend to all of a single person's needs; imagine how exhausting it would be to single-handedly tend to the needs of three! Some days, her parents felt well enough to pitch in. But most days, the responsibility fell solely on Gemen. From childhood into womanhood, Gemen dutifully carried out this responsibility, to the exclusion of nearly everything else.

"Then, one fateful morning, Gemen went to

rouse her mother. Only her mother didn't rouse. She had passed in the night - quietly, peacefully, and without warning. Gemen wept alone over her mother, gazing upon her face one final time. Her mother's face no longer appeared pained. It was relieved, relaxed, even youthful. And altogether beautiful.

"Gemen roused her father and told him the news. They cried together and then spent the day just sitting together, breaking from all of the duties of the household to fondly and lovingly remember their wife and mother. They shared stories. They admired her beauty, both in life and now in death. Toward the end of the day, Gemen's father told her how much her selfless service had meant to them over the years. And when he laid down that night, he looked deeply into her eyes and told her how much he loved her. That night, in his sleep, he breathed his last.

"When morning came, Gemen didn't even go to rouse him. Somehow, she knew. In the span of two sunrises, she had lost the only two people she had in her life. Aged beyond her years (though her years themselves were reasonably advanced), she spent the remainder of the day grasping the reality of this new situation. Alone. Without the responsibility of caring for her parents to fill her time.

"She slept that night, and in the morning, she set out to bury her parents. It was a long hike from her hut by the bay to the mountainside of the Old Grove, which was at that time the entirety of the Grove of Ancestors. Gemen slid her arms under her mother, who was surprisingly light. She was able to inch her way out the front door before having to stop and catch her breath. But even in the time it took to catch her breath, her mother's weight became more apparent. She needed to set her down and rest.

"After resting, Gemen bent down to pick her mother back up, but couldn't lift her above her knees before having to set her back down again. She quickly realized that there was no way she was going to get her parents to the hillside. The only option she had was to slide them into the sea. She grieved the thought of letting their memory slip into the ocean, gone forever. Ashamed that the reason they had to be buried this way was because she was too weak to carry them. She grabbed her mother's ankles and started to drag her step by step. Every few steps she had to stop and catch her breath.

"A young man who was wading into the bay to cast his net happened to see this scene unfolding. Up to that point, we watched with a morbid curiosity, unsure of how to strike up a conversation with a stranger carrying a corpse. But when he saw Gemen change course from the hillside to the ocean, he dropped his net and went running to her, calling for her to stop.

"They spoke for a while that day. He learned her story and her recent dilemma. He had a family of his own that was waiting on him. But he was afraid for Gemen what it would mean if he left her. So instead of fishing, he helped Gemen carry her parents up to the hillside and bury them. It took the entire day, through sunset. They finished that evening utterly exhausted. The young man went back to his family. Gemen spent the night alone.

"The next morning, Gemen awoke and stepped outside her hut. To her surprise, someone had already been out fishing and was on the shore cleaning their catch. Gemen watched for a while, wondering who would be out so early. The person finished cleaning the fish and began heading up the shore toward Gemen's house. She noticed it was the same young man who had helped her the day before. He approached her, handed her a couple of fish, and took the rest back to his family.

"Over the next few days, the young man continued that routine. Then, one day, Gemen walked outside of her hut to see the young man building a hut a short distance down shore. His family was with him. When the hut was finished, he and his family moved into it. They immediately began including Gemen in their lives, learning how to share life together and rely on one another. Gemen took the children gathering and weaving everyday while their parents took care of the other duties. At first, it simply felt like a bigger family. But over time, as more families took notice of the two huts by the bay and began relocating themselves to the shore, it began to feel like something new and different. And exciting. It wasn't long before only a few people were doing the fishing for the entire group of huts on the shore without expecting a trade for their catch. Meanwhile, only a few people were carrying water for the whole group. Only a few people were gathering for the whole group. They all began sharing meals together by the fire. It had many of the characteristics that had come to define families, but it wasn't a family. It was a community. It was the beginning of a village.

"Everyone depended on everyone else. Everyone provided some value, even if it was simply playing with the children or maintaining the huts and common areas. More and more people caught the vision for this way of life and were building huts along the bay. When there wasn't any more room around the fire pit, people started building new fire pits with huts encircling them. More and more huts with more and more fires fanned out from those first two huts on the shore.

"While the legacy of community belongs to everyone in that generation who was willing to give up their sense of self-sufficiency and privacy in order to gain something far greater, we remember Gemen today. In the span of a single day, she lost her entire family; in the ensuing days, she gained a community. She epitomizes why community is so vital. We will need community like this when we land on that distant shore on the far side of the horizon.

"As you leave here today, and in the days to come, I encourage each of you to take note every time your life is touched by community – whether it's the food you eat that someone else caught, or wood that someone else cut providing you heat and a place to cook, or simply sharing a laugh with a neighbor that you know as well as you know yourself. Let this sense of community fill you deeply, and carry it with you away from this place."

Chranit stops speaking. As if to fill the silence, the wind gusts through the forest causing the branches of Gemen's tree to slowly sway, rubbing and tapping against one another. There are so many of them. Tangled and twisted and wrapped around one another, it's hard to tell where one begins and the other ends. Cutting this tree down will be an arduous, painstaking process. Maybe that's why Chranit selected it, hoping that our fragile, intricate community would be equally as resilient in the days, months, generations to come.

I rise and find Brisa to continue our conversation from the beach. We start down the mountain together. Slowly through the forest. Quietly admiring the canopy of the Old Grove, how the branches of the trees touch and brush past one another, connecting them to one another in the most subtle, natural way. Like the branches of Gemen's tree. Like the ripples of which Chranit is so fond of speaking. Across lives, across time.

"I can't imagine how lonely it must have been," I throw into the silence. "For Gemen. Down by the bay. All alone."

Brisa thinks about this for a moment before simply saying, "It still happens."

"I don't think it does. I think that was the point Chranit was trying to make. That one of the reasons we live in a community is so stuff like that doesn't happen."

"No, you're right. I guess I meant that it's still possible for people to feel lonely even if they're living in the middle of a village."

"You?"

"Sometimes."

"Right now?" I ask, opening myself up for potential disappointment.

"No, not now. Not ever when I'm with you, Uri. I feel like we didn't get to finish our conversation from earlier. About the sadness, the darkness, the falling. I never feel any of those things when I'm with you. You make me feel secure. You help me hope for better things. Sometimes I feel like I could spend my entire life with no one but you and never feel lonely for a moment of it." She sounds like she is about to say more, but cuts herself off.

My heart is racing. The way it does when I stand at the crest of one of the mountains and gaze out across the ocean on a windy day with the clouds racing overhead. Yet despite this exhilaration, the only words I can find to respond are an unimpressive, "Me too." In all the times I've played this conversation through my mind, I've always had more to say than *me too*.

"I know," Brisa says with a smirk, unfazed by my lack of eloquence.

We walk for a while longer, allowing the sounds of the ocean and the wind and the island to fill the air between us. When we finally turn toward our homes, the air becomes filled with the sounds of the village. People playing with other peoples' children. Water carriers returning from the mountain with water for themselves and their neighbors. Fishermen mending their nets together. Meals shared in groups around fires. It's hard to tell where one life ends and the next begins. Chranit was right. We need one another. Braided together like ropes, we are one another.

Chapter 11

The Fifth Moon

"What's on your mind, Uri?" The words float past my ears. I hear them, but my mind doesn't capture them. "Uri?" The sharpness of my name catches me this time.

"What's that?" I shake off the distraction.

"What's on your mind? You keep staring out at sea. What's distracting you?" Chuan tilts his head toward me with genuine concern.

"I –" Brisa. Lately, it's always Brisa. But I'm not quite sure I want to get into all of that with Chuan. "I don't know. I guess I'm just day dreaming."

I return to my work, fastening a plank in place. But Chuan doesn't let me brush him off so easily. "You are a dreamer. But you aren't dreaming right now. You're lost somewhere. I've been around you long enough to know the difference. So where are you lost today?"

His words are like an unexpected poke from behind, the kind that awakens you to the reality that you are a part of other peoples' lives just like they are a part of yours, that other people think about you just like you think about other people, that you occupy their thoughts and memories and observations just like they occupy yours, that just because you aren't reaching out to them doesn't mean they aren't reaching out to you. It's comforting. Flattering. Scary.

"I don't know, Chuan. Maybe it's more of what we were talking about last month. We point our boats to the horizon. The wind carries us past it. Then what? What will life will be like on the other side of the horizon? What's on the other side of the horizon…for me?"

Chuan stops what he is doing and squints at me like he's trying to understand. Then with a dramatic look of realization, "For you and Brisa, you mean."

He sees right through me. No point in denying it. "Sure. For me and Brisa."

Chuan nods again, this time thoughtfully. "Our lives have been on hold ever since this ordeal began, haven't they? For some reason, we feel as though we can't go on living our normal lives until we've made it safely to the other side. I see it all over the village. I even see it in myself. We feel like we owe it to each other not to move forward individually until we can all move forward collectively. But no one has ever mandated this, Uri. We've each taken this burden on ourselves. If you and Brisa had wrapped your lives around one another on this side of the horizon, they would be wrapped around one another on the other side of the horizon as well; but if things are uncertain between you on this side of the horizon, they will be uncertain on the other side of the horizon as well. So why wait? Why prolong it? If you are certain, why not move forward?"

His words splash me like cold water. It's true. No one has ever directed us to put our lives on hold. And, yet, everyone has put their lives on hold. Why? I'm reminded of the story of Gemen. Community. Commitment to one another that surpasses even our commitment to ourselves. "I guess I've just felt like this is our duty right now. Like we need to get off of this island and nothing should distract us from that. Why should we be preoccupied by anything less urgent?"

Chuan shrugs. "Urgent. Why should this journey be any more urgent than the rest of our lives? Who knows when death will come? Who knows when love's day may pass? Over on the other side of the island, they aren't waiting. They're going about their lives. They haven't stopped focusing on the things that matter for each day. You say you don't want to be preoccupied by moving forward with Brisa, but I've been watching you all morning be preoccupied by not moving forward with her. So what's the difference?"

Chuan stares at me for a moment before returning to his work. I'm stunned. I want to be upset with him, but I have this annoying suspicion that he's right. So, instead, I'm feeling upset with myself. And confused. Go for it? Wait for the horizon? Love pulls me toward Brisa's house – go for it. Duty pulls me toward the horizon – wait. And I'm caught between the two.

I glance toward Brisa's house. I glance toward the horizon. And somewhere in between, my eyes pass a boat covered with builders. They sweat and strain in the sun. Surely they'd rather be resting in the shade. But they're out here working. Because they know that it's more important for the boats to be built than it is for them to indulge themselves.

Maybe Chuan is wrong. In eight months we'll be gone. What's eight moons in a lifetime of a thousand moons? It can wait. We can wait. To arrive at a new land and live freely together. Nevertheless, his words have planted themselves deeply in my mind. There's no escaping them now. Even as I convince myself I can wait, I feel a tug in my chest toward Brisa's door.

And I can't escape something else that he said. About the people living on other side of the island. They've been quiet for a couple of months now, ever since the rotting fish incident. If it weren't for the pillar of smoke on calm days, it would be easy to forget that they're even over there. Every day, a few people from their village come over with baskets full of berries to meet a few people from our village. They all carry the baskets of fish back to the other village. Then the group from our village returns with more baskets of berries. That's the sum of our interaction with them.

I wonder what the group talks about as they carry the fish back to the other village. The exchange crews are the only people from the two villages who have any interaction with people from the other village. Do they talk about the typical village gossip? Or do they talk about more meaningful things like the horizon, or how ridiculous it is for our tribe to be torn in two? Or do they continue to debate the issues that split us in the first place? Or do they walk in silence? Already strangers. Already two separate tribes who just happen to share an island. Counting down the days until they won't have to share it anymore.

That last possibility is unbearable to me. It makes my stomach sick even to think about it. The thought that we might have dissolved in such a short span of time. We may have differences that we can't reconcile, but we are a family, a community, a tribe. We can't have lost that so quickly. I need to know.

I turn to Chuan. "What did you say about the other side of the island?"

Chuan looks puzzled, trying to recall his own words. "Just that they are going about their lives the way we would be going about ours if we weren't so preoccupied by trying to escape this island. And maybe they have the right idea."

"How do you know?"

"We're so obsessed with this ideal of 'duty to the tribe' that we aren't allowing ourselves to move forward with our own lives. But I feel that our real duty to one another is to give one another the freedom to move forward with our passions and aspirations, rather than expecting one another to repress them. It's unrealistic. It's unhealthy."

"No, I mean how do you know about how the other side of the island lives?"

"Oh. I don't. But why wouldn't they keep going about their lives? For them, their greatest weapon and their greatest defense against us is to go on living life as though nothing has changed. As though we aren't here. As though we were already gone. Forget about us and move on."

"Doesn't that make you sad?" I ask.

"Sad? I don't know about sad. They did this. They're the ones that split from us. It's a shame. But I don't know that I feel sad about it."

"I just can't stand the thought of us falling apart like that. We've lived together for forty generations. And then, overnight, everything comes crashing down. How did we let that happen so easily? And why isn't anyone doing anything about it?"

"It's more complicated than that, Uri. It goes deeper than leave or don't leave. Deeper than use the trees or don't use the trees. It cuts straight to peoples' hearts, exposing very personal beliefs in a very public way. What is a tribe? Is it an identity or a geography? Which things do we value and what are we willing to sacrifice in order to preserve and obtain those things? Is the Grove of Ancestors a timeless testimony to enduring values or a vast supply of wood? Do legacies exist on their own, independent of our existence and opinion, or do they exist simply because we allow ourselves to believe they exist? Do we set the course of our lives according to the Seen or according to the Unseen? There are no easy answers. No clear right and wrong. Just a mess, and a bunch of people trying to work through it as best they can."

I don't understand most of what Chuan is saying. "So because there aren't any easy answers, we just won't bother trying to find them?"

My frustration must be audible. Chuan exaggerates the calmness in his voice, over-pronouncing each word, "No, I'm saying that's precisely what this whole mess is about – the search for answers."

I still don't understand. Seen. Unseen. Search for answers. None of it makes sense. "So does that mean that everyone on the other side of the island only cares about the Seen?"

"No."

"And everyone on our side only cares about the Unseen?"

"No."

"What then?"

"I believe that we're all trying to figure out what we believe. Even Abis and Chief Sangra. Until this crisis, we didn't really have to come to any hard conclusions. We could be comfortable in an endless search for elusive answers. But this crisis changes things. It demands that we find an answer to what we believe."

"What do you believe?" I demand.

"Me?" Chuan pauses and looks up to the sky. "I believe that some Unseen things are pretty important. But no point in getting carried away over them. In the end, it's the Seen things that we come to depend on for survival. Food. Air. Touch."

"Then why are you on this side of the island? Why spend all day every day building these boats?"

"Because some kid who I never paid much attention to spoke up at a Council meeting about these crazy dreams he was having. A boat unlike anything that anyone had ever conceived. There's got to be something special about that. No chance that I would miss out on being a part of it. Besides, there isn't much for a boat builder like me to do on the other side of the island."

• • •

On the morning of the fifth full moon I arrive early, hoping to catch Alver who coordinates the exchange trips between our village and the other village. I search the crowd for him, keeping my conversations with others brief and light. When I finally see him, he's already in conversation with someone else. How did I miss him?

I cut a direct path toward him, trying not to be too obvious that I'm seeking him out directly. No luck. As I step within an arm span of him, he looks up from his conversation flustered.

"Hi Uri," he says warily.

"I was wondering about the exchange trips," I say a little too eagerly.

Silence. "Yes?" He prods reluctantly.

"So…" For as much time as I've spent anticipating asking Alver if I could join the exchange trips, I hadn't really thought through the conversation itself. In this awkward moment, I'm wishing I had. "If you ever need any help, feel free to call upon me. Mehan and I used to carry baskets of berries back and forth across this island every day. I'm up to the task and happy to help."

Alver studies me for a while. I may be the first person to make such an offer to him. "But aren't you building boats?" He asks.

"Yes. But I have no clue what I'm doing out there. They could afford to lose me for half a day if it would help you."

"Okay," Alver says politely. "I don't know if we'll ever need to take you up on your offer, but it's good to know that we have you if we need you. Thank you, Uri."

I don't know how to end this conversation. Fortunately, Chranit strolls past us, stealing our attention. As we follow him across the grassy plain, I glance over and happen to see Brisa. I pick my way through the moving sea of people to meet her. She sees me approaching and smiles, "Uri." I love the way my name sounds through her lips.

I smile and echo back, "Brisa." We walk close to one another. The distant sound of crashing waves catches my ear, drawing my attention toward the horizon. The sight of the sunrise evokes the memory of my conversation with Chuan. About the horizon. About love. Duty. Waiting. Moving forward. Seen. Unseen. His words are still fresh in my mind, reinvigorated now by Brisa's presence.

We ascend the mountain to the Old Grove. Take our seats uphill from the tree at which Chranit stops. "Beauty," Chranit begins. "Why do we observe the colors of the sunrise and perceive beauty? The grass. The mountains. The trees. Ocean waves. Lightning storms. Dancing flames. The beauty of it all. Why are these things beautiful to us? Something inside of us recognizes them and responds. And when we respond to the beauty around us by creating a beauty of our own, we call it art.

"These trees are windows through which we can perceive the principles that govern our world; in much the same way, art is a window through which we can perceive the principles that govern our hearts. The longings. The vulnerabilities. The joys and the sorrows. Art is a window for all of our senses. The beauty revealed to us in this world and the beauty we discover through art allow us to comprehend things that are beyond us. Things that are older than this world. Things that are bigger than the skies. Things that are vaster than the sea. Things that never change or fade or perish.

"Art has been part of our culture since before we arrived at this island. Music, visuals, dance, foods. They've all had their place in our tribe. But in the twentieth generation, a man named Oskus elevated art to a focal point. As a child, Oskus commonly stained slats of tree bark with berry juice to make pictures. He shaped remarkable sculptures in the sand of the beach. He was always humming a tune, drumming a beat, dancing a step. He invented stories of imaginary people who lived in imaginary lands. And he'd take you there with him.

"But as he became a man, he became less interested in imaginary people and more interested in real ones. Less interested in imaginary lands and more interested in the one that he inhabited. Less interested in making up his own stories and more interested in telling histories. He spent most of his life pondering ways of using art as a means of conveying the histories he grew up learning. Songs. Dances. Music. Costumes. Props. Performances. And as he felt age begin to set into his bones, he decided to share it with others. He wanted to bring the history of our tribe to life in a way that people would be able to experience it with all of their senses. He wanted the whole tribe to come together to share in an experience unlike any other.

"He picked the evening on which the sun pauses and moves backward in the sky to be the evening on which the tribe would pause and look backward in time. For the months leading up to it, he worked tirelessly with different groups throughout the tribe teaching and rehearsing music, dances, skits. Everyone knew their role, but no one quite knew what the whole thing would look like when it came together…except Oskus.

"On the evening of that first performance,

they were astonished as they experienced the history of the tribe unlike ever before. Our ancestors' voyage to the island, the early days of war, the establishment of peace, the construction of the village, the founding of the Council, the Great Storm, the Great Fire, and many other major events. He depicted daily life on our island and the things we value most. That night, he gave everyone a glimpse into the things that have made us special as a people and what a long, difficult path we have traveled to arrive where we are. And to this day, on the evening of the day in which the sun pauses and moves backward in the sky, we pause and move backward in time. We've added to the performance as notable events have occurred since that original performance, but it is still essentially the same.

"In the twilight of his life, he was asked by one of his students to explain art. He thought about it for a few moments before responding, 'Art? It gets messy. And then it gets beautiful.' How appropriate for us to remember that phrase during this trial of our tribe or during any other time when life becomes messy. Perhaps something beautiful is being fashioned within you if only you will let it."

The branches of Oskus' tree dangle in the breeze. Heavy and hollow. They inhale the wind, and exhale a deep, wooden hum. They knock against one another with slow, gentle, hypnotic clanging. The sounds are beautiful on their own, but they can be harnessed and made even more beautiful. I remember Choko taking me out here when I was a child, as I had seen many fathers do with their children. He sent me climbing the tree in search of a branch that fit my hands perfectly. When I found one, he had me cut it and bring it down. Then, with his precise stone cutter hands, he carved a flute and began to teach me how to play. Note-by-note. Beat-by-beat. He would shape my fingers into the right positions to show me how to make just the right sound. *Blow. Good. Now you try.* But I didn't want to learn notes. I wanted to learn entire songs. *Songs are simply notes strung together,* he would tell me. *Learn the notes and the songs will come naturally.* The songs never came. I was too impatient. Too distracted. Too something to focus on the notes and let the songs come naturally.

I still love the sound of those flutes. It takes me back to a very old place. A place that has been a part of me since before I can remember. In the sway of its sound, I feel tranquility. I need them now more than ever before. We all do.

A strong gust of wind comes rushing through the forest. The branches of Oskus' tree respond with their moody humming and rhythmic gong. It's a song. Not like the songs we play on handmade flutes, but one from some hidden, mysterious place. Stillness in the air. Except for the wind. And the windsong. Captivating the hillside.

Haunting.

Lingering.

Beautiful.

Legacy.

Chapter 12

The Sixth Moon

"You're overcooking your fish. Why do you always overcook your fish?"

That voice. In the days that I gathered berries alongside that voice, it sounded like that of a boy. Today, it sounds more like that of a man. Has my voice changed that much, too? It doesn't sound any different to me. But, then again, people are always telling my how much taller I appear every time they see me and I never feel any taller than the last time they said it to me.

"I like it well-cooked," I shoot back over my shoulder. "Don't ever try to give me your mushy fish. I'll throw it right back at you."

"Bleh," Mehan bends down to inspect my fish before surmising, "Way too dry."

"What? You prefer to eat your fish raw?" I ask. He sits next to me and tosses a fish on the fire pit.

"No. Just the perfect amount of juice between each flake. Squishy. A little clear."

"Sounds raw to me." He's too caught up in the thought of his perfectly juicy flakes to hear me.

It feels so different speaking with Mehan lately. Conversations with Brisa have gotten sweeter. Conversations with everyone else have remained mostly as they've always been. But conversations with Mehan have become more distant, contrived, abrupt. Has he changed? Beyond the voice? Sure, he's taller, more angular, and much stronger. But through it all, I still see my favorite berry-picking companion. Focused, ambitious, always in a hurry. So why do our conversations feel so different? Is it because I've somehow changed?

"How's watching?" I ask, genuinely curious but mostly just trying to make conversation.

"It's fine," he shrugs. "The watching part is pretty boring. But I'm learning some great skills."

"Like what?"

"Like how to run faster. How to climb faster. How to blend in with my surroundings. How to move without being noticed. How to fight. How to use weapons. Stuff that will be important to know if we ever need to defend ourselves."

I wince at that last part. "Our tribe has never needed to defend itself. Who even knows how to do these things in the first place? Who would know how to fight with a weapon? Who would know how to blend in with their surroundings?"

"Different people show us different things. Like fishers teach us how to use the spears the way they use spears to stick the fish they catch. It was actually a former gatherer who taught us about blending in with our surroundings, since the berries we gather are always blending in with their surroundings. You study the berries, you learn their tricks. But mostly we just learn all of those things by practicing with one another."

"Do you actually think you'll ever have to use those skills?" I ask skeptically.

"That doesn't matter, does it?" Mehan replies defensively. "If we ever need them, we will have them. That's the important thing. Better to have the skills and never need them than to need them and be unprepared."

I can't think of a counter to his argument. I don't like it, but I don't know how to argue it. Except to say, "Well I hope you don't ever have to use them."

Mehan pauses before soberly replying, "Me too." He stuffs a pinch of fish into his mouth. Closes his eyes in pleasure. "Perfect. Juicy. Flaky. Perfect." He savors his first bite for what seems to be an excessive amount of time. Then he continues, "Besides, even if we don't need those skills on this island, we may need them when we arrive at our destination. You never know."

This isn't the first time I have heard

someone mention this possibility, but it frightens me to hear it so matter-of-factly flow from Mehan's mouth. The thought that all of the pain of splitting our tribe, building these boats, and sailing into the unknown could end with us in the throes of war with an unfamiliar enemy is more than I can handle right now, so I change the subject. "I didn't see you at Chranit's last legacy talk."

Mehan shakes his head, "Didn't go."

"Or the one before that."

"Haven't been in a while."

"Why not?"

"Got to stay behind and guard the village."

"These stories matter, Mehan. They are our identity. And when we're gone soon, we won't have a chance to learn from them anymore."

"When we're gone, we'll just have to carry the stories in our hearts. I already carry our stories in my heart. I don't need to listen to yet another story about bravery. I need to be brave. That's why I stay and watch while all of you go to the hillside."

"You have always been brave, Mehan. It's part of who you are. But what about things like mercy? How can we know what it means to be merciful unless we learn about what mercy is?"

Mehan grows irritated. "You don't think I know how to be merciful?"

"No, I'm just saying that we all need to–"

"While you peacefully fall asleep tonight,

unafraid of being attacked, I hope you remember that the only reason you can do so is because I'm out there watching." He rises to his feet. "My bravery *is* mercy!" With that, he spits into the fire and walks away. The boy I've known so well, becoming a man I hardly recognize.

• • •

The morning of the legacy talk, the crowd is especially light. I double-check the sun to see if I'm just really early. No, there should be more people here by now. Some sort of sickness has been going around the village. Many people have found that the best way to deal with it is simply to stay in their huts until it goes away. Perhaps that's why our crowd this morning is less than half its usual size.

I notice Alver approaching me. "Good morning, Uri," he greets me. "I honestly didn't think we would need to take you up on your offer to help. But with this sickness going around, two of our carriers and all but one of our backups are laid out in their huts as we speak. We have an extra spot to fill. Does your offer still stand?"

"Of course." I try not to sound too eager.

"Good. Find me after the legacy talk. We'll go down to the shore together."

"Sounds good."

I scan the faces in the small crowd, stopping short upon one face in particular. Mehan's. I can hardly believe it. He's here. Aloof. Jaded. But here. And the spear that has become a permanent fixture in his hand lately is conspicuously absent. I break my stare quickly, for fear that he might notice me noticing him and change his mind out of spite. Whether he's here because he's genuinely interested or because he feels guilty after our last conversation doesn't really matter. He's here. The boy I know isn't completely lost.

Chranit makes his way to the front of the small crowd, surveys it, grimaces at its small size, and leads us to a tree in the Old Grove.

"Two generations after Gemen, our ancestors were just learning what it meant to live and function as a community. They desired to take to the seas in order to fish and to move people and materials around the island. But it had been generations since we had built boats or sailed the sea. They had become lost arts to our tribe. Sadly, several skills that had once been so familiar to our earliest ancestors had been lost over generations due to lack of use.

"A group of people from the newly formed village came together to reinvent and relearn all that had been lost. They decided to begin with reestablishing our mastery of the sea. Our ancestors who sailed to this island had been very accomplished seafarers; so it seemed appropriate that in rediscovering our ancestors' way of life, they should begin by relearning something that had been so central to their way of life.

"Over the span of nearly a generation, this group worked on constructing and maneuvering a seaworthy vessel. They had to relearn boat shapes, building techniques, sail making, knot tying, tacking, and nearly everything else related to boats and boating. A few anecdotal stories had been passed down through the generations as well as an armful of engravings that depicted the vessels and their way of life. But for the most part, they had to figure everything out for themselves.

"After countless failed attempts, the group was finally able to fashion a seaworthy boat. It was crude, but it sailed. And it became the template for the fishing boats we use to this day. They became comfortable sailing this boat around the bay and were ready to try it on the open sea by sailing a full circle around the island. One morning, they gathered along the shore, launched the boat, and watched it leave the bay with a few of its members aboard. It turned out of the bay, followed the length of the island, turned around the far end of the island out of view, and was never seen again.

"No one ever discovered what happened to the boat or its crew. Today, we might suggest that strong currents swept it away, or the wind, or hidden obstacles lining the ocean floor. But they didn't understand those things back then. They only understood the laws and perils of sailing around the bay, which (as is common knowledge to us today), are very different from the laws and perils of sailing out into the open sea. And they realized on that day that if they ever wanted to sail the open sea, they would need to understand it much more intimately than they did.

"There was a debate within the village about whether or not it was worth the cost. On one side of the debate, people felt that the loss of the sailors' lives already outweighed any benefits that stood to be gained. On the other side of the debate, people argued that the endeavor was about more than simply boats and sailing, it was about our relationship with the world around us. They argued that with the loss of the crew, it had become about our tribe's resolve, that all great adventures involve risk, even adventures of the mind. This side's loudest proponent was a woman named Kyo, who felt that the tribe not only owed it to themselves, but also to the sailors they lost to master the seas.

"Kyo made it her life's focus to understand the vast, deep, mysterious forces at work beyond the island. She studied the wind, currents, tides, waves, even ocean life. She studied the patterns in the stars, moon, and sun. The more she studied these things, the more she realized how connected they all were. And while our tribe didn't master the seas in her lifetime, she made many observations and discoveries that continue to inform us to this day.

"And most importantly, she represents the belief that the better we understand the forces at work around us, the better we can understand ourselves. It was upon this foundation that our tribe was able to rediscover much of the forgotten knowledge of our ancestors; it was upon this foundation that we discovered new knowledge. And it was also upon this foundation that the elder tradition began, as the stories of our tribe were gathered and shared.

"Kyo's legacy is one of unending learning and exploration. When we arrive at the new land, there will be much to learn. And there will be much to remember. Let us carry the example of our ancestors and Kyo to always reach higher. Never stop learning. Never stop exploring. Never stop being curious. Never become so content with the way things are that you feel there is nothing new to learn or discover. There are always new things to learn and discover. New ways to challenge ourselves and one another.

"Notice the branches of Kyo's tree, how they all jut upward out of the trunk. Every one of them reaches higher. None of them sits level with contentment or downward in regress. Every one of them stretches for the heights. And every one of them draws our eyes toward the heights with it."

Chranit turns and focuses on the upper branches of Kyo's tree, tilting his head as far back as he can. Every head on the hillside does likewise. Admiring the heights of Kyo's branches, I recall my last conversations with Mehan. About bravery and mercy and always allowing ourselves to be open to the lessons of the trees. I'm glad he came to this legacy talk about Kyo, who was never closed from learning something new. I'm glad he could hear this. Maybe Chranit lends a credibility that I can't.

As I rise to my feet and stretch in preparation for the exchange trip that's ahead, I feel an elbow dig into my back and brush past me. Mehan. He doesn't stop or turn, maintaining a brisk stride. The boy. I smile to myself.

Downhill, I notice Alver motioning for me to join him. We head back toward the village. Alver explains the routine while we walk. Three members from their village will meet three members of ours with baskets of berries. They will leave the berries. All six of us will carry baskets of fish over to the other village. There, we will leave the fish as well as the members of their village, pick up three more baskets of berries, and carry them back to our village. Simple.

When we reach the shore just outside the village edge, I see six baskets being loaded with fish. Several fishers are wading out into the bay, casting their nets and hauling their catches back to the shore.

"The boat fishing crews are just now getting started." Alver explains. "If we waited for them to go out and bring their catch back to the shore, we would get too late of a start on our day. We already get late enough of a start on legacy talk days as it is."

As I watch the fishers fill the baskets with bay-caught fish, I begin to wonder if I've misunderstood Alver's instructions. Bay-caught fish are much smaller than boat-caught fish, but they take nearly as much time to clean and prepare. The same amount of work for a lot less reward. Is this enough to feed their entire village for an entire day? Just as I open my mouth to ask Alver this very question, I am interrupted by the arrival of the members of the other village.

They approach us and set three baskets of berries at our feet. They don't say anything. They don't even look at us. Almost defiant in their aloofness. Two other people follow shortly behind, both of them carrying spears. One of them is Degi, strutting arrogantly, as though he were the chief of the entire island. He sees me standing by the baskets of fish and cocks his head to the side inquisitively.

Alver comes from behind us. "Okay, it looks like we're set." He nods toward the fish.

The three from our village as well as the three from their village each line up behind a basket of fish. We bend down and pick up our respective baskets in unison. Without another word, Alver leads the procession toward the far side of the island, flanked on one side by two watchers from their tribe and the other side by two watchers from our tribe.

No one says a word.

As we crest the ridge of the grassy plain, the group stops and sets down their baskets. I do likewise, though I'm not really in need of a rest. They stretch their backs and rub their arms, taking in the sun and the ocean breeze. No one says a word. Something about it makes me uncomfortable. It doesn't feel as though they've simply run out of things to talk about. It feels as though they're intentionally not speaking to one another.

"So, how have things been?" I casually ask to no one in particular, hoping to break through the tension. The simultaneous glares of ten people bearing down on me. Especially Alver. I panic and try to deflect attention from my intrusion by swiftly bending down and picking up my basket, relieved to see everyone else do the same. Alver rolls his eyes and turns to lead the group the rest of the way. From here, the walk is mostly downhill to the pillar of smoke rising from the far side of the island.

Though the sun is just past its highest point in the sky as we enter the village, the air suddenly seems cloaked in a veil of darkness. A foreboding haze in the air, as if the air itself doesn't want me here. A dense stillness, heightening my caution. The village is empty. A few smoldering fires. Some thatched huts. No people.

Alver stops at a certain place and we set the baskets in front of him. As soon as our baskets touch the ground, people begin emerging from their huts. Something isn't right. I recognize them, but I don't. I recognize their eyes, but I don't recognize the darkness that fills their eyes. I recognize their faces, but I don't recognize the hollowness in their expressions. I recognize their bodies, but I don't recognize the slowness in their motions. They're frail, lethargic, defeated. Familiar, yet foreign.

I had noticed the thinness of the carriers that met us, but it didn't strike me as odd until now, seeing an entire village full of people more emaciated than them. It's eerie. They don't even feel like the people I once knew. It's as though some imposter tribe happened to wash upon our shore and settle here.

They shuffle from their homes to the freshly delivered baskets, picking out two fish apiece. I could eat two bay-caught fish as a snack. A light meal. Something to hold me over until dinner after a long, hard day of work. Not a meal. Certainly not enough for an entire day. But for them, this is their entire day. This is all of the eating they will do until six more baskets arrive tomorrow. One for lunch, one for dinner. Some berries in between. As sweet as berries are, they don't fill a stomach like fish do. Each person patiently waits their turn, picks two fish from the basket, and moves out of the way of the person behind. Lifeless. Expressionless. Hopeless.

It isn't at all how Chuan speculated it might be. These people aren't moving on with their lives. They're barely hanging on to their lives, staving off death. Is this why they've been so quiet for the past few months? It's all I can do to choke back tears. And I'm suddenly aware of a set of eyes fixed fiercely upon me. I feel them, but I don't turn to acknowledge them. Degi. He must be reading the revulsion on my face, the pity in my eyes. He knows my thoughts. He wants this image to burn itself into my mind. To haunt me. To devastate me. He wants me to react. The satisfaction of seeing me overwhelmed by what has become everyday life for him. It takes every bit of strength not to give in.

Abis emerges from his home. Though he, too, is thinner than I remember, he has somehow maintained his imposing stature. He will not be defeated. He makes his way over to Alver and they quietly talk with one another. Does Chief Sangra know about this? Surely this must be some sort of oversight. Perhaps someone miscalculated how much fish their village would need. Or perhaps this is Alver's doing. Perhaps he is concealing the village's condition from Chief Sangra. I need to know. At tonight's Council meeting, I will find out.

I scan the faces huddled around the baskets. Former playmates. Former neighbors. Former family. Former family? No, I can't allow myself to think that way. Always family. My family. Our family. And then, I scan past a face that nearly brings me to my knees. A young woman that I know, that I've known for as long as I can remember. Prem. The sight of Prem sends my mind flashing back to carefree days. Sitting in trees. Splashing in the surf. Shaping mountains in the sand. Chasing. Playing. Wandering. Some of my earliest memories involve Prem by my side. Some of my fondest memories.

Prem clutches something tightly to her chest. As she leans over to pull two fish out of the basket, I catch a glimpse of it. A newborn baby. Her baby. The forty first generation. The future of this island. And with this glimpse, I surrender to the reaction that Degi was hoping to evoke. Tears pour down my face. The beauty of a baby, marred by wretched circumstance. The hopefulness that comes with a new life, quelled by the hopelessness of this situation. In the collision of amazement and sorrow, I weep. The conditions into which this child was born. It isn't the life I've known. It isn't the life this child should know.

I want to go to Prem. Hold her. Hold her baby. But any intention of that is stolen away as Alver firmly taps my shoulder and points back toward our home village. I pick up a basket of berries in a ruin of tears.

We make the long walk back to our village.

No one speaks the entire way.

• • •

The Council meetings have become so routine by now that I find myself getting distracted during the conversations. The very same conversations that Mehan and I once hid in bushes to hear now seem rote, even meaningless, at times. The same issues. The same debates. The same resolutions. I understand the importance of the discussions, but I think back to those nights of hiding in bushes and I wonder what I found so fascinating about them. Why was I so eager and excited to hear them?

This meeting is no different from the others. Reports on the status of the tribe. Village administration. Trivial controversies. And finally, the question that closes every meeting, "Are there any other matters to discuss?"

I straighten in my seat at the question. This is my chance. After spending the entire meeting up to this point clouded by memories of the other village, I have some matters I would like to discuss. Sunken eyes. Protruding ribs. Vacant expressions. Two fish per day. Prem. Her baby. Our family ebbing away on the far side of the island. "Yes." I assert resolutely.

Every head in the room swings in my direction. Chief Sangra nods, "Go ahead, Uri."

"How are things at the other village?"

One of the other Council members is quick to jump in. "Things must be going well. They haven't harassed us in months."

"And why haven't they?" I shoot back. "Is it because they've suddenly decided that they want peace?"

Chief Sangra interjects, "They don't want peace. Not as long as we're on this island. Not as long as we occupy this village. Not as long as we control the supply of fish. They want us gone. They may remain peaceful until we leave. But we shouldn't be lulled into the illusion that it's because they desire peace."

"But how can we know that they don't want peace?" I ask innocently.

Chief Sangra sounds annoyed in his reply, "Surely you haven't forgotten so easily, Uri.

The way they split our village. The way they harassed us in the months after the split. What makes you think they could potentially want peace, when they are the ones who have been creating strife?"

"Well, if they don't want peace, then what else would explain why they suddenly went silent four months ago?"

Chief Sangra's eyes narrow. He suspects something. "What's really on your mind, Uri?" His directness catches me off guard.

I survey the room, prepared to expose everything that I saw today to the perplexed eyes staring in my direction. But I happen to see Alver nervously wringing his hands and tapping his foot. He knows what's on my mind. And he's regretting that he took me on the exchange trip. He looks anxious, but he doesn't look guilty. Somehow, I can tell that he isn't responsible for whatever is going on in the other village. But, then why does he look so anxious? I scan back toward Chief Sangra. His eyes are set on me like stone. Like solid, jagged stone. Something I've never seen in his eyes before. Something that causes me to recoil.

"I –" The intensity of his glare. I withdraw any hint of accusation from my voice. "I guess it just makes me sad to think that they don't want peace. It was only a few months ago that we were one village and everything was fine. And now they aren't."

Sangra slowly replies. “It's a sad thing, indeed. If there were a way to make peace, we would have made it a long time ago.” His eyes give me no relief.

With that, Chief Sangra concludes the Council meeting. As the Forum unloads, I'm confronted with a myriad of stares. Confused stares. Annoyed stares. Judgmental stares. Curious stares. Impressed stares. Only one affects me, though: Alver's disappointed stare. I'm angry at myself for even speaking up in the first place. And I'm angry at myself for restraining myself once I did. Something about Alver's nervousness and Sangra's glare caused me to doubt myself.

I sulk back to my house where I spend the rest of the night not sleeping.

Chapter 13

The Seventh Moon

The night drags on. Though the nightscape outside my hut is perfectly serene under a perfectly full moon, my mind has been a restless and raging storm. It began with thunder. Reliving the confrontation with Sangra at tonight's Council meeting. The things I should have said. The things I would have said if I were braver. After the thunder came the gales. The gusting onslaught of the faces I saw at the other village earlier today. Downcast faces. Heavy faces. Sunken faces. But one face keeps coming back to me more than all the others. And that face has brought on the torrential rain of memories. The young mother. Prem.

Prem was Brisa before there was Brisa.

The childhood of my childhood was a constant string of adventures with Prem. Adventures on the mountains. Adventures in the bay. Adventures across the grassy plain. Some adventures were battles. Others were quests. All of them took us somewhere fantastic. To islands beyond the horizon. To the tops of the clouds, which were islands of their own floating through a sea of air, each a new adventure awaiting its heroes.

But on one of the days when Brisa's dad came over to be a little piece of a dad for me, he happened to bring Brisa with him. That day changed everything. From the first moment I saw Brisa, I was captivated by her. I don't know that I understood love at that age, but it was some form of love. A seedling of love. Some irresistible force that drew me toward Brisa and Brisa toward me. And in drawing toward Brisa, I drew away from Prem. We were still friendly with one another, but the wider the gap between us grew, the more awkwardness filled the space.

A few months before the tribe split, Prem wrapped her life around a young man and moved to the other side of the village to live with him. Apparently, when the tribe split, they followed Abis...which puzzles me. Though it had been a long time since Prem and I exchanged so much as a friendly greeting, I still feel as though I know her fairly well. And from what I know of Prem, I can't understand why she would follow Abis. In our adventures through the Grove of Ancestors, she was always so enchanted by the stories that the trees proclaimed. Sometimes, we'd pretend that we were the people in the stories that the trees memorialized. Like we were the ones shaping and leaving the towering legacies. The affection she felt for those trees couldn't have so easily been replaced by a willingness to cut them down, could it? Unless - as my mind focuses on the memory of baby in her arms - she was pregnant at the time of the split.

She must have known that she was pregnant before the split. And perhaps the proposition of carrying an infant across the indefinite sea was more than she could bear. Abis' vision might be disheartening to her, but it's safe. And that matters to a brand new mother. In our village, she would have had to put her life on hold like everyone else, then embark toward the sunrise for an unknown length of time toward an unknown destination. And there's always the possibility that we won't make it. But in Abis' village, there are no unknowns. Life goes on.

It was that very notion that inspired me to ask Alver if I could join an exchange trip to the other village. I wanted to see for myself. Discouraged by stalling my life with Brisa, I wanted to see life in a village where people lives weren't stalled. Where people continued living. What I discovered was so very different from what I expected. They may not have placed their lives on hold, but they are hardly moving on. There's too much frailty. Too much darkness. Too much staleness. Chuan didn't anticipate that. No one did. No one could have. Except Chief Sangra. Except Alver. Except the three carriers and two guards from our village that assist Alver. And now, except me.

People should know. This isn't right. Something needs to be done. Something needs to change. Am I the right person to tell them? And will making the situation known only end up making things worse for Abis' village? Worse for me? Would anything even improve at all?

This tempest of thought keeps me awake through the night. Until the slightest beam of sunrise pierces my hut, dissipating the thunder and the wind and the rain in my mind. But while the storm has calmed, it left devastating wreckage in its wake. I peel myself from the ground and stumble outside, the first one awake. My head is pounding. I trudge toward the fire pit and sit by the embers to gather my focus. The smell of yesterday's fish makes me nauseous. A couple of fish lay at the bottom of the basket by my feet. Their lifeless eyes staring up at me judgmentally. Though these fish might be eaten this morning, the extras are typically returned to the sea. The thought of these excess fish being discarded while the other village starves adds to my nausea.

And then, a realization. These fish don't have to be wasted. They wouldn't be noticed. They wouldn't be missed. I grab the basket and tiptoe away from the village as quickly as I can. The sunrise and the moonlight discretely lighting my way. Rather than cut across the middle of the island where too many people might see me, I follow the shoreline. Penja is already standing his watch for the day. I consider trying to sneak past him. But if he saw me, he would know that something was up. Best to try and play it casually. That way if he decides to stop me and ask questions, I can give answers that would make the whole incident perfectly forgettable.

I stroll confidently down the shore with the basket clutched closely to my side. I look over at Penja a stone's throw away from me. He doesn't recognize me at first through the dimness of the dawn light and startles into a defensive posture. I nod at him and give a slight wave. He leans his head in and squints his eyes before recognizing me. I make my stride as unsuspicious as I possibly can. He raises the end of his spear off the ground as if to return the wave. One of the benefits of having a reputation as a wanderer is that no one suspects anything unusual when they see you wandering.

I continue following the shoreline all the way around the mountain. It's the longest possible route to the other side of the island, but also the least conspicuous. If anyone knew where I was going right now, there would be consequences. Though unspoken, it's plainly understood that no one is to have any contact with the other village, much less to physically go to the other village, much less to go alone. Here I am doing something unimaginably worse than all of those. I'm aiding the other village. Bringing them fish when we already have an arrangement to provide them fish. It's only a few fish, nothing significant. But the quantity is irrelevant. Be it a day's supply or a single fin, it's the act that's subversive. The reality of this becoming weightier in my mind with each step I take. I hold onto images of Prem, her baby, and all those emaciated bodies for the resolve to keep moving forward.

The sun climbs in the sky as I pick my way through the heavy trees and brush on the seaside slope of the mountain of the Old Grove. I've forgotten how treacherous some of the remote places on the island can be. The abundance of berries all around me reminds me of gathering trips with Mehan. Of simpler days, when a trek all the way around the mountain was undertaken as an act of exploration or fun, rather than an attempt to evade suspicion.

As I round the mountain and the other village comes into view, I crouch down and seek out the most hidden vantage point on the mountain slope that will still allow me to see the village. People are going about their daily routines. I watch, fascinated. In a sense, it feels like I've sojourned through the wilderness only to arrive at another island. A foreign island.

With foreign people, whose lives look so much like ours and, yet, somehow so different. The gauntness. The slowness. The countenance on their faces. Different. And yet their huts, their routines, and their movements are exactly like ours. Because they are ours. They are us. We are them. Nothing changes that.

It's the subtle differences that strike me most. Like how they pass each other by without acknowledging one another. Like how they eat their meals in silence, without stories or laughter or even so much as simple conversation. Like how they walk so intently, more focused on their task or destination than the path they are on. No unnecessary motions. No meaningless chit-chat. No impromptu stops to share a hug or a laugh or an act of kindness. The differences are subtle, but significant. And they tell me everything I need to know about life in this village.

I watch for a while, mesmerized by this foreign twin tribe, until Prem eventually emerges from a hut, holding her baby, accompanied by the young man with whom she moved to the other side of our village to wrap her life around. They are roughly my age, but seeing them together with a child, they seem so much older. They walk out of sight.

Suddenly, it dawns on me that I haven't thought through my plan very well. Now what do I do? I successfully sneaked out of my village, successfully navigated around the ocean-side of the mountain, and successfully found a vantage point from which I have a good view of their village. Now how do I complete the crucial last step of sneaking into their village without being noticed? I deliberate for a while before deciding that this was a bad idea. There's no way I could sneak in right now without being noticed. And I hate to think about what would happen if I were noticed.

Finally, with much frustration, I give up. What was I thinking? I retrace my steps back around the mountain, dumping the fish into the sea along the way. The sun is well into its descent by the time I reach my village. I stroll down to the shore and join the boat builders at work. When Chuan sees me, he innocently asks me where I've been all day. I don't think he suspects anything, but his question reminds me that people notice when I'm gone. If I'm ever going to attempt my valiant act of subversion again, I'd better wait a while. And I'd better have a plan next time.

• • •

How to move without being noticed.

Listening to Mehan extoll this skill, I was cynical. Cynical of its need and cynical of his motivation for learning it. But since my uneventful visit to the other village earlier this month, it has been planted in my mind.

I remember using this skill as a child. Escaping undetected after a great prank. Stealing cupped handfuls of berry wine from the huts of the men who made it. Sneaking to and from the Council meetings (though I'm fairly certain now that we were much more noticed than we gave ourselves credit for.) But I never thought about perfecting this skill as a man. Until I sat in my vantage point from outside of Abis' village and couldn't devise a plan to deliver the fish the final few steps to Prem without being noticed.

Having played through all of the possible scenarios in my mind, it's clear that the only way I will be able to sneak into and out of Abis' village is under the cover of darkness. I don't know the layout of the village well enough, or their routines, or where there watchers are placed to chance it during the day. The trek from our village around the ocean-side of the mountain requires nearly half a day. That means in order to have darkness as my cover, I will either need to leave my village in the middle of the night or return to it in the middle of the night. If I return in the middle of the night, I will miss the evening meal and my absence will be noticed. My only option, then, is to leave my village in the middle of the night, returning around midday, where my absence will be relatively unnoticed and easy for me to explain away. Only one obstacle remains, then: sneaking out of my village at night without being noticed. The watchers are on heightened alert during the night. They watch closely for shifting shadows. They listen closely for every aberration from the rhythmic rolling of the tides. They smell every change in the wind. And what they can't see or hear or smell, they try to feel. Their senses are keenly tuned for suspicion. If they catch me sneaking out in the middle of the night with a basket of fish, I won't have any easy explanations. I must find a way to move past them without being noticed.

I watch the sun slip below the ridge of the grassy plain, wondering if Prem and her family are watching it complete its ultimate descent beyond the horizon. Stars gradually appear in the sky. The brightest first, followed by their less luminous neighbors. I search the sky for the moon, but it's nowhere to be seen. It has been fading for the past few nights. Tonight it must be empty. The mystery of the changing moon. In its fullness, it illuminates the island almost as clearly as the dawn light. In its emptiness, the sky shimmers with a special kind of brilliance while the island lays cloaked under a faint veil of starlight.

Cloaked under a faint veil of starlight?

The darkness on the evenings of empty moons hides the mountains, hides the trees, hides the rocks; why wouldn't it hide me?

Allow me to move without being seen. I could leave the village tonight, sneaking past the watchers under the cover of darkness, the faint veil of starlight guiding my steps. If I left early enough in the evening, I could arrive at the other village before sunrise, sneak in, leave a basket of fish by Prem's hut, and return to my village by late morning, by which time, the watchers wouldn't suspect anything.

It could work. If I have any hope of doing this small thing for Prem and her family, this is my best chance.

As the evening meal winds down and people retreat to their houses, I go to mine and wait. I wait for the speaking and stirring to fade into silence. I wait for the firelight to sink dim. I wait for sleep to overtake the village.

Then I move.

I move quickly, mindful of the placement and impact of each step. Grab a basket of fish that I hid earlier in the evening. Sneak down to the shoreline where it's dark, where my silhouette doesn't stand in contrast to anything, where the sand muffles the sounds of my movements and crashing waves drown out anything that the sand doesn't conceal. The waves, the darkness, the sand beneath my feet. I'm hidden even to myself. How to move without being noticed.

As I get close to the watchers' line of sight, I crouch as low as I can until I'm practically crawling on my stomach. I can't hesitate. I can't look back at the watchers. I just need to move. If they notice me and I get caught, I'm just going to have to deal with the consequences. But I can't let myself be distracted by that possibility. I need to focus. I need to go for it.

I go for it. My heart racing. My arms shaking. My breath wavering. I stay low for as long as I can, until the sandy shoreline narrows, narrows, narrows to the point where grass meets rock and rock meets sea. When the sand is gone and I stub my toe on a rock, I shoot up to my feet. I bite my lip to hold back a yelp. I'm way beyond the village. Way beyond the watchers. Way beyond the point where I need to worry about moving without being noticed. But I have to keep moving, because I need to be on the other side of the mountain before sunrise, where the darkness becomes my friend once again and I shudder to consider the consequences of being caught.

I dust the sand off my legs and body. Stretch my limbs. Pick up the basket. And keep moving. The faint starlight provides only enough light for me to see the ground immediately around me. The black contour of the mountain carving out a swath of stars. I continue to follow the shore until the rocks transition to small cliffs and a slight misstep could send me into the sea. Pick my steps slowly, carefully, steadily. Rounding the mountain, I use the trees to guide my steps. I brace my hand on a tree, search out the next nearest tree, and move directly toward it until my hand is safely braced once again. I rely on the contours of trees and rocks against the starry sky. It's slow. It's tedious. But it's safe. And on a night without the moonlight to illuminate a treacherous path, you choose safety over speed.

As I pick my way from tree to tree, I feel the brush grow thicker and thicker against my legs as they begin to itch and run warm. I know this pain. When Mehan and I would gather over here, we sometimes caught ourselves in thorns. In the daylight, they were easy to spot and avoid. Here in the blackness, there's no way to see them. I just have to endure them.

Step-by-step, tree-by-tree, the horizon gradually fading from black to deep blue. It won't be long before the sun begins to rise. When the mountain blocks the place where the sun rises from my view, I know it's behind me and the other village is near. Without a sandy shoreline to muffle my footfalls here, I step gently down the mountain, past my vantage point, toward Prem's house. No one in the village is stirring yet. I tiptoe toward the door of Prem's hut and place the basket by the frame. As I pivot on my back foot to turn around, a sudden rustling from inside the hut paralyzes me. I want to run away. But I'm too shocked and nervous. Prem juts her head outside her hut. She gasps, readying for a scream. Then she stops herself. Narrows her eyes at me.

"Uri!?" She whispers frantically.

I don't say anything. Despite all my planning and all my contingencies, I hadn't anticipated this.

"What are you doing here?" She whispers again, this time harshly.

"I thought you'd be asleep," I whisper back, stunned to be having this conversation.

"I have a baby. I never sleep. What are you doing here?"

I look down toward the basket of fish. She follows my eyes, then looks back up at me confused, expecting an explanation.

"I saw you and your baby when I brought fish on an exchange trip. I want to help you."

The confusion remains. "Help me do what?"

"Fish. I'll bring you fish. Every empty moon. Every half-moon. Every full moon. Er, I guess it will have to be the day before the full moon since we have legacy talks the day of every full moon. But you will have to leave a basket outside the village for me so I don't have to risk my life sneaking into your village every time. Can you do that?" I point toward my vantage point slightly up the mountainside. Dawn is breaking. Prem nods, unsure of what to make of all this. Another rustling sound from inside her hut. I don't wait or say goodbye. I scurry up the hill and out of sight as quietly as possible. When I'm a safe distance from the village, I ease my stride. My heart, racing. My breathing, quick.

The stark silhouette of the mountain to my left. The open sea to my right. The oranges and pinks in the sky and on the water before me. I've never watched the sunrise from this spot on the island before. It's one of the most stunning views I've ever seen. Were my heart and breath not already exhausted, the sight of this sunrise would have stolen them from me.

The ascendant morning light guides my path back around the mountain, through the trees that had been my guide and the brush that had been my adversary in the darkness. My legs are streaked and swollen from the thorns. When I've rounded the mountain and the cliffs transition back into rocks and the rocks transition back into sand, I wade out into the water and wash the dried blood off of my legs. It stings. But as I think about Prem and her family having a little more to eat today, the pain seems like a small sacrifice. It won't solve all of her problems, but maybe it will allow her and her baby to sleep a little more soundly with full stomachs just for tonight.

I return to my village. Past Penja, who waves when he sees me. To the shore to join Chuan and the other builders. It isn't even midday yet. No one asks me where I've been.

Perfect.

• • •

The half-moon greets me as I rise to greet the sun. Knowing that Prem has left a basket for me, I'm not concerned about the time that I arrive at her village. I just need to leave my village at an inconspicuous time in the morning and return before the evening meal. I grab a couple of fish. Wave to Penja on the way out. Make the long walk around the mountain. Go to my vantage point. Find the basket that Prem left for me. Drop the fish in the basket. Retrace my steps back home. Wave to Penja on my way back in. Join the builders on the shore. No one questions where I have been.

Perfect.

• • •

The day before the full moon, I do the same. Sunrise. Fish. Penja. Mountain. Vantage point. Basket. Leave.

But this time, something different.

As I turn to leave, my legs go flying out from underneath me, slamming my back against the rocky hillside. The stars in my eyes clearing, I find myself looking up the shaft of a spear that follows directly into Degi's furious eyes.

"What are you doing here?" Degi growls through clenched teeth.

Clouds in my mind. Throbbing body. I can't answer.

"Why are you here? To steal from us? To spy? To hurt us? I'll kill you on this very spot, Uri."

I gasp. I wheeze. Weakly lift my arm and point downhill toward the basket of fish.

Degi quickly shoots a glance downhill. "What's in the basket?"

I sputter a raspy, "Fish."

"Why fish?"

I want to tell him the whole story, hoping that in hearing my good intentions, he would realize that this is all just a big misunderstanding and let me up. But after multiple attempts at speaking, the only two words I can muster are, "Prem. Baby."

Degi doesn't know how to react, the expression on his face alternating between rage and confusion. "We don't need more fish, Uri. Prem doesn't need more fish. Her baby doesn't need more fish. Fish won't solve the problem. Your tribe is the problem. Your presence on this island. Your hoarding of the island's resources. Your abuse of our tribe. These are the problems. A basket of fish fixes nothing."

"I know. Just trying to help." Relieved I can speak in full sentences again.

“No,” Degi replies coldly, “you weren’t.”

“Yes I was,” I retort back, sounding as offended as my strained, raspy voice will allow.

“No you weren’t,” Degi quips back. Keeping his spear pointed at my neck, he crouches down by my side and leans close into me like he’s telling me a secret. But rather than whisper, he speaks loudly, firmly, his voice more sinister than I’ve ever heard it before. “You do this for yourself. Not for Prem. Not for her baby. Not for my tribe. You happened to come here on an exchange trip and you were sickened by what you saw. I watched your face. I saw your revulsion at the conditions you have forced us to live in. And you felt guilty. But rather than doing something that might actually change anything, you’re just doing enough to appease your own guilt. You did this for *yourself*, Uri. Don’t try to fool me. Don’t try to fool yourself by believing that bringing a couple of fish over here makes you any less responsible for our plight. You are responsible, Uri. Everyone in your tribe is responsible. And the only way to fix this problem is for all of you to be gone.”

Degi’s words pierce me more deeply than the spear in his hand ever could. I have no defense. Tears pour from my eyes like blood from a gaping wound. “No. You’re wrong!” But maybe he’s right.

Degi withdraws his head. Rises to his feet.

"Go home, Uri. Don't ever come back here. Ever. Soon your tribe will be gone. And our tribe will be just fine. There will be peace on this island once again. The problem will be fixed. And you can forget your guilt just as quickly as we forget you."

I slowly work myself to my feet. First, I lift my head. Then my shoulders. I slide my hands to push my torso upright. Roll to my knees. Eventually to my feet. I ache everywhere. Degi watches, pleased with himself.

I shoot him one last glare before turning to walk away. As I take my first step, Degi calls out, "Hey, Uri."

I turn, disdain in my eyes.

"Tell Brisa 'hi' for me." He snickers and walks away.

Heat rushes down my neck as a sloppy kind of anger rises in me. I want to unleash all of it onto Degi. But I don't stand a chance against him with his spear. So instead, I clench the anger in my fists, in my jaw, in my throat, and I walk away as quickly as I can. When I'm a good distance from their village, I scream. I roar. I stomp. I punch trees. And then I weep.

I'm utterly helpless. Helpless against Degi with his spear. Helpless against the hunger that plagues Prem and her baby. Helpless against the hatred between our villages. Helpless against the crisis of trees. Helpless against the careening of time toward that final full moon when we will board twelve boats and chase the place where the sun rises. I'm helpless against them; yet, I've had a hand in all of them.

When my tears are exhausted, when my throat is raw, when my hands are throbbing, I concede to my helplessness and stagger the rest of the way back toward my village. Painful step by painful step. Degi's words ringing in my ears. One word in particular: guilt. I'm appalled by his accusation that my trips have been motivated by guilt. But I can't think of any other explanation for it. Love? I don't love Prem. Fear? No. Compassion? I had thought so. I'd like to think so. But is it really compassion if all I'm doing is dropping a couple of fish every so often in a basket that's hidden away on a mountainside? Doesn't compassion require more personal investment in the object of one's compassion? That's the way the legacy trees have always made it seem.

Maybe there's more guilt in my actions than I realize. How did Degi see through me like that? He saw something in me that I couldn't even see myself. I've always thought of Degi as somewhat of a brute. All action, little thought. Perhaps there's more to him than I realize. Or perhaps he just has some innate understanding of people like Mehan does. The two of them are really quite alike.

I pass Penja on the way back into the village. Hide my pain behind a smile and a wave. He waves back. It's well past midday, but instead of going to the shore, I head straight for my hut and don't come out until the following morning just before we depart for the legacy talk.

• • •

On the morning of the full moon, we follow Chranit up the mountain toward the Old Grove. Sit uphill from the tree at which he stops. He begins, "Today, we reach back to the early days of our tribe to learn about the origins of a value that our tribe holds in the highest regard: Justice."

Justice. The very sound of the word makes me cringe. It stirs up images of Prem, Degi, the multitude of hungry faces. Guilt. Compassion. The accusation that I'm not doing anything meaningful about the plight of their village. All the rage that I felt toward Degi resurges in my chest. I stand up. Chranit pauses mid-sentence surprised by my disturbance. I step over people, making my way back down the mountain. A thousand eyes on my back. I don't care. No, that's not true. I do care. I care that they have stopped listening to Chranit and are watching me walk away. I care that they're seeing me stand up for Justice. I care that they're curious as to why. I hope they ask me so I can tell them about the things I've seen. And I hope they will join me in standing up for Justice, too. I wish Degi could see me now.

I pass Mehan on my way out. He looks at me and shrugs as if to ask what's going on. I shake my head slightly and keep walking. Not sure of exactly where I should go or what I should do to pronounce my great act of rebellion, I head straight to my hut and stay there for the rest of the day. Perhaps my absence will force people to think about Justice and our tribe's unjust dealing with the other village for themselves. Then I can re-emerge at tonight's Council meeting, which should be ablaze in debate, to take my stand against Chief Sangra and whomever else is responsible for the conditions at the other village.

Throughout the day, I hear sets of feet accompanied by hushed voices outside my door. But no one ever prods me to come out. The crack of light in my doorframe gradually fades darker throughout the day as the sun completes its arc and the only light remaining is that of the flickering fire. People gather for the evening meal. I remain in my hut. When the conversations around the fire begin to lull, I know it's time for the Council meeting to begin.

I roll out of my hut quickly, trying to take a path to the Forum that will avoid interaction with anyone else. My legs quiver as I walk. I can't tell if it's from nerves, or lack of eating, or Degi's attack yesterday. All three are taking a toll on me. Deep breaths and clenched fists hold them at bay. Stay composed.

I hesitate for a moment before crossing the threshold into the Forum, prepared to face the uproar that my abrupt exit from the legacy talk is sure to have stirred. I walk in and take my usual seat. No one treats me unusually. Sangra opens the meeting in the usual way. We discuss the usual things. After the usual amount of time, Sangra asks if anyone has anything else to discuss. As usual, no one says anything.

What's going on? Why isn't there an uproar? About me defiantly walking out of the legacy talk? About Justice? About the way we're treating the other village? Why isn't there so much as a spirited debate?

As Sangra begins his motion to conclude the meeting, I rise to my feet. "Wait!" I shout.

Sangra looks at me with a smile. "Ah, Uri. I take it you're feeling better?"

This hits me unexpectedly. "Feeling better?"

"I heard you got sick at the legacy talk this morning, abruptly left, and spent the rest of the day in your hut. Must have been pretty bad. Quite a few folks were worried about you. And we were worried that last month's sickness was about to start making its rounds again. I'm relieved to see that you're feeling better."

"No. Well. I." I'm stunned. Annoyed. Insulted. My grand act of protest was misinterpreted – intentionally or unintentionally – as a stomach illness. This whole day, rather than debating Justice and change, the tribe has been wondering when they should come check on me. I shake off this distraction, accepting this wrinkle as a second chance. A second chance to make my point. And a second chance to decide whether or not I even want to make the point. If I'm not willing to deal with the consequences of raising this issue, I have an opportunity in this moment to play the whole thing off as a sickness. But if I am willing to see it through, this moment is my opportunity to speak openly and directly to a captive audience of the island's decision makers. I waver between the two in my mind for a moment of a moment. The course of my life in the balance. I see both paths in front of me. The easier path is much more appealing, except for the weighty disappointment that I would carry with me forever.

Here it goes. "I wasn't sick. I walked out of the legacy talk because it was wrong. Chranit was speaking about Justice. About how much we value Justice. And yet I've seen firsthand how our tribe is not only failing to uphold Justice, but is possibly even suppressing it. I couldn't sit there and listen to something that I knew was untrue. Not only untrue, but wrong."

Murmuring in the Forum.

"Uri, what are you talking about?" Chranit

calls to me from across the room.

"Earlier this month," I call back to him, "I took it upon myself to sneak over to the other village. I saw how they live. They're hungry. We don't give them enough fish. They barely have enough to survive."

Sangra interjects. "We make an even exchange with them, Uri. Six baskets of fish for six baskets of berries. And we have to distribute those six baskets of berries across five times as many people as they have to distribute their six baskets of fish."

"But we have an endless supply of fish available to us. We can always go out and catch more if we need more."

"And they can always go and gather more berries."

"But, Chief, a handful of fish is so much more filling than a handful of berries. I can eat berries all day long and still be hungry. If they need more food, they should be getting more fish, not more berries."

"And they are welcome to go fishing for those fish if they choose."

"You can't fish off that shore. Not by boat. Nor by wading. Otherwise, why would they need to depend on us for fish in the first place?" And in my last question, everything suddenly fits together. Depend. This dependency was created by Sangra so he could control their tribe. It isn't an oversight. It isn't a miscalculation. It isn't even a severe punishment, as I had suspected it was. It's something far more intricate. Sangra knows that whoever controls the food on this island controls the island. The other village may not regard him as their chief, but by controlling their food, he can effectively control them as a chief would.

I feel foolish for being blind to that until now. Sickened that I have been part of something so cruel. My stomach churns as I ask, "Who set the terms of the exchange? Six baskets of berries for six baskets of fish. Who set those terms? Them or us?"

"They agreed to those terms," Sangra says sternly, no doubt wanting to silence me, but aware that he can't do so without arousing the suspicion of the Council.

"But who set them?" I press. "Did the other village even have a choice in the matter?"

"They have always had a choice, Uri. They had the choice to stay with us through this crisis or to separate from us and deepen it. They chose to deepen the crisis. After they chose to separate, they had the choice to maliciously threaten us or to let us carry out our task in peace. They chose malice. They had the choice to steal from us, to vandalize our homes, to scatter putrid fish throughout our village. The terms were much more favorable for them at the outset of this crisis. But they have ratified these new terms through every reprehensible thing they have done. *They* must live with the consequences of their actions, not us!"

The Council is becoming uneasy with the tension in the room. Silence. Shifting in their seats.

"But what about Justice?" I ask feebly, a final effort to plea my case.

"What about it, Uri? They harass us, we do nothing. They attack us, we do nothing. Soon our people are afraid and demoralized; meanwhile, there is no limit to the other village's oppression. Is that Justice? Would you rather have it that way?"

I have nothing to say to this. No better solution to offer. Though I still feel the heavy conviction in my heart that our actions are wrong, I have no way of articulating it. So I answer with a quiet, defeated, "No. But they are still our brothers and sisters."

"They will always be." With that, Sangra abruptly motions for the meeting to adjourn. Council members look at one another, confused by the harsh dispute that they just witnessed. I rise to leave, disheartened. But as I do, I hear Sangra's unmistakable deep voice. "Uri." I turn to him. He motions stiffly with his finger for me to come to him. My knees become shaky. I walk toward him. He doesn't acknowledge me until the Forum has cleared and we are alone. When it's just the two of us remaining in the center of the Forum, he motions for me to sit across from him.

Sangra inhales deeply and exhales with a groan, looking at me like he's not sure what to do with me. "Why am I here, Uri?"

He says it like a statement, so I don't answer. But after an uncomfortable amount of time passes, I realize that it might have actually been a question. "I –"

"Why do we need a chief? We have the Council to govern the tribe. We have judges to arbitrate disputes. We assign duties to ensure that everything necessary to sustain our tribe is accomplished. We have families that care for one another. All of these things go on without my involvement. If I were to step away, it would all continue to run smoothly. So what purpose do I serve?"

I've never really questioned this before. We've always had a chief. It's just an accepted part of life in our tribe. To imagine our tribe without a chief is to imagine the sky without stars. So why does the sky have stars? "I guess you hold it all together."

Sangra shrugs his eyebrows as he considers my response. "That's very perceptive of you, Uri. But not quite. I don't hold it all together. The trees of the Grove of Ancestors – the legacies they reveal to us – are what hold it all together. So my role as Chief is to constantly point our tribe toward the trees. I must be a continual reminder, a sun that remains permanently fixed above the Grove of Ancestors, a living tree in the midst of our village whose branches point everyone toward the hillsides. Do you understand this?"

I nod.

Sangra nods and continues. "Our tribe is special, Uri. I don't know if people appreciate how special we are. Trees grow in the places where we die. The first time this happened, it shocked our ancestors. This sort of thing didn't happen in the place where they came from. It's special and mysterious. And, ironically, it's the reason why we're embarking on this journey away from them. They're so special that it's better for us to leave them than it is for us to cut them down for common use. In leaving them, we will certainly lose sight of each individual legacy that the trees proclaim. But we establish an enduring legacy that will be handed down to every generation that follows us. It might be the most important legacy of all: that it's the unseen things, not the seen things, which define who we are and what we strive for. It isn't an easy decision, but I'm convinced that it's the right decision. Can you appreciate that, Uri?"

I nod again.

"I wish Abis could appreciate that, too. At least enough so that he wouldn't feel compelled to create trouble for us while we prepare for this great and fearsome journey. But he couldn't. He can't. For him, the island is what holds everything together. Our tribe's identity is this island. And he will fight for it. He would sacrifice the trees in order to remain on this island. But you and I understand that it isn't the island that holds us together – it's the trees. In Abis' obstinacy, he was prepared to sabotage everything. The threats, the dead fish, these were just the beginning. He would have made it impossible for us to leave. Until we had no option but to stay on this island with him, desolating the mountainsides for survival, reducing the size of our tribe, laboring to restore balance between tree growth and consumption. And it likely wouldn't have even worked out in the end. In an effort to preserve some things, we might have lost everything. And I couldn't bear that possibility. My purpose as chief is to not allow that. My purpose is to ensure that we uphold the virtues and legacies that the trees proclaim. Nothing can stand in the way of that."

I find his words both moving and disturbing. "But what if, in upholding the virtues and legacies of the trees, we violate the very virtues they proclaim?"

Sangra looks perplexed by my question.

"Like Justice," I try to explain. "The trees proclaim Justice. But what if, in trying to uphold Justice, we find ourselves behaving unjustly. Like we're behaving toward Abis' village?"

"Their village threatens Justice for us. If the only way for Justice to be upheld for the whole is for it to be taken away from the few who threaten it, then it's an unfortunate but necessary sacrifice."

"But then what good is Justice as a virtue if the only way to uphold it is to undermine it?"

Sangra shifts in his seat, visibly frustrated by my persistence. "So what would you do, Uri? Let's say you're the chief. What would you do in this situation?"

"I don't know. I would try to find a way to uphold Justice for everyone."

Sangra leans forward. "That's another thing about being chief, Uri. There's no room for 'I don't know.' You have to know. Always. Even when you don't. And you have to fight for what you know. Always. I know that Justice is worth preserving. And I made a decision that will preserve it. In the end, if Justice endures, then it was the right decision."

I'm at a loss. My mouth is open, ready to counter him, but words aren't coming. I don't agree with him, but I don't have anything else to offer that might persuade him otherwise.

Sangra continues, "Uri, you showed poor judgment in secretly visiting the other village. It was dangerous and it could have caused a lot of problems for everyone in our village. In order for this Council to retain the trust and confidence of our tribe, it must be comprised of people who demonstrate sound judgment. I need you to step down. You have many gifts, Uri. And your contribution to the design and construction of those magnificent boats can never be overstated. But I can't allow you to serve on the Council any longer. Do you understand?"

His words come like a punch to the stomach. I nod slightly, afraid that if I nod too much the tears in my eyes will come pouring out. Sangra nods back solemnly. He rises from his seat, walks over to me, tenderly touches my shoulder, and walks out of the Forum. I sit alone for a while, allowing the swirling dust to settle in my mind, hoping that this distraught feeling settles with it. It doesn't.

As I leave the Forum, I glance up at the moon resting in its fullness. Calm. Steadfast. Unaffected.

How I wish I could be more like the moon.

Chapter 14

The Eighth Moon

I had expected to wake up the morning after my last Council meeting feeling depressed. But I didn't. Nor the next day. Nor the day after that. Instead, I've felt strangely relieved. Even happy. From time-to-time, a wave of resentment or embarrassment or frustration washes over me when I think back to that meeting. But never shame. And that has made all the difference. I stood for my conviction. And I feel no shame in that. Where I've failed Brisa, Mehan, even myself by not fighting for what's important, at that meeting, I finally fought for something. I lost. But I fought.

"Uri!" Chuan snaps at me, pulling me out of my thoughts. I look up to him from the stack of wood in front of me to see his annoyed expression. He gives me an over-exaggerated shrug. I hand him a couple of planks. Since the Council meeting, Chuan has been especially short with me. I'm pretty sure it's due to my confession that my recent absenteeism from boat building was not only intentional, but was spent doing something so objectionable. It made him look bad as supervisor of the boat building crew. And it wounded him even on a more personal level. Two months ago, he was encouraging me to move forward with my life. Move forward with Brisa. Instead, I went away from that conversation and took a definitive step backward. If I regret anything about my actions, it's the way they have changed things between me and Chuan.

I look out across the bay. Twelve boats in various stages of building. A few are complete. A few are little more than frames. Most are somewhere in between. They are beautiful along the bay. Like a little village all to themselves out in the water. I scan them all the way from one end of the shore to the other. I scan past the last boat and continue up the beach, past the treeline, past Brisa, past –

Past Brisa?

I dart my eyes back to her. Standing there looking at me. Curiously. Invitingly. I glance back over to Chuan who is muttering to himself as he wrestles one of the planks into position. He's fine without me.

As I approach her, I notice the corner of her mouth drawn into the most subtle smile I've ever seen. So beautiful.

"Walk?" She asks. I glance back over my shoulder to see grumpy Chuan still wrestling with the same plank. He won't notice my absence for a while. Back to Brisa.

We walk out of the village, across the

grassy plain toward the ridge. For the entire ascent, we simply enjoy one another's company in silence. As we reach the crest of the ridge, we stop. Ocean in front of us. Ocean behind us. Mountain to our left. Mountain to our right. We take it all in through slow, deep breaths.

From the ridge, you can see both villages. Brisa's attention falls on Abis' village and the subtle smile turns into a subtle frown. She stares for a few moments before the subtle smile returns and she playfully says, "So, I hear you've been stirring quite a bit of controversy at the Council meetings lately."

I laugh, surprised that she heard about the Council meeting. And glad that she did. "Someone needs to bring some excitement to those meetings every once in a while." I say with as much dissidence as I'm capable of.

She laughs again and enquires, "So tell me what happened."

" At the Council meeting?"

"No, everything! Tell me the whole story. From the beginning."

I try to think when the 'beginning' was. The crisis of the trees? The conversation with Chuan? The exchange trip? Caught up in the moment, I just begin at the exchange trip. "Well, remember a couple of months ago when that sickness was passing through the village?"

"Of course."

"I had offered to Alver to fill in if he ever

needed help on the exchange trips, since Mehan and I used to make that trip every day when we were gatherers. Well, it turned out that he needed help one day during that wave of sickness. So I went. Brisa, I wasn't prepared for what I saw during that trip. The people in Abis' village don't look like themselves. They're hungry. They're tired. They're empty."

"Why?" She asks.

"They don't have enough food. And we are their main source of food."

"But I see baskets full of fish go over there every day."

"I know. It looks like a lot when it leaves here. But when you see how many people it needs to feed, you realize that it isn't much at all. And they are bay-caught fish, so you have to figure that half of what's in those baskets is bones."

"Why aren't we giving them enough?"

"I guess it's some sort of punishment for the things they did after the split – the stealing, the rotting fish, the threats. Some sort of way to keep them under our control."

"I never realized," she trails off, absorbed by some thought.

"Neither did I, Brisa. It wasn't until I went over there and saw for myself. And the thing that stuck with me most was seeing a young mother holding her baby close to her bony chest as she picked through the baskets to find two small fish. That was the turning point for me. I knew I needed to do something."

"A baby?" Her voice turns to surprise. It's amazing how something that was once so common can so quickly become something so novel. Like a baby. We used to welcome several new babies into our tribe each month. But for the last couple of months, there have been no new babies. And no new pregnancies. Another testament to how we've put our lives on hold. "Whose baby?" She asks.

I've always sensed an awkwardness between Brisa and Prem. Brisa has never expressed disdain toward Prem, but there's something about the way she gets so quiet anytime I mention Prem's name. I proceed delicately, "Do you remember Prem?"

"Prem?" She repeats quickly. Her face flushes red as she looks away from me. "I didn't realize she had a baby."

"Neither did I. Until I went on that exchange trip with Alver."

Something about this piques Brisa. She furrows her eyes, looks up at me with a confused expression. "Wait. I heard that you snuck over to the other village on your own. But you just said you went with Alver." She allows that to hang between us for a moment, begging a response.

A warmth rushes over my body. This is tricky. At the Council, in order to protect Alver,

I had only told everyone about my sneaking over on my own. Now, in order to protect Brisa, I only told her about my trip with Alver, not realizing that she knew about my solo trips. My stomach sinks. I know how this conversation is going to end. I can't cover this up with a lie. Not to Brisa. "Both are true."

"Both?" She asks sharply.

"I did go over with Alver. But when I saw the conditions of the village, I decided that I needed to do something about it. So I began carrying extra fish over there on my own from time to time."

"Extra fish? They just let you walk into their village with extra deliveries of fish?"

"No. I had to do it secretly. No one from our village could know. No one from their village could know."

"If no one from their village knew, how did they get your fish?"

"Prem was the only person who knew. I had her hide a basket for me outside of the village where I could leave them."

"You and Prem did this together in secret?" She looks like she's about to cry. Or vomit. "Why didn't you tell me? Why would you share a secret with Prem that you couldn't share with me?"

"I was afraid you'd be upset if you knew."

"That makes it worse, Uri!" Her breathing becomes quick and shallow. "How do you really see us? Because I thought I knew. But then you go and do something like this and suddenly I'm not so sure anymore."

The pace of my voice becomes more frantic, "Nothing has changed, Brisa. My feelings for you will never change. I didn't mean to hurt you. I never want to hurt you."

Tears in her eyes. Tears in my eyes. If it weren't for the tears, I'd be afraid that all hope was lost for us. A painful silence. She puts her hands on her head, looks like she's about to say something, stops herself, closes her eyes tightly, turns, and walks away.

• • •

The eighth sunrise on the morning of the eighth full moon as the tribe gathers for the eighth legacy talk. I almost don't go. I haven't seen Brisa in nearly a month. The day after our argument, I picked some flowers off of a tree and laid them at her doorstep. But I never heard from her. I miss her every day.

Chranit leads the way as he always does; however, today he cuts up the mountain toward the New Grove. When we're seated uphill from him, he begins.

"We've told some extraordinary stories over the past seven months. These stories are our stories. The things we do. The things we value. The things we strive for. They've all been shaped by stories like these. But there's a danger in focusing solely on extraordinary stories like these. A danger that we would allow ourselves to believe that our legacy is only meaningful if it's equally as extraordinary, or that all of the stories worth telling have already been told. But the lush mountainsides bear witness to a different truth – the truth that every legacy matters. That there's power even in the ordinary. That even a simple, common legacy like kindness can be told a thousand times and never lose its splendor. That the legacies never fade or change.

"Does the ocean fall away? Do its tides rest? Does its saltiness fade? Of course not. And though I've watched these waves crash against the shore my entire life, I find their beauty no less enthralling today than I did when I was a child. Each wave beautiful in its own way. In just the same way, we can sit on this hill and be captivated by the towering legacies of people just like ourselves who spent their entire lives striving for the same virtues that we do. They may not have rescued people from a great fire, or united us in some pivotal way, or ignited a revolution. In fact, we may never know most of their names. But their collective presence reveals this captivating truth that there are unseen things in life that are greater than any of us. Greater, even, than the sum of every life that has ever graced this island. That new trees grow with each passing life shows we haven't exhausted the limit of these unseen things. Maybe they are limitless. Unending. Unchanging. Unfading. Inescapable.

"Consider these two trees behind me. You probably don't know these trees. Or the names of the people that preceded them. If it weren't for the legacy stones at their base, neither would we. But this we know: that they lived in the thirtieth generation, that their names were Mila and Caru, that they left a legacy of love for one another. And we know what their trees proclaim. The lush, abundant leaves. The way in which branches reach from one tree to the next, entwined in embrace. And most notably, their fragrance. Sometimes I come to these trees just to smell their fragrances. Sweet. Dense. Unique among the other fragrances of the forest.

"What do these trees teach us about Love? That it is life-giving. That it fills all spaces just as its leaves and branches flourish abundantly. There are no barren spots. There are no places separate or hidden. That it produces life, rather than detracting from it. And that it draws people into it. The fragrance of deep, abiding love is attractive to everyone who encounters it.

"So I invite you to learn from Mila and Caru and to powerfully live out the lesson of their legacy in your life. Don't assume that a life that seems ordinary is somehow less important or less beautiful. Learn love from these trees and love likewise in your life. Love, like all legacies, requires commitment to something greater than oneself, forsaking many of the immediate, seen things in order to attain this greater unseen thing. And the more you commit yourself to it, the more you realize that its depths have no bounds."

Almost immediately after concluding, as the seated crowd rises and chatters, Chranit looks directly at me. Silently beckoning me. I walk over to him. When I'm within earshot, a sly grin graces his face and he calls out to me, "So my storytelling was more to your liking this time, Uri?"

I know what he's referring to, but I'm embarrassed, so I act confused in hopes that he will leave it alone. He prods me again, "I'm relieved that I was able to hold your attention through the entire story. When you walked off last month I was afraid I had lost my touch." The sly grin grows. He winks and motions his head for me to walk with him.

The two of us walk down the hill of the New Grove toward the center of the island. His steps are slow. I keep finding myself ahead of him and having to pull myself back. It isn't his age that slows his steps; it's his nature. He simply isn't in a hurry. So why am I? I slow and shorten my stride to match his, consciously measuring every step.

I've forgotten how the island looks and smells and sounds and feels when you aren't in a hurry. On gathering trips with Mehan I was never in a hurry. On walks with Brisa I was never in a hurry. Our leisurely pace takes me back to those days. Before we were building boats. Before there weren't enough trees. Before the tension, the conflict, the injustice. When the far side of the island was overrun with berries and no one on our island was starving. In those days, Mehan and I would walk together. He was always in a hurry. In my wandering, I never understood why. Now I find myself in a constant hurry and I don't understand why either. But I find the hurry escaping me with each step of Chranit's slow, mindful pace.

"What's on your mind, Uri?" He finally asks.

What's on my mind? Brisa. Degi. Sangra. Prem. Chuan. Boats. Fish. The horizon. What isn't on my mind? What isn't broken right now? The very mention of his question causes the hurry to return to me once again. I look at him as my breath shortens and my heart quickens. But in his quizzical, sincere eyes, I find myself brought back into unexplainable stillness. A calm. A comfort. A safety. The clutter of images scatters from my mind and I'm able to focus.

"Do you remember last month's Council meeting?" I ask.

"Yes. Vividly. You had quite a bit on your

mind that night, didn't you?"

The hurry rises to my defense. "If you had seen what I saw Chranit, you would know. You would have done the same thing-"

"Slow down, Uri. Take me back further. What compelled you to sneak over to the other village in the first place?"

I think back to my first trip with Alver. But I need to go even further back than that. To my conversation with Chuan. To the fear that Brisa and I were putting our lives on hold for no good reason while the other village was carrying on with their lives. The fear that we were missing out on precious time. "Chranit, remind me why we are leaving this island."

"We won't survive if we stay. You know that, Uri."

"Maybe we could. If we used the trees of the Grove of Ancestors. If we cut back on our need for trees. If we planted lots and lots of new trees. If our tribe could find a way to grow smaller. Maybe we could survive."

"So many 'ifs'," Chranit says as though it's only half a thought, leaving us walking in silence for a while before he continues, "Trees grow; trees are cut down. People are born; people die. Clouds pass overhead, never to be seen again. Waves crawl up the shore and melt into the sand. Day; then night. Then day again. Stars shift places in the sky. The moon grows; the moon fades. Though the island doesn't change, everything upon its face is constantly changing. Do you understand these things, Uri?"

"Yes."

"Good. That is the first great truth: every visible thing passes. But there's a second great truth: every invisible thing endures. Unseen things that you can't see or touch or hear or smell or taste. You can't carve their image. You can't carry them in a basket. You can chase them, but you can't capture them. And, yet, as intangible as they are, they can be perceived by everyone. Not only perceived, but attained. They have weight. We frame our lives around them. Do you understand this?"

"I think I do."

"Well, let's think back to the Council meeting. You spoke of Justice. What does Justice taste like?"

I give a short, knowing laugh as I try to think of how to answer that.

He smiles and continues, "What does Justice sound like? Can you carve me an image of Justice? Have you ever walked out of your hut in the morning, taken that first deep breath of the day, and gotten a big whiff of Justice?" We're both chuckling by this point. Then Chranit's tone becomes serious again. "Why, then, would you criticize the Council for something that you can't even apprehend?"

The hurry. "But I can! If you could have

seen the village for yourself, Chranit, you would understand!"

Chranit holds up his hand to still me. "Unless…unless you can, indeed, apprehend Justice. Maybe you can't perceive it with your senses, but you can perceive it. And something deep down inside of you reacts, responds, stirs. It's those kinds of things, Uri. The second great truth. The Unseen things that we can't explain directly; we can only explain them indirectly by describing the way they give meaning to the Seen things. The Unseen things that endure while the physical things pass. And that raises some profound questions about the mysterious nature of Unseen things. Where do they come from? Why do they matter? Why do they endure? We don't know. All we know is that they are real and they demand our attention. Do you understand better now, Uri?"

"Yes."

"So, let's bring it all back to your question. Why are we leaving the island? The answer can be found by contemplating the two great truths: every visible thing passes and every invisible thing endures. The Grove of Ancestors is this rare, sacred place where the invisible things somehow become visible, allowing us to apprehend them even with our senses. The trees shouldn't cause us to confuse the Seen with the Unseen; rather, they should help us understand the Unseen more clearly by providing us with tangible glimpses into Unseen things. But if we stay on this island to cut the trees down for common use, we would be confusing the Seen with the Unseen. And we might never be able to recover from that confusion."

"I don't understand. Aren't we also confusing the Seen for Unseen by refusing to cut the trees down?"

Chranit starts to respond then refrains, pursing his lips as he considers my challenge. "You may be on to something there, Uri. But if we are to err, isn't it better to err on the side of the enduring things, rather than the passing things, especially since the plan to err on the side of the passing may ultimately fail?"

"What if we don't fail? What if we are able to change?"

Chranit stops. Looks deeply into my eyes. Compassion in his. "Let me show you something, Uri." By this time, we have crossed the grassy plain and are at the fringe of the Old Grove. He looks uphill, finds his bearings, and leads us deep into the Old Grove. "Not many people know what I'm about to show you, Uri. In fact, almost no one else knows about it. But you're in a fragile place. And I feel that knowing it might be helpful for you. My heart would break if we lost someone as special as you along the way."

We walk up the hill, the trees becoming

taller and thicker. The valley, the village, the ocean shrinking farther away as we climb higher. Chranit doesn't slow or speed his pace. Each step exactly like the last. Each breath exactly like the last. He stops at a tree close to the top of the mountain. Even from this point, we can look out across the top of the other mountain, the lake within its mountaintop bowl shimmering brilliantly in the sunlight.

"The island that our ancestors lived on was very different from the island that we live on today," he explains. "The mountains were bare. The valley was forested. No house or boat or fire pit stood. Most people are aware of that. But what most people aren't aware of is that the island was also full of creatures."

"Creatures?" I ask. "What does that mean?"

"Living things. Like fish and insects. But they weren't fish or insects. They were somehow different. Bigger. Of a different kind of flesh. No one alive today is exactly sure what they were like. Some walked on the ground with legs. Some flew through the air with wings."

My head hurts trying to imagine these creatures, fascinated by the very suggestion. All I can picture are giant bugs or fish with legs. Finally, I shake my head in frustration. "What happened to these creatures?"

"Apparently their different kind of flesh was very appealing to our ancestors. Just as we catch fish, they caught these creatures and ate their flesh, wore their skins, used their bones. But after a few generations, people began to notice that the creatures became harder and harder to come by. They realized that they were hunting the animals more quickly than they could be replenished. So they tried to stop. They tried switching to a diet of only fish and berries. But to no avail. The few remaining creatures dwindled until they disappeared entirely. And once they were gone, they were gone forever. Some things, once they're gone, they're gone forever." Chranit becomes somber, almost tearful. After a few moments, he leans down and brushes the top of a legacy stone with his fingers. He looks up at me, inviting me to lean in and see for myself.

I study the stone closely. A figure like a circle, with four lines protruding from its bottom and a smaller circle adjacent to a side of the top.

"That's one of the creatures. This man was a hunter." Chranit says. "Like a fisherman, but instead of fish he caught creatures. His legacy is that of provision, of providing for the needs of others even at the expense of himself."

He leads me to the next tree and brushes the legacy stone at its base with his thumb. Another circle, but instead of four lines protruding from the bottom, two slanted lines begin in the middle of the circle and meet together at a point just below the circle.

"Is this a flying creature?" I ask.

"We think so. It certainly isn't a fish." We gaze at the crudely etched flying creature for a few moments before Chranit continues, "And it wasn't just creatures, Uri. Some of the plants that grew on this island when our ancestors arrived no longer grow here either. We've changed the island, Uri. And yet we seem powerless when it comes to changing certain things about ourselves."

That last sentence causes me to wince. "But we have changed. Isn't that what your legacy talks are about? How we've changed?"

"Yes. But they're about how the Unseen things have changed us. Not about how we've changed ourselves. There's a difference. I don't fully understand it myself. In the absence of transformation, we seem destined to tread the same well-worn paths."

There's a truth to his words that I can't deny, no matter how much I want to. I ponder this before returning to the flying creature inscribed on the legacy stone.

After a while, Chranit says, "I think I understand why you went to the other village. And I think I understand why you felt the need to challenge Chief Sangra at the Council meeting. You understand the sacredness of the Unseen, and yet you struggle because you feel that our commitment to the Unseen is somehow causing us to neglect the sacredness of the Seen. I respect this. I will speak to Chief Sangra personally. Perhaps he will be more receptive to your concerns if it came from someone else and in private."

Chapter 15

The Ninth Moon

One month.

It's been one month since I last saw Brisa. More than a month, actually. In as long as I've known her, I've never gone this long without at least seeing her. Without her, I ache. I ache every time I relive our last conversation and the hurt I saw in her eyes.

I need to see her.

I leave boat building early so I can sit outside the weaving hut and catch her as she leaves. I sit with my back against the doorpost, debating in my mind whether I should apologize when I see her or simply be content to leave the past in the past. The sun shines directly into my eyes. I close them and allow my other senses to speak to me. Immediately I'm calmed by the warmth of the sun. It's amazing how the sun can be to my eyes a source of discomfort, while simultaneously being to my skin a source of comfort. And how this same kind of duality plays itself out so frequently in life. Like Brisa. The greatest source of happiness; the greatest source of heartache. Love.

"Uri?" I look up behind me through the doorframe, but she isn't there. Did I imagine her voice? "Uri." She says again. I swing my head the other direction, next to the weaving hut. I scramble clumsily to my feet. Steady myself. Smile. She is skeptical and unamused.

I try to speak, but the sight of her leaves me speechless. "I … Hi."

"Hi," she responds plainly.

"I've-" I hesitate. Don't hesitate, just say it. "I've missed you so much. I can't stand for us to be apart like this. How can I make things right?"

"Where have you been for the last month?" She asks with exasperation in her voice. "Why did you wait so long to do this?"

"I left flowers," I offer, realizing how pathetic the gesture truly was as the words leave my mouth. She rolls her eyes. Nonetheless, I try to plead my case, "I thought you'd be too upset to speak with me."

"Probably. You should have tried anyway."

This doesn't seem fair. She was the one who walked away from our last conversation. Shouldn't she be the one to reach out to me? But even I'm wise enough to know how this conversation would end if I suggested this to her right now. So I choose contrition. "I'm sorry. For everything. I've had a lot of time understand how the things I did must have hurt you. I can see it clearly now. And I'm sorry."

"Don't ever lie to me again. I forgive you. I'm sorry, too." She leaves it at that.

"How have you been?" I ask.

"Mostly sad."

"Because of what I did?"

"Because of us. Because of what you saw in the other village. Because our time on this island is drawing to an end so quickly. Because we're stuck here waiting without really knowing exactly what we're waiting for."

"The moment this whole thing began, everyone suddenly stopped living and started waiting," I add.

"I'm tired of waiting," she says. The longing in her voice, in her eyes.

"I'm tired of waiting, too, Brisa. The reason I wanted to go see the other village is because of a conversation I had with Chuan about waiting. He said that we don't have to wait, that the other village wasn't waiting, that they were moving on with their lives. I wanted to see it for myself because I was frustrated with having to wait for us. For our chance to wrap our lives around one another. I'm ready, Brisa. I'm ready for it to be our time. To move forward. Together."

Her eyes are sparkling with tears. She looks like she wants to say something, but the words won't come out. So instead she just smiles and nods. I pull her as close to me as I possibly can.

"Uri, I want that, too," she says, "but we need to keep waiting. Just a little longer. Until we make it to the other side of the horizon."

Surprised. Exasperated. Frustrated. "Brisa, we've been waiting! How can we move forward if we wait even longer?"

"We can still move forward. In our hearts. In our minds. But I have this feeling that if we move forward in a more public way, we will cause more problems than we realize."

"Problems? What kinds of problems?"

She loosens her embrace. "I know no one has directed everyone in our village put their lives on hold. But the reality is that everyone has. And if we decide suddenly to be the only ones who stop waiting, people will notice. And if people notice, you know that some will feel envy, bitterness, judgment. I don't want something that should be joyful to be marred by those other things. I know my dad, for one, would be upset with us for being so selfish at a time like this."

"I'll talk to him."

"No. That won't change anything. You know him. It's just a few more months, Uri. We're so close; let's not allow something that's supposed to be happy become a thorn."

I cringe my eyes. "So we just keep waiting? Nothing changes?"

Thoughtfully, Brisa offers, "No, something has changed. This is a different kind of waiting.

It's waiting, with the expectation of something better. This kind of waiting doesn't make me sad. It makes me excited. It makes me…giddy."

"Giddy?" I laugh.

"Yes, giddy." She proudly stands by her choice of words.

I pick up her hand and wrap our fingers together. Kiss her cheek softly. Water in her eyes. Wind in her hair. There are moments in life where, even as they're happening, you know you'll never forget them as long as you live. This is one of those moments. This moment, this emotion, this embrace. They'll be with me forever. And for that, I'm giddy, too.

• • •

The early morning walk up the mountainside to the New Grove for another legacy talk has new meaning. Brisa was right. It is a different kind of waiting. Now, every full moon is a month closer to the moment when Brisa and I will be freed from our wait, free to love openly, free to begin living our lives together. Now, the horizon is a doorway to new adventures with Brisa rather than a daunting unknown. Now, boat building is an act of love, rather than a burdensome chore. I approach the work every day with a newfound vigor, which Chuan seems to appreciate, as he has stopped being abrupt with me.

Chranit leads the village through the trees with measured steps, stops at a tree, and allows us to fill in the spaces uphill. "In the forty generations we have been on this island, we've encountered tragedy, adversity, discord, and uncertainty. There were times where, even in hindsight, it's amazing that we survived. But here we are. Strong.

"With each setback, one wonders how we have managed to survive, heal, and grow back stronger than before. The answer is in a simple word: hope.

"It was hope that launched our ancestors from their native land, setting sail for a brighter future. It was hope that established peace after years of war. It was hope that sustained us through months when the skies refused to give up their rains. It is hope that allows us to look at the horizon and imagine a new life for ourselves across the other side. And, if I may be so bold, it is hope that has led some of our brothers and sisters to make the decision to stay on this island.

"Do you understand the power of hope? Hope is the trust that there is purpose behind everything. It's the expectation that someday we might be able to take hold of that purpose for ourselves. And in that trust and expectation, our tribe has found something worth striving for.

"One man in particular comes to mind

every time I hear the word hope. He lived during an event in the twenty fourth generation that nearly washed our tribe off the face of the island. If it hadn't been for this man in particular and the hope he inspired, we may not be here today.

"It began on an unremarkable morning. Azim was down on the shore working on boats just as he had on every other unremarkable morning prior. But on this otherwise unremarkable morning, Azim noticed something remarkable. Something wasn't quite right on the shore. Something wasn't as it should have been. The beach was much broader than it normally was. It resembled low tide, but he had never seen the tide anywhere near as low as it was that morning. It reminded him of the moments between waves, after one crashes and the next one pulls the water back down the beach. The bigger the wave, the more it recedes. It was in that thought that he was struck by a suspicion: could this somehow be caused by a giant wave on its way to the shore? If so, he realized that it was going to be enormous.

"Instinctively, Azim knew that if it was going to be a giant wave, people would need to get out of its way. He ran up the shore to the village, calling out to every hut and person he passed to get as high as possible, leading them to the hillsides. As people joined him in running up the hillsides, Azim's fear came true.

An enormous wave engulfed the shore and crashed onto the island. It washed over the entire village. It raced across the valley. It crawled up the mountainsides. Those who were fleeing kept climbing, climbing, climbing. No looking back. And then, as quickly as the wave came, it receded down the hillsides, the village, the shore, and was gone.

"Azim and the others who had fled with him looked around. A group of roughly fifty people. Exhausted, stunned, confused. Fifty people, out of a village of several hundred, standing there on the mountainside, speechless. Fearful that another wave would come on the heels of the first. Anxious to get back to the village to help any survivors. After much time passed and no other waves came, they mustered the courage to go back down to the village.

"But the village was gone. In an instant. The wave had transformed the place where the village once stood into a sandy, muddy, littered shore. Fallen trees. Ocean debris. Rocks. Pieces of huts. No people.

"There was silence. And then there was weeping. Weeping at the loss of loved ones. Weeping at the loss of their homes. Weeping at the loss of everything they knew. Guilt. Despair. Hopelessness. For days and days and days they wept together, too overcome with sorrow to do anything else. They began to grow weak from a lack of food and water. Some of them didn't care. They welcomed death as a way to be rejoined with those they lost. To be relieved of the weight of their sorrow.

"After so many days of sorrow, Azim was walking through the place where the village once stood when he noticed something in the mud at his feet. He crouched down to investigate it. A tiny, green speck sticking out of the mud. He leaned in closely. Grass. It was a blade of grass. A sliver of green pushing its way out of the mud and mire. It was insignificant. And yet, it was profoundly significant. This blade of grass wasn't welcoming death. It wasn't allowing itself to be crushed under the wreckage. Somehow, it found a reason and a purpose for which to persevere. To persist. To overcome.

"The sight brought Azim to his knees. He lowered his head all the way down and pressed his lips against that little blade of grass, as if to kiss it. Somehow, that tiny blade of grass reminded him that life was worth sustaining. That there are forces at work other than the force of devastation alone. And if a tiny blade of grass could find a reason to persevere through the struggle, perhaps he could, too. That tiny blade of grass saved Azim.

"Immediately, Azim set himself to work building a fire pit next to the blade of grass. When the fire pit was arranged, he built a fire.

Once the fire was lit, he realized how hungry he had become. So he looked for a net. Eventually, he found one tangled in some brush. He carefully picked the net out of the brush and began walking toward the bay. On his way, he noticed that several people had already seated themselves by the fire he had built. A boat builder by trade, he had spent nearly every day of his life building and mending fishing boats; and yet, he had never actually fished. It looked easy. But he quickly learned that it wasn't. After casting his net many times without any luck, he felt a hand on his shoulder. Her turned and was pleasantly surprised to see one of the fishermen. Together, they were soon able to pull in a small catch of fish and haul it up to the fire.

"By the time they returned to the fire, the group huddled around it had grown in number. Some people had even taken to the task of clearing the area around the fire pit. That night, the group ate together. No one spoke, but they were eating again, and they were together again. And in being together, sharing a meal, they began to feel like some semblance of a tribe once again.

"Over time, more debris was cleared. Huts were rebuilt. More fires were built. Boats were rebuilt. Skills were taught and relearned. Families were pieced together out of the survivors. Children were born. And a new generation was formed. This generation understood hope differently than any other generation before it or since. They had lived it in the deepest, most visceral kind of way. Hope to fight through even the fiercest opposition. Hope to endure like the unseen forces at work in the world endure. Hope that blades of grass will grow out of ruins."

As Chranit delivers the very last word of his talk, a cool drop of water splashes on my shoulder. I reach up to touch it. And just like that, as though Chranit had planned it, the skies open up and rain comes pouring down. One of those rains with drops so big, they pelt you. One of those rains where the clouds are spotty and sunbeams dart between the raindrops in a glowing haze. One of those rains that's so thick, it's almost hard to breathe. Chattering in the forest, overwhelming every other sound.

Perhaps on any other day, the rain would have sent people seeking shelter. But not today. Today, with a story of hope fresh on our minds, we let the rain wash over us. Some stretch out their arms. Some dance. Some laugh. Some open their mouths capture the drops in their mouths. To taste it. To allow the rain, like hope, cleanse them inside and out. Because these days we need hope. Maybe more than any of us have needed it before.

Rain down.

• • •

Why does it seem like so many legacies are born out of tragedy?

Isn't that life? Tragedy.

I gasp awake. Open my eyes and roll out of my hut. The rain has cleared. It is late afternoon now. I laid down in my hut after lunch and must have fallen asleep. Mehan. Was that Mehan speaking in my sleep? In a dream? I stretch, trying to rouse myself to go down to the shore to build boats. But I can't shake Mehan from my mind. So instead, I walk out to the edge of the village toward his usual watching post. I recognize him from afar - his sturdy posture squared with the middle of the island watching, waiting, ready.

I approach him and place my hand on his shoulder. He jumps forward and whips around in my direction, startled. When he sees that it's me, he relaxes and puffs deep breaths of air through his cheeks. Regains his composure. Shakes his head at me. Then smiles. "How's it going, Uri?" He manages to ask congenially.

"Did I startle you?" I ask, perplexed by his reaction to my greeting.

"A little," trying to downplay his reaction.

"I was able to sneak up on you? A watcher? Perhaps we need to find another assignment for you, my friend."

"It's called watching, not listening. You snuck up from behind. If you had come from the front, I would have spotted you all the way across the island."

I sarcastically nod and roll my eyes, "Of course you would."

We share a smile, then shift our attention back toward the ridge of the island. The clouds roll up from behind it and fly overhead. Remnants of the clouds that had earlier brought the rains. Reminding me of Chranit's legacy talk. Hope.

"Chranit had some good things to say today," Mehan says without shifting his gaze, apparently reminded of the same.

"I didn't see you there."

"I was late. Came in through the side. Anyway, I've heard Azim's story before. But in all the times that I've heard it, I've always thought of it as a story about a giant wave destroying the village. I never thought of it as a story about hope. I like that."

"Me too," I agree. "Until the last nine months, it was easy to hear some of these stories and focus only on the story. But every story is also a legacy, isn't it? They're twisted together. Like the legacies would be meaningless without the stories and the stories would be meaningless without the legacies. They give meaning to each other. And to focus only on the story or only on the legacy is to miss the point entirely." I stop myself to reflect on my own words, not quite sure where they came from, but impressed with myself for being responsible for them.

I think back to Azim's story. How the village discovered hope only because a great tragedy nearly stole hope away from them forever. I'm reminded of my conversation with Brisa after Poshar's story. About cruelty, suffering, legacy, tragedy. "Mehan," I ask as a vague fog starts to form in the back of my head, "why does it seem like so many legacies are born out of tragedy?" This sounds familiar. Why? The fog encroaches. This isn't a memory. But it feels like one.

Mehan, without hesitation, replies, "Isn't that life?" Tragedy. "Tragedy." The fog envelopes my mind, causing me to feel light-headed, like I'm stepping outside of myself. Mehan looks at me, concerned, and asks, "Are you okay?"

"Yeah." I place my hands on my head to clear the fog. "I just–" Mehan wouldn't understand. "I just remembered part of a dream, that's all."

Mehan chuckles. "You and your dreams. Your legacy. The man who dreamed of boats." Mehan pauses for a moment and embellishes, "Those magnificent boats."

I look at him, a little thrown off by his

unusual kindness. "Do you really think that will be my legacy?"

"Sure!" He declares. "They're amazing, Uri! And they're going to save our tribe. Our kids' kids' kids' kids' will tell the story about the boy who had a dream that changed the course of history. Why wouldn't that be your legacy?"

I don't want to be contrarian, especially with Mehan in rare form, but I'm unconvinced. I've been wrestling with this since my conversation with Chuan where he suggested the same notion. "I don't know. I guess I don't feel like they're truly mine to claim. I didn't really have anything to do with those dreams. They just happened to me. Is that a legacy? Don't you have to do something for it to be your legacy? Does it count even if you had nothing to do with it?"

"Of course it counts."

"I guess I just feel like I ought to have a more active role in whatever my legacy ends up being. Or at least it would be nice to be conscious while it's happening."

I didn't intend for that to be funny, but it causes Mehan to laugh. First small, then big. I haven't seen him laugh this way in a long time. The boy. I join him, allowing it to take me back to days when Mehan and I could innocently share a laugh. As the laughter exhausts itself, Mehan wipes the corner his eye and challenges me, "Fair enough. Okay, Uri - what do you think your legacy is, then?"

"I don't know. That's my problem. I look at my life and I can't really tell."

"I'm sure you will figure it out. We still have a lot of adventures ahead of us. Something will turn up."

"What about you?" I ask.

Mehan shrugs, "I don't know. Maybe for being a great warrior."

We stand for a while in silence, watching the clouds launch themselves over the ridge. My mind drifts back to his comment about tragedy. "What did you mean when you said that life is tragedy?"

"Isn't it?" He asks matter-of-factly.

"I don't think so. Our lives are mostly happy."

"Not lately."

"Sure, not lately. But up until this crisis began they were. Did you honestly feel like your life was tragedy?"

Mehan takes a deep breath, keeping his eyes fixed on the ridge. "I spend a lot of time standing here, Uri. Right here. Looking at that ridge. Nothing exciting ever happens. When you stand in the same place doing the same thing every day of your life, your mind gets to thinking. If you think about our lives for long enough, you realize that most of what we do in the course of a day is done simply to keep ourselves alive. Getting water; drinking.

Catching and gathering food; eating. Tending fires; cooking. Building and maintaining huts to sleep in; sleeping. That's all fine. But here's the thing, Uri: who has ever lived forever? It ends the same for everybody. Eventually. We work so hard to keep ourselves alive only to die someday. Tragedy, right?"

"So much for hope, then." I say ironically, disturbed by his disparaging summary of life.

"No, well–" he catches himself. "There's room for hope in there. We spend so much of our lives delaying death. But you can't delay death forever. And that's tragic. But the greatest tragedy of all comes if you spend your entire life focusing on the things that delay death, as though you could delay it forever, only to arrive at death having missed out on the things that never die. That's what the tragedy should ignite within us. The tragedy of death should cause us to be dissatisfied with spending all of our time postponing death, instead focusing on the things that never die. Standing here day after day watching and thinking, that's what I realize the most. The trees point us to things that never die, so that our lives don't have to be tragic.

"That's where things like hope come in. And honor. And beauty. And justice. And on down the line of the things that the trees teach us. The tragedy of death should inspire us to search for things that never die. And when we find those things, we should embed them into everything we do in our life. Like when we find Hope, we should embrace it; we should share it with others when they're downcast; we should do even the most common, mundane things in life with Hope in every thought and motion. Because when we're dead and gone, it's only things like Hope that will have mattered."

As he says those last words, I become aware that my jaw is hanging open. This is a Mehan I've never seen before. Not the boy. Not the watcher. Something entirely different. "Who are you?!" I ask. Mehan becomes self-conscious and furrows his eyes. "I mean, how did you become so wise? A few months ago we were picking berries together. Now here you are, teaching me with a kind of wisdom that is typically reserved for chiefs and elders."

Mehan half-smiles, uncertain if he's being made fun of or not.

"Seriously," I reiterate. "It's amazing."

"Uri," I hear from close behind us, startling me. Mehan was right: it's hard to hear someone sneak up on you from behind out here. It's Chranit. "I've been looking for you," he says between breaths.

"Am I in trouble?"

"No. I have news."

Chapter 16

The Tenth Moon

Desperation changes things. In obvious ways, but also in not-so-obvious ways.

Obvious ways: the tension, the arguing, the worrying, the distracted looks on peoples' faces.

Not-so-obvious ways: Chranit persuading Sangra to re-evaluate his stance toward Abis' village. Sangra quietly commissioned a special exchange trip to bring them extra food, baskets, ropes, wood, water, and other supplies. But just one trip. And don't bring Uri. Don't involve Uri. Don't mention Uri. Don't make it look like Uri had anything to do with it. While I haven't mentioned my subversion or what I saw to anyone other than the Council and Brisa, word of it has spread throughout the village through whispers the way that all secrets always do. No one has confronted me about it, and as far as I know, no one has confronted Sangra either. I'm told that Sangra, aware of the whispering, commissioned this trip to preemptively redirect the focus off of me and onto him in a positive way.

Desperation.

As long as something is being done, I can't be too upset about the intentions or motivations behind it. It won't end the other village's suffering. But it will ease it slightly, temporarily. Exactly three months from today, we will leave this island. Until then, this special exchange trip will help. Somehow. A little. And maybe it imparts some small sentiment of unity and goodwill.

On the morning of the tenth full moon, we gather at the edge of the village as we always do for legacy talks. Only this time, something is different. Fifteen people carrying full baskets for the special exchange trip. They will come with us to the legacy talk and continue on to the other village afterward.

Brisa walks over to me and sets down a basket full of ropes. When she heard about the special exchange trip, she immediately went to Chranit and volunteered. She wanted to see the other village for herself. I want to be happy about it - happy that she gets to see what I saw and happy that she gets to be a part of providing them aid - but, instead, all I feel is this nagging worry. Degi's last words to me ringing in my ears. The thought of what he might say or do when he sees her. Maybe nothing at all. Maybe he was just trying to get under my skin. But maybe something. And I can't escape this worry that he might do something.

Chranit leads the village across the valley to the Old Grove. High up the mountain we climb; higher than any of the legacy talks have taken us yet. He stops by a tree that can be seen all the way from our village. Its bright, white flowers stand out among the other trees. And when the sun hits them, they shine like the sun itself.

"The ocean," Chranit begins, "brought our ancestors to this island. It provides us with fish. It extends out to every horizon. It cannot be controlled or conquered. It is a deep, dark unknown. A mysterious, inescapable force. Much like death. Believing that we emerged from the sea, that our days were governed by the sea, and that we returned to the sea in death, our ancestors buried their dead at sea.

"Every individual life was believed to be a passing current in a vast and ever-changing expanse of currents. We appear; we flow; we dissipate. Just like the currents. Just like the waves. Just like the tides. Burying at sea was our way of returning our dead to the expanse to be absorbed back into that endless cycle.

"But then something curious happened. In the third generation after our ancestors arrived on this island, two people died on this hillside and their bodies weren't buried at sea. And in the exact places where their bodies rested on that otherwise barren hillside, two trees grew. That event changed everything.

"In the ensuing days and years and

generations, our ancestors abandoned the practice of burying their dead at sea in favor of burying on the hillsides, where trees unexplainably grew in the places where people were buried. Four generations after those first two trees grew, a small grove of trees now sat atop this barren hillside. A man named Sophe sat in this grove day after day, pondering the mystery of the trees. He gazed out across the ocean, pondering the way in which the tides move with such precise predictability. How he could tell on any given day when the tide would be high and when it would be low. Never breaking from this predictable pattern, no will of their own. No authority. No purpose. Instead, they seemed subject to the will of the forces around them. Upon reflection, the sea didn't seem worthy of the esteem our tribe once paid it.

"After pondering the sea, Sophe lifted his gaze and pondered the sky. Could the mystery of the trees be solved in the sun? The moon? The multitude of stars? Could it be these things that govern and sustain the world? But the more he reflected on them, the more he realized that they were no different than the waves and tides, bound to endless cycles and repetitions, bound by a power and a will superior to theirs.

"After pondering the sky, Sophe lowered his gaze to the ground beneath him. Could the island itself be the great governing force behind it all? Fixed in place, with the waves and the sun and the moon and the stars venerating it through countless repetitions. Yet, he recalled, our ancestors had come from another land, vaster than this island. If there are greater islands upon the waters, then no single island could be the governor of the patterns and rhythms of the world.

"After pondering the elements around him, Sophe wondered if, rather than explaining life through a single force, the mystery could be understood through the sum of all of the forces working together. The sea, the island, the luminaries in the sky. Could all life emerge and exist from the balance of these forces hanging together in tandem? But what could bring all of those forces into agreement? And wouldn't that force – the force that brings them into agreement – be the greatest force of all, the one most deserving of our attention? And what force was that?

"After pondering the myriad of forces, Sophe considered the possibility that there were no forces at work at all, and all things are simply fleeting gatherings of sand and water and light. Or if there happened to be some force at work, it was utterly indifferent. But if that was the case, where did things like justice, dignity, and love come from? If the forces that govern life are indifferent or absent, it seems that life itself should be indifferent as well. And when he looked into the eyes of another person, or suffering, or joy, he didn't respond with indifference. Instead, he responded with honor, dignity, and empathy. Why did these things matter in an indifferent world? He couldn't explain it. If life is a forgetful accident, he couldn't bring himself to approach his life as though it were, no matter how hard he tried to persuade himself to do so. Something deep inside of him demanded that he acknowledge the inherent value and worth of all people and all things.

"Finally, Sophe returned to pondering the sum of the ocean, sun and moon and stars, and abundance of life on the island. He considered the tiniest details etched into the most hidden places. There was an order, a rhythm, a dance to it all. Vast and intimate. Connected and distinct. Seen and unseen. What sort of force could give it all order? What sort of force could hold it all together? What sort of force could fill the spaces in between with beauty, laughter, love, and even sorrow?

"Sophe never solved these mysteries. But he concluded that the explanation for these mysteries was also the explanation for all of life and legacy, for every seen and unseen thing, for the trees themselves. And he concluded that the part of us that can perceive these mysteries is the part of us that endures just as they endure. And so, this great ancient sage helped us to see the unseen and orient our lives toward perceiving and pursuing and apprehending these enduring things."

Chranit turns toward Sophe's tree in quiet contemplation. Children rise to their feet to play one last time under its shade as the adults ponder Sophe's mystery. The group of fifteen makes its way to Alver. When they're all gathered with baskets in hand, Alver motions and they walk down toward the other village.

I watch Brisa intently until she becomes obscured by trees, my stomach churning with anxiety. Turning back toward the group dissipating from the legacy talk, my eyes meet Mehan's a short distance down the hill. He looks at me. Looks in the direction of the group of fifteen. Looks back at me with an expression of concerned confusion. Then starts following the group of fifteen. Quietly, staying a measured distance behind them. Spear in hand. He disappears into the trees.

• • •

Some days end so quickly I'm convinced the sun skipped ahead in the sky when I wasn't looking. It almost always happens on days when I'm with Brisa. Other days drag on so slowly, I'm convinced the sun stayed in place when I wasn't looking. This is usually the case on days when I build boats. Lately, all I do is build boats.

Since this morning's legacy talk, I've been building boats under a lethargic sun. Waiting. Anxious. Mind racing. Every few moments, I glance inland to see if the group of fifteen has returned.

"Uri! Hello, Uri. Are you there, Uri?" I turn toward the sound of Chuan's voice. "Hi there," he says with a sarcastic sweetness. "Do you realize that you're actually slowing us down today? We would actually be working faster as a group if you *weren't* here right now. That's really quite an accomplishment."

"Sorry."

"Don't be sorry. Just focus on your work or move out of our way."

At least Chuan's talking to me again. I bend down to pick up a plank when I'm jolted back in the other direction by the sound of Brisa's frantic voice. "Uri!" I spin around to see her fearful, tear-streaked face. Wide eyes. Out of breath. Panicked.

"What? What's going on? Are you okay?" Degi's face flashes in my mind as I race down the beach to her.

"Mehan," she gasps.

"Where is he?"

"It happened so fast." She looks like she's about to cry.

I put my hands on her shoulders to focus her thoughts. "What happened? Where is

Mehan?"

"At his house."

"Is he hurt?"

"No." She shakes her head, sobbing.

"What's wrong then?"

"Degi." She squeaks out before clasping her hands over her mouth to contain herself. In between sobs, she is able to compose herself just long enough to say, "Degi is dead."

I grab her hand and pull her behind me as we run into the village. A small crowd of people has gathered just outside of Mehan's hut. At the center of the crowd, Mehan sits on the ground with Alver crouched beside him. With one hand, Alver squeezes Mehan's hand; with the other hand, he braces Mehan's back. The look on Mehan's face. I can't explain it. He wants to cry. Or scream. Or run far away. Maybe all of those at the same time.

Whispers scamper through the crowd. All eyes are on Mehan. Everyone has this uncomfortable look on their faces like they want to do something but they aren't exactly sure what to do. Help him? Leave him? Say something? Do something?

I wedge my way through to the center and crouch down beside Mehan, opposite Alver. Lock eyes with Alver. Then with Mehan. "Everything's going to be alright," I say hopefully, not even really aware of what I'm saying or what might be helpful. Mehan turns his head the slightest bit in my direction, but doesn't focus on me. Instead I follow his line of sight toward Brisa. Tears flowing from her eyes. She looks back at Mehan intently.

What happened?

Suddenly Sangra comes bursting through the crowd and kneels directly in front of Mehan. "Are you okay, son?" He asks caringly.

Mehan utters a simple, weak, quivering, "No."

Sangra shouts, "Alver, you stay here with us. Everyone else, leave."

We look at one another. Stunned. Confused. Hearing, but for some reason not reacting.

"Leave!" Sangra booms.

We startle and scatter. I cling to Brisa. "Brisa, you have to tell me. What happened?"

"Uri, it was horrible."

"What? What was horrible? Degi is dead. Mehan is in shock. That's all I know. The last time I saw you, you were leaving the legacy talk with Alver. Mehan was following behind. What happened from there?"

"Mehan wasn't supposed to follow," she says through a trickle of tears, her voice more calm, her breathing more controlled. "When we arrived at the other village, Abis met with Alver while we set the baskets in the middle of the village. That's when people started coming out of their huts. Uri, it was exactly as you described it. I was looking at these people and I was thinking to myself, *these can't be the same people who were living in our village just a few months ago*. I was looking all around the village, amazed and appalled all at the same time. That's when I saw this girl about our age, standing at the door of her hut on the outskirts of the village with a baby in her arms. It was Prem.

"I wanted to talk to her, to see her baby. So I walked toward her, past the crowd, past the cluster of huts. Then suddenly, out of nowhere, someone steps right in front of me. It-" She stops shortly. Places her hand back over her mouth. The tears start flowing again. I pull her into me tightly. "It was Degi," she blurts out. "He asked me why I was there. He touched my arm. He asked where you were. He told me to be quiet as he started to pull me out of sight. I wanted to scream but I was frozen. The look in his eyes-" Her voice gives way to uncontrollable weeping.

Suddenly I'm not holding Brisa anymore. I'm holding an echo of the little girl that I used to play with. Crying the way she cried that time that she fell out of a tree and couldn't move her arm for the rest of the day. The pain. The fear. Echoes of the weeping from that day. I hold her closer, tighter, stronger. I want to take her tears away. Take them onto me. All of the hurt. All of the fear. All of the sadness. But they're hers.

And all I can do is helplessly hold her and hope that in holding her, she can feel safe enough to let go of those things herself.

When the weeping subsides and her breathing becomes regular again, she continues, "I was so afraid. But then, out of nowhere, Mehan came bursting through the trees behind Degi like a storm. It happened so fast. The next thing I knew, Degi was laying on the ground with Mehan's spear sticking out of his chest. And there was Mehan standing over him. Stunned. Shaking. Mouth gaping. I grabbed his hand and we ran. As fast as we could, we ran away from that place, across the island, back to our village. We didn't stop. We didn't look back. We just ran and ran and ran until we got to his hut. Then I came to find you." With that, Brisa folds herself back into my arms, crying a gentler cry than before. I place my hand on her head, trying to be strong. But by this time, I'm crying too.

The sun falls low. The moon hangs over head flaunting an apathetic gaze.

Nothing will ever be the same again.

Chapter 17
The Eleventh Moon

Sunrise bursts over the horizon, carving twelve silhouettes against the fiery reds and oranges that paint the sky. Twelve boats nearly complete. Two awaiting their masts. I've come to love these boats even as I've come to loathe them. They represent everything that has been wretched about the last twelve months; yet they are our salvation. Saving our tribe from the same fate that befell the native trees and the creatures that once flew and crawled across this island. The boats bring hope; the boats bring sorrow. Just like the sunrise.

The other village didn't bury Degi in the Grove of Ancestors. Instead, they laid his body on the crest of the ridge across the center of the island at a spot that could be seen by both villages. Then they started piling rocks around him. Rocks and rocks and rocks. High and wide. Their entire village spent the entire day piling tear-stained rocks, until the pile was so high and wide that it became a hill unto itself in between the hills of the Grove of Ancestors. Every sunrise since, the sun gleams off of the pile of rocks, starkly contrasted against the muted grass and hills and fading twilight sky. It serves as a reminder of Degi, Mehan, and the struggle that has come to define life on the island.

Every sunrise, Mehan slips further and further into this dark place inside of himself. Every sunrise, Brisa joins him by his side and goes to that place with him. Every sunrise, the anger of the other village swells. Every sunrise, we draw closer to our final sunrise. Hope. Sorrow. This is what the sunrise has become.

I walk down to the shore. Chuan's unmistakable profile: hands on his hips, admiring the boats, surveying the work that needs to be completed for the day. All of the boat builders take a rest day every now and then. Not Chuan. Every morning, he stands on the shore before anyone else rouses, greeting the sun, hands on his hips, planning the day. Then he works tirelessly until the sun surrenders to the night. What used to be a sleepy job - boat builder - has become the most exhausting, most intense, most complex job of all. He used to spend his days making minor repairs to boats or slowly building new boats over the course of several months. He would spend entire afternoons sailing a boat around the bay to ensure its seaworthiness, or to test some minor modification he made to its design. Lazy days. Simple work.

Now, the job has become every job on the

island combined into one, requiring the strength of a carpenter, the skill of a stone cutter, the endurance of a water carrier, the attentiveness of a gatherer, the precision of a weaver, the discipline of a watcher, the focus of a fisherman, the patience of a care giver, the vision of an elder, the leadership of a chief. And in addition to it all, Chuan is trying to perfect the art of building a boat that is unlike any other anyone has ever built before. Then he must teach this art to others, most of whom don't have prior experience building anything, much less a boat.

In the span of a few short months, Chuan has had to become all of these things. The magnitude of this feat strikes me as I stride toward his powerful silhouette carved in the sunrise alongside the twelve boats. I begin to feel guilty that I haven't shown him more respect or gratitude as he has made this transformation. I've been too caught up in my own turmoil. He wanted me to come alongside him in this adventure, but I resisted him. And then I betrayed him.

"They're beautiful," I say from a few feet behind him.

He casually looks over his shoulder at me. "They're the most beautiful things I've ever seen."

"Beautiful and dreadful," I elaborate. It's a thought I had been keeping to myself. I don't know why I felt the urge to share it now, with Chuan of all people.

"Dreadful?" He asks curiously, mildly bothered by my suggestion.

"Well, you know, just how the whole matter has divided our tribe."

Chuan nods. "Yes, that has been dreadful." He pauses, thoughtfully. "It's too bad we didn't see this crisis coming generations ago. Maybe we could have done things differently." Another thoughtful pause. "But dreadful isn't the right word. If all of us tried to stay on this island, there's no way we could have survived. But maybe a tribe Abis' size can survive. Maybe they can make the decisions that should have been made generations ago. So maybe having a small portion of our tribe stay on the island while the rest of us seek out new lives in a new land is the best alternative, after all. That way, we won't leave the island completely vacant and forgotten. Some of our brothers and sisters can stay and enjoy this beautiful land with its majestic grove. The place that our tribe has inhabited for the last forty generations. The legacies of our ancestors can continue to be taught and enjoyed and honored. Those are good things, right?"

I've always considered the difference between our village and Abis' village as the difference between good and bad, right and wrong, never considering them as complements of one another. I'm not sure what to make of Chuan's way of thinking.

Chuan continues, "It's easy to be upset with the other village for their decision, isn't it? After all, we're the ones making the tough choice. We're the ones taking the big risk. Since the beginning, we have made it all about who is right: Chief Sangra or Abis. Which plan is best? Who is more virtuous? But I'm starting to think differently. I'm starting to think that either plan on its own would have ended with an unfortunate outcome - either the complete abandoning of this island or the slow death of our tribe - but both plans taken together actually give us the best possible outcome, don't you agree?"

I turn his words over in my mind before conceding, "I guess I do." Amazed at my own admission. Amazed that no one has ever suggested this before. Ashamed that I didn't think of it myself. Discouraged that, in light of all that has happened in the last month, it's doubtful that anyone can be persuaded to see this perspective for themselves.

We stand there in silence, the sun now fully revealed, the sky less fiery than when our conversation began. "Hey, Chuan?"

"Yes?"

"Thank you." The words fall out of my mouth. A hundred different meanings to them. A hundred different reasons to thank him.

Chuan places his hand on my shoulder, giving me some small awkward hope to face another sunrise.

• • •

The moon is growing. It will be full again soon. I've hardly seen Brisa since it was full last. I haven't seen Mehan at all. Mehan spends his days and nights hidden away in a hut that isn't his own to protect him from someone who might sneak over from the other village to reciprocate Degi's fate upon him. This isn't Mehan's choice, but he's in no condition to put up a fight about it. Brisa sits by his side much of the day, sharing in his mourning. She began sitting by his side because she said she wanted to keep him from slipping away. But I'm afraid that instead of her holding him steady, he is slowly pulling her away with him. Something about her countenance. Her voice. The way she walks. I'm losing her.

Each day, I become more consumed by this fear that she and Mehan will go to this dark place together and never come back from it. And I will have lost her forever. I want Mehan back. But I want Brisa more, even if it means losing Mehan. I hate myself for even having the thought. But it's there. I can't deny it.

After dinner, beneath a growing moon, consumed by my obsession, I sit by the fire closest to Brisa's hut. Most of the village has retreated to their huts after the evening meal and are drifting to sleep. But I can't sleep. Tethered to a restless mind. I don't know why I chose to sit by this particular fire. My feet led me here. And, somehow, just knowing that Brisa is close, even if she's asleep, comforts me.

"What are you doing here?"

I leap to my feet. "Brisa! I was just–" She hasn't been in her hut all this time, after all. "What are you doing out so late?"

She shifts her weight and folds her arms. "Mehan still has trouble falling asleep. I sit by him until he does. Most nights, it isn't until late."

"How is he doing?" I ask, trying not to fixate on the thought of the two of them alone in his hut at night.

Brisa shrugs. "He's starting to talk a little. That's an improvement. But you wouldn't think it's an improvement judging by the things he says." Her gaze becomes flat, like she's replaying some of his words in her mind.

"Like what?"

Brisa starts to answer but stops herself. "Why are you here, Uri?"

"I haven't seen you in a while. Just wanted to see you and make sure you were okay. What kinds of things does Mehan say?"

"Thank you for checking on me, but I'm fine," she replies bluntly.

Struck by her sudden shift in tone, I feel the need to defend myself. "Look, I didn't expect to see you tonight. I've just been missing you and I can't sleep and I needed a place where I could sit and gather my thoughts."

"And of all the fires in the entire village, you just happened to sit by mine?" She asks accusingly.

"No, I sat here because I wanted to be near you. Even if I couldn't see you or touch you or hear your voice I just wanted to be somewhere close to you. But if my being here bothers you, then I suppose I should leave." I turn to walk away.

"No," She calls out. I stop and turn back toward her. She rubs her eyes in frustration. Exhaustion. "You don't bother me. I'm just really tired, Uri. I spend all day trying to be supportive for Mehan. I guess I just don't have much left for anyone else afterward. Even for myself."

"It's a good thing that you're doing for Mehan. I'm glad he has someone by his side. But aren't there other people who can be there for him too?"

"Maybe. But it doesn't matter. I need to be the one by his side because it's my fault that he got this way."

"Wait, what?" I interject.

"I was the one who left the group to go see Prem. If I had stayed with our group, Degi wouldn't have had an opportunity to attack me. If Degi hadn't attacked me, Mehan wouldn't have had to attack Degi."

"Brisa, you can't think that way. Degi chose to attack you. Mehan chose to attack Degi. This has more to do with the two of them than it has to do with you. You realize that, right? It's not your burden to carry."

She nods. Sniffs back a tear. "I still need to be there for Mehan until he's himself again. Responsible or not, I was there. Mehan risked everything to save me. Now he needs someone to be there to save him. I can't let him down. I hope you understand that, Uri."

I don't want to. But I do. The strength in her eyes. A facet of Brisa that I've never seen before. And I've never loved her more than I do in this moment. There are so many things I want to say to her now.

I love you.

Don't lose yourself trying to save Mehan.

When can I see you again?

But the only thing that comes out as I lean in and kiss her cheek is a simple, heartfelt, "Thank you." Another thank you with a hundred meanings and for a hundred reasons.

• • •

"Walk with me."

The voice rips me from my sleep. I try to sit

up, but my shoulders are pinned to the ground. I thrash my feet fearfully, trying to squirm free.

"Uri!" The voice again, in a yelling whisper. "Stop making so much noise!"

Mehan? I stop thrashing and try to get my bearings in the darkness. The faintest blue creeps in from under the door. Not quite dawn yet. The shadowy figure crouched over me certainly resembles Mehan's, though I'm having a hard time believing he has somehow emerged from his hidden dark place just to come sit on me while I sleep.

He releases his grip on my shoulders, quietly helps me to my feet, and tugs my hand to lead me outside. We walk to the outskirts of the village without saying a word. My mind acclimates to wakefulness, filling with a myriad of thoughts and questions for my shadowy companion. Like why he's finally out of his hut for the first time in a month. And where he is taking me at such an odd time of the day. The eleventh full moon illuminates our steps. I wonder if he is taking me to the gathering spot for the legacy talk early. But when we pass by the spot without saying a word or even breaking our stride, I realize he has something else on his mind.

When we're a safe distance from the village, Mehan turns to me. "I'm sorry I couldn't get to Brisa faster. I was distracted by the condition of their village. I lost track of

Degi. I lost track of her. Maybe if I hadn't lost track of things, I could have intervened sooner. I could have protected Brisa. I could have stopped Degi without a fight. Maybe things could have gone differently."

He hangs on that last thought, causing a familiar protective instinct to rise up within me. He needs to have this guilt taken away from him; otherwise, he will cling to it forever and it will crush him. "Mehan, you have nothing to apologize for. Nothing! The condition of the other village isn't your fault. Brisa going to the other village wasn't your fault. Degi attacking Brisa wasn't your fault. You went so you could protect her. And she needed your protection. You did the right thing, the brave thing. I'm so grateful that you were there since I wasn't allowed to be there myself. I can't imagine what could have happened if you hadn't been there. If it hadn't been for Degi, none of this would have happened. You didn't kill Degi; you protected Brisa. Don't let anyone, even yourself – especially yourself – convince you otherwise."

Mehan nods, swallowing back tears. He glances uphill in the direction we're walking. I trace his line of sight directly toward Degi's burial place and start to grow uneasy at the thought of going to that particular place with this particular person. Why are we going there?

"I heard some good news the other day," Mehan says with tranquility returning to his voice.

"What's that?"

"I heard that they started bringing boat-caught fish over to the other village. See? You made a difference. A couple of months ago you were telling me that you didn't think the boats were your legacy because you wanted to have an active role in shaping it. Well here you go! Your legacy. You fought for that. You made people aware."

"Yeah, but it isn't going to solve the problem. They still don't have enough to eat, even with six baskets of boat-caught fish."

"But it's better than it was. The boat-caught fish will sustain them just a little more. You made their lives better."

I weigh his words apprehensively, but I'm flattered nonetheless. Whether the change came as a result of my actions or because Sangra wanted to placate the village doesn't really matter in this moment. "Thank you for helping me see that, Mehan."

As we draw nearer to the pile of rocks that comprise Degi's mound, I realize that it's even larger than it appears from our village. The tension grips me more tightly. Not so for Mehan, who only seems to grow calmer. "Uri?" He asks.

"Yes?"

"I had been trying so hard to live more like the people in the legacy talks. Then I went out and killed someone. I hadn't planned on killing anyone. But in the mess of the moment, I wasn't thinking about my legacy; I was only thinking about the mess and the moment. Has this become my legacy now? Murderer? In forty generations we haven't had a murder on our island. Is there any turning from that?"

"You were protecting Brisa, not seeking to harm Degi. Why would Degi's death define you any more than Brisa's life?"

He nods slowly, pensively. "I take back what I said in that conversation a couple of months ago. About my legacy being that of a great warrior. Fighting isn't a legacy. Not one that I want anymore. I don't want to be remembered for fighting. And maybe it's too late for that. But it's never too late to be brave." Mehan says that last word as we come within an arm's length of Degi's mound. My apprehension turns to anxiety, as I fear how the other village might react if they were to spot us right now.

He places his hand on one of the stones, letting his fingers drag across it as he walks along its perimeter. Then he stops, crouches down, places his forehead on one of the stones, and closes his eyes. For a while, neither of us say anything. Me – confused, nervous, distracted. Mehan – lost in deep, deep thought. Finally, Mehan repeats himself, "It's never too late to be brave."

He rises, walks over to me determinedly, and embraces me tightly. "Uri, thank you."

"Thank you?"

"For showing me the power of legacy. I hope we see each other again." He releases his embrace and begins stepping away from me.

"What's going on, Mehan? What are you doing?" Panic in my voice.

"I'm going to make things right. Or as right as they can be."

"What are you saying? What does that even mean? What are you going to do?" I start walking after him.

"Don't try to stop me, Uri. I'll pin you down again."

"You aren't thinking clearly," I protest. "I don't know what you're planning to do, but I know that we have no business being up here. Why don't we go back to the village and talk it over."

"Not thinking clearly? I've been thinking about this every day for a month. I have to do this, Uri. If I don't, I will spend the rest of my life regretting it. Either wish me well or step away. I won't let you stop me."

I imagine myself trying to stop him. But every way I imagine it, Mehan prevails and our final memory together is full of bitterness. So instead of trying to stop him, I exhale, drop my shoulders, choke back the swelling in my throat, and simply say, "Goodbye. Brother."

He walks over to me and embraces me again. I return the embrace, more tightly than I've ever embraced another person. The swelling in my throat rises into my head sending tears down my face. I've grown up with sisters, but he's the closest to a brother I've ever known. And in some ways, somehow, it's the most powerful relationship of all. We eventually pry ourselves apart. Mehan smiles at me, walks to the other side of Degi's mound, and runs down the hill toward the other village.

I have no clue what, exactly, he plans on doing. But I know it can't end well. And as I watch him descend the hill, I feel a piece of myself descending with him. Until he's gone. And I'm alone.

Heading back downhill toward our village, the sunrise now hanging above the horizon, a crowd gathered at the edge of our village, I do my best to conceal the wetness and the puffiness from my eyes. Chranit makes his way to the front of the group just as I slip in. He leads us to the top of the Old Grove, even higher than we climbed last month.

When we're settled uphill from the tree at which Chranit stops, he begins, "Two words come to mind as I reflect on legacies: *elusive* and *powerful*. Elusive because they can't be touched or heard or seen in the same way that the other things in our lives can be. And without this kind of tangible presence, it's so easy for us to forget them, or to deny them, or to fail to see their power. Which brings me to the second word: powerful. Powerful because they have the ability to shape an entire tribe for generations upon generations upon generations.

"Like that image of ripples across water. Long after the rock has sunk out of sight, the ripples continue to radiate out across the surface of the water. There are moments when the elusive becomes tangible and is made powerful and sends ripples out for generations to come. That's what these legacies are about. But over time, even ripples across water begin to fade, don't they? They flatten. They spread. Eventually they are absorbed back into the surface. It's no different with legacies. If we aren't seeking them, if we aren't instilling them into our lives, they fade. They don't cease to exist, but they cease to exert their power over us. And they become elusive once again.

"This is the reason why we come to these trees to remember. We remember them that we might be able to perpetuate their power. In our lives and in the lives of those around us. In this way, the ripples will continue radiating out forever. In a few short months we will leave this island and these trees, never to return. It means that each of us will have to work even harder to be trees to one another. We must proclaim these powerful, elusive legacies to one another. By the way we go about our daily routines. By the way we respond in crisis. By the way we teach our children. By the things we celebrate. By the way we honor those whose ripples have affected us. Otherwise, the last forty generations and our dangerous journey will have been in vain.

"When our ancestors first came here, they were immediately at war with one another. They split into two villages. The chiefs of each village governed with tight control so as not to show any signs of weakness to the other chief or to their own people. This sustained them in times of war, but when the villages finally made peace in the third generation it only produced strife.

"Two villages which had been ruled by their own chiefs for over three generations now had to give up control and find common ground upon which to establish a single tribe. The first chief they selected to lead this new society had descended from one village and largely favored those people in his counsel and decisions to the neglect of the other village. That chief was eventually overthrown by those who had been part of the neglected group. They replaced him with a chief from their village. This second chief led exactly as his predecessor had, only this time the roles of favored and neglected village were reversed.

"Eventually that chief, like his predecessor,

was overthrown. By this time, whispers were circulating around the tribe of splitting once again. Perhaps all that was needed was for someone to turn their whispering into shouting and that split would have occurred.

"Fortunately, before the whispering had the opportunity to grow any louder, someone was able to shout a different vision. It was spoken through the voice of a man, Ziba, who had been one of the first children born on the island after our ancestors arrived. By this time in his life he was quite old and he had spent most of his life witnessing the battles and factions of the two villages. But he also understood that we came to this island as one tribe. One village. One people. Just as he was born into one tribe, he never stopped believing that we were meant to live together as one tribe and he longed to see us united as one tribe again before his death.

"He realized that where the other chiefs had failed, it was in their desire to control. They sought to control every facet of the tribe. This control may have served a purpose in times of war, but it served as a wedge in times of peace. In the chiefs' desire to control, they imposed their own prejudices and short-comings upon the tribe.

"Ziba saw the divisiveness that this caused. He saw how it led to certain groups being favored and others being neglected. He saw how the chiefs lived in far better conditions than anyone else in the village. He saw how their flawed decisions created angst. If these two villages were going to become one tribe once again, and if that tribe was going to survive, Ziba knew that chiefs needed to exist for a purpose other than satisfying whatever whims arose in their minds.

"The elusive and powerful truth by which the other chiefs had failed to allow guide their lives and decisions was the idea that all people have the same inherent worth. No single person is more valuable than any other; no group is more valuable than any other. Perhaps the other chiefs understood this truth, but they didn't let it guide them. They had lived as though their position as chief meant they had a greater worth. They had made decisions as though the village from which they had descended was somehow greater than the other.

"The first thing Ziba did after being named chief was require that both of the old villages be dismantled. As long as two villages stood and the chief resided in only one of those villages, people would continue to feel like two separate tribes, rather than one. The existence of two villages also made splitting seem like too convenient of an option. Ziba feared that relocating everyone to one of the villages would foster a sense of superiority in one group over the group that was forced to relocate. So he decided that the best option was to start fresh, as though they were their ancestors arriving on the island for the very first time. He designated all of the bay area where our village stands today as common area. People began settling across the entire island. Of course, if you recall from our legacy talk several months ago, this had its own shortcomings that wouldn't be addressed until Gemen's generation. But what Ziba's plan accomplished was that it rid our tribe of the idea that we were two separate villages, two separate people groups, two separate worths.

"The other significant thing that Ziba did was establish the Council, where wise men and women from throughout the tribe would make decisions on behalf of the tribe. The chiefs before him had made their decisions in isolation. Some of those decisions were good, but most were flawed and self-serving. The Council allowed many voices to be heard in each decision and for many minds to consider and select the best possible course of action.

"Ziba's legacy sent out ripples so strong, they can be felt even to this day. If we continue on in his legacy, nothing can divide us. An ocean may rest between us, but we will forever be one tribe. On the other hand, if we forget his legacy, we might all remain on this island but still be forever divided."

Chranit's story ends in solemnness. A

stillness in the air. The branches of Ziba's tree spread out wide from its sides. They gradually bend downward like the roof of a shelter. A shelter in which all are welcome. A shelter in which all are safe.

Safe…I hope Mehan is safe.

Chapter 18

The Twelfth Moon

Brisa wasn't at Ziba's legacy talk yesterday morning. She wasn't in the hut with the other weavers in the afternoon. She wasn't around her hut in the evening. This morning as I walk down to the shore, I see her standing among the trees. Waiting for me. I smile at her.

She smiles back quickly before her expression nervously turns to worry. "I spent all day yesterday looking for Mehan. I think he might have done something stupid."

"I know."

"How?" She asks suspiciously.

"He came to me yesterday morning. Early. He woke me up, led me to Degi's mound, and forced me to watch him leave."

"And you let him?" She accuses as she pushes me. "Why didn't you stop him? Why didn't you warn somebody? Why did you just let him go and get himself killed?"

"I didn't 'let' him go. He was set on going. Even if I had tried to stop him, I wouldn't have been able to."

"It doesn't matter what he's set on doing, Uri. He's unstable. Whatever it takes, you stop an unstable person from hurting themselves!"

"I tried to stop him, Brisa. But there wasn't anything I could have done to stop him. He was so set on this decision. He wasn't going to let anything stand in his way. And you know, as hard as it is for me to admit, I understand his reasons for going. I get it."

"There's nothing to 'get', Uri. Except that Mehan is dead and you didn't do anything to stop him." Her anger turns to sadness as she says that last part.

"Brisa, that isn't fair! Yesterday morning I woke up with Mehan on top of me. Yes, physically on top of me. He walked me up to Degi's mound. And as we walked, we talked. He wasn't desperate. He wasn't unstable. He wasn't confused. He was clear. He knew exactly what he was doing. And as he explained it to me, I realized that it was something he truly believed he needed to do. He spoke of bravery. He spoke of honor. If he hadn't gone, he would have spent the rest of his life like the person you sat with in the hut for the past month. A shadow of himself. Sick with regret and guilt and shame. He had an opportunity to change all of that and he did. Would you rather for Mehan to have remained trapped in a long life full of pain and sorrow, or to die young but full of bravery and honor?"

Brisa's gaze becomes long, pensive. "I kept hoping time would heal him. That if he stayed in that hut for long enough with enough people who loved him by his side, eventually he would be fine."

"Maybe for some people that would have been the case. But you know Mehan. That month in the hut with people who loved him by his side allowed him to find perspective. He needed that time. And I'm so glad you were there to give it to him, to help him heal. But time alone isn't enough for a person like Mehan. All his life, rather than letting things happen to him, he caused things to happen around him. Why should we have expected it to be any different in his death?"

By this time, I'm crying too. Brisa crosses her arms and leans into me. I wrap my arms around her. We stand there for a while, quietly mourning the loss of our friend. When she finally pulls herself away from me and begins walking back to the village without looking at me or saying anything, I want to chase after her. But I'm too afraid of fanning the embers of her resentment. So instead, I stand here watching her longingly. Hoping, once again, that I haven't lost her.

• • •

The month drags on, bogged down by anticipation of the twelfth full moon. The twelfth legacy talk. The twelfth mast of the twelfth boat.

At this point, the boat builders have narrowed into three groups: one group putting the final touches on the eleventh boat, another group preparing the twelfth boat to receive its mast, and a third group staging materials and supplies so the completion of the twelfth boat can move quickly and smoothly once the mast is in place. It amazes me how quickly the work moves as the number of groups dwindles and the number of people in each of the remaining groups increases. Things that used to take days when the builders were scattered across several small groups are now being completed within a single day.

But the accelerated pace of work only heightens our anticipation. After the twelfth moon, the three groups will merge into a single group and work furiously to finish the twelfth boat so we can depart on the thirteenth moon. No one knows what happens after that. How long will we be at sea? Will we find another land? Another island just like ours? Full of trees. And water. And berries. And fish. And creatures that crawl. And creatures that fly. Will we be able to do things right this time? Forty generations from now, will our distant descendants enjoy a land abundant in everything needed to sustain them? Will they tell stories about a great journey that their ancestors took to deliver them there? Will they continue passing down the same stories that have been passed down to us? What new stories will they discover along the way?

It sounds wonderful – a return to life exactly as we knew it before we were shaken by this crisis. But it's all based on what we already know. It's the unknown things that nag us, that whisper doubts into our ears as we try to fall asleep, that give us pause every time a sunrise catches our eye reminding us of our impending journey to that spot where the sun rises. Such a place might not exist anywhere else. We might arrive somewhere worse. We might arrive somewhere far more wonderful than anything we can imagine.

Around the village, there's a shared feeling among nearly every person. It's a feeling we actually don't have a word for. The feeling you get when you run down a mountainside as fast as you can, until your feet are hardly catching you and you're practically falling. Your stomach rises into your chest. Your arms flail out of control. It's part fear, part excitement, part freedom. We don't have a word for it, but we all know it. And we all try to describe it any time we talk about the twelfth moon drawing near.

When the morning of the twelfth moon dawns, the feeling is so manifest in the air you can almost see it. You can almost touch it. It's on the faces of every person gathered and awaiting Chranit. It's in the pace and volume of their murmuring. It's in the way people get lost in the sunrise.

When Chranit appears, utter silence.

We follow him up to the Old Grove. To the very top. The only thing between the place where we stop and the blue sky is a steep bluff that crowns the mountain. Without any room to sit uphill from the place where Chranit stops, we all fill in the space downhill. It's awkward trying to sit on the mountainside and focus our attention uphill without sliding backward. But we brace ourselves on rocks and trees and one another and are able to make it work.

When the rustling dies down, Chranit begins. "Peace. Over the last twelve months, we've walked backward through our tribe's history, honoring some of the legacies that have had the greatest impact on our tribe. We are who we are today because of those legacies and countless others.

"Perhaps we would have split back into two tribes if it hadn't been for Ziba. Perhaps we wouldn't have our deep sense of community if it weren't for Gemen. Perhaps we wouldn't dare to sail beyond the horizon if it weren't for the hope and perseverance shown to us by Azim. Love, art, justice. Those trees, and countless others who echo their legacies throughout the generations, have not only become a permanent part of this island, they've become a permanent part of us.

"Today we remember the life and legacy that started it all. As was explained during Sophe's talk, our ancestors didn't bury their dead underground when they arrived at this island. Where they came from, trees didn't grow in the places where people died. So it never dawned on them to consider changing their ancient tradition of burying at sea. Meanwhile, they were at war.

"It wasn't until the third generation that everything changed in the span of a moment. It brought an end to the war. It established a new tradition. It forever changed our understanding of who we are as a tribe and what we strive for. And it all began with Peace. Peace was the first legacy to be proclaimed from the trees. Upon Peace, every other legacy has been proclaimed since. You can't have Justice without first having Peace. You can't have Healing without first having Peace. Without Peace, there is only the war and strife that gripped our tribe for three generations.

"The wars of the early generations were waged over land, over resources, over pride, over misperceptions, over false assumptions. We weren't going to survive as a tribe if the wars continued. Even if one side had won the war, the strife that ruled the hearts of the people would have eventually consumed whatever portion of the tribe remained. That was our course; that was our destiny. And it seemed there was nothing we could do to avoid it. Then something curious happened. In the third generation, two trees grew on this barren hillside and everything changed. The unshakable strife was shaken. The unwinnable war was won. Peace was the victor. And our hearts were the spoils.

"A young girl born in the third generation saw the strife that gripped the island. It not only gripped the relationships between the villages, it gripped the relationships within the villages as well. People hurt, undermined, and argued with one another as a way of life. This young girl, Santi, knew that this wasn't the way we were intended to live, but she didn't know how to change it.

"The only thing she could think to do when strife broke out among her fellow villagers was to secretly lay a flower on the doorsteps of the offender and the offended. In her mind, flowers were the opposite of strife. Whereas strife was imbalanced, flowers were balanced. Whereas strife was imposing, flowers were inviting. Whereas strife was ugly, flowers were beautiful. She would crouch down over flowers and study them, looking for answers to the strife that was all around her. She didn't find answers, but she figured that maybe if other people were confronted with the beauty and balance of flowers they would see what she saw, and maybe they could find the answer for themselves.

"When the rampant strife became more than she could bear, she would sneak away from her village, up to the peak of the highest mountain on the island. From the top of the barren peak, she could look out across the entire island and the entire sea. The villages and the turmoil that encompassed them became hidden by the treetops, so the only things she could see were mountains and clouds and ocean surf. This is the way the island was intended to be. Peaceful. Serene. Everything in harmony with everything else. She would sit up there as long as she could, because she knew that the moment she returned to the village, she would be thrust back into the reality of strife.

"On one particular day when she escaped to the peak, she was shocked to find another person already sitting up there. A boy, roughly her age, whom she didn't recognize. She nearly fell backward in surprise, letting out a yelp that nearly startled the boy off the other edge of the cliff. They caught themselves and warily examined one another. A lifetime of strife between the two villages had led each of them to assume the worst in the other. But instead of seeing the malice that they expected to see in the face of their enemy, they saw reflections of themselves. Reflections of their own fear. Reflections of their own kindness. Reflections of their own discontentment with the discord that had become a way of life for both of their villages.

"Seeing himself in the eyes of Santi, the boy smiled at her. Santi smiled back. The first of many smiles they would share. They spent the rest of the day together. He, too, had come to the mountain summit seeking refuge from the strife in his own village. They talked about strife. They talked about peace. They talked about life. And they wondered aloud together how two villages so alike in nearly every way could possibly have so much enmity between them. By the end of the day, they both felt an unspoken, intoxicating connection between them. In the company of someone who was supposed to be their enemy, they experienced the greatest peace they ever had. In the company of one another, the only strife they felt was that of an unwanted goodbye, as the descending sun demanded that they part ways and return to their villages. They conceded to the sun, promising to return to the peak to see the other again.

"Their meetings atop the peak became more and more frequent, as often as possible without being noticed. Over time, their conversations became less about the difference between peace and strife, and more about the similarities between peace and love. On one occasion, Santi brought flowers and explained how their beauty was reminiscent of peace. From that day onward, the boy brought flowers to Santi every time they met.

"Months passed. With each meeting, it became more and more painful for them to say goodbye. When they were apart, they thought about each other constantly. People around them noticed that something was different. Santi spoke to others of love, but never revealed the object of her love. Weren't it for the war between their villages, they would have wrapped their lives around one another. But they knew that if they made their love known, they would be forever separated. Only their closest friends were even aware that they went to the mountaintop to escape the strife, and even those friends didn't know that they had found companionship atop the mountain.

"One fateful day, as they sat atop the mountain peak drawing out their time together until the last possible moment, a storm started moving in. Even while the storm was in the distance, the winds atop the mountain became fierce. Each gust considerably stronger than the one before it. They realized that the winds were only going to get stronger as the storm moved in and they didn't want to get caught in the storm.

"With the winds mounting and whipping against them, they began to carefully climb down. Santi stepped onto a craggy footing. The wind surged. She lost her balance and began to fall. The boy dove to grab her. They linked fingers, but their momentum sent them both tumbling over the edge, down the face of the cliff, hand-in-hand.

"They never came down from the mountain that day.

"When the villages realized that their children were missing, each one assumed the other village was responsible. They yelled. They accused. They vowed vengeance. The tension between the villages had never been more strained. Weapons and armor were fashioned. Strategies were formed, anticipating the day that the tension would reach its breaking point.

"Then one day, several months later…breaking point. People from both villages were drawing water from the mountain. It was common for both villages to draw water at the same time of day. Generally, they kept a safe distance apart and tried their best to ignore one another and the tension between them. But this time, for whatever reason, the tension became words. Words became threats. Threats became actions. Actions became injury. Injury became a battle cry. After word of the skirmish returned to the villages, they girded up for combat to decide the victor of the war once and for all. And one morning, the people of the villages lined up within eyeshot of one another. They stomped their feet loudly. They shouted. They rattled their weapons. And then, silence. The silence was like the silence before a storm, like the silence before a crashing wave, like the silence before a bending branch snaps. The front lines took their first step forward. The Last War was underway.

"But then, as quickly as the war had begun, the strangest thing happened. White flakes began to trickle through the treetops, landing on warriors' weapons, landing on warriors' armor, landing on warriors' faces. Slowly at first; then constant, like a sun shower. Everyone stopped in their tracks, looking up through the treetops, marveling. Beams of sunlight through the canopy of trees, dancing and shimmering through the gentle rain of petals floating and spinning down. And a new silence filled the air. Silence like the silence at night, like the silence in a baby's rest, like the silence after the storm has passed.

"And then the sound of weapons dropping. And then the sound of curious footsteps through the forest toward the place from which the petals were falling. Both villages ascended the barren mountainside, their eyes fixed on this very spot where we sit today, to find two trees adorned in white with flower petals streaming down.

"At the foot of the trees, the two villages met. But war wasn't in their eyes anymore. Amazement. Wonder. Sadness. Bewilderment.

There was something so familiar about the petals. Santi's village recognized the flowers as the very same kind that she would leave on their doorsteps from time to time. The boy's village recognized them because, after he had gone missing, they had found dozens and dozens of the same flowers in the corner of his hut – some old and dried, some fresh.

"Could it be? The trees stood like perfect twins. Tall, though still young. Somehow, no one had ever noticed the trees before. Yet everyone who stood there that day felt this strange, unexplainable kinship and connection to them. Both villages were aware that their beloved lost children had sought refuge atop the mountain, but neither realized they had sought refuge in the company of their enemy. Until that moment. These two trees represented something beautiful in the midst of the ugliness and afflictions of the villages and their war. Bringing calm. Bringing peace. Bringing rest. Drawing their attention away from the circumstances of their lives toward the truths that transcend life.

"There was no battle that day. Or ever. Their hearts had been pierced by a weapon that no hand can wield, nor armor can resist. Both sides were conquered that day – indeed, it was the Last War, but for reasons no one anticipated. And things would never be the same again. From that point forward, they regarded the island and their life on the island as something significant. From that point forward, they became enamored with these truths that transcend life and the legacies they leave behind. From that point forward, they buried their dead on the mountainside and watched a lush grove flourish where there had once been desolation and emptiness. Generations passed and this entire mountain filled with a dense forest. When it was full, they began to bury the dead on the other mountain, and it has nearly filled as well. Thousands of legacies have been proclaimed from these hillsides over the generations. But it all began here. With these two trees. And conquering Peace where there had once been war and strife."

As the last word departs Chranit's mouth, the forest all around us comes alive with shuffling footsteps. We look around frantically, trying to discern the source of the stirring. People from the other village emerge from among the trees and shadows in every direction. Members of our village jump to their feet or brace themselves where they're sitting or cover any children that happen to be close to them. Prepared for a fight.

The other village stops at the edge of our group, surrounding us. They wait. We wait. A palpable apprehension grips the mountainside. And then, from out of the stillness, a lone set of footsteps emerges through the wall of people around us.

Mehan.

Mehan alive. Mehan unharmed. Mehan looking exactly as he looked the last time I saw him. Maybe even more himself than the last time I saw him.

An audible gasp echoes off the bluff. Everyone nervously scans the faces of the opposing group. Have they come to fight us? Have they delayed killing Mehan so they could do it here, before our eyes? Are they going to use him as a bargaining point for negotiating with us? Countless questions running through everyone's minds. Why are they here?

Finally, as though to provide a single answer to every question, Mehan smiles. Almost on cue, the procession from the other village converges onto our group. Laughing. Hugging. Weeping. People kiss the faces they haven't been able to kiss since the night that our tribe split. They hold the hands they haven't been able to hold. They say the words they haven't been able to say. They tell each other how much they've been missed. They remark at how tall the children have grown. In an instant, all of the things that divided us evaporate and we feel like one tribe again. Abis walks over to Sangra and the two begin quietly talking. A short distance away, Prem stands among a group of girls our age who are eagerly awaiting their turn to hold her baby.

Mehan is lost in a mob of people who have spent the last month grappling with his death. Now they are grappling with the surprise of his life. As though they just received him back from the dead. People who thought they would never see his face again kissing his face. People who thought they would never be able to hold him again clinging to him. People who thought they would never have another chance to tell him that they loved him clamoring for their voices to be heard over each other.

I study the faces of the members of the other village. Though still thin, life has returned to them once again. Emotions. Expressions. Color. I want to know what happened. I want to know why we're standing here atop a mountain embracing each other like family when only a sunset ago we were bitter enemies. I want to know where we go from here. I want to know why Mehan is alive.

So many questions.

But for now, I just embrace the joy of the moment, as white petals slowly flake away from Santi's tree.

Chapter 19

The Last Moon

It doesn't seem real. None of it seems real – the last fourteen months, that we'll be leaving less than one month from now, the reconciliation of our villages yesterday, Mehan alive. Every day since the first of this crisis has brought its own pain. Every day, that is, until this day. When I woke up this morning, it all felt unreal, as if I was awakening from a wild dream. Maybe I'm still napping on the hillside waiting for Brisa to finish weaving while the fishermen do their masterful work just beyond the bay. Maybe in a moment she will shake me awake and listen patiently as I tell her about this horrible, wonderful dream of leaving this island, and building boats, and our tribe splitting, and legacy talks, and Mehan being brave, and the two of us deciding to wrap our lives around each other on the other side of the horizon. And after I finish recalling everything I can, we will share a laugh of relief. And then we'll take a walk through the Grove of Ancestors and plan the rest of our lives on this island together.

But, no.

It isn't a dream. It's real. Every bit of it is real. Every wonderful thing. Every horrible thing. There's no escaping any of it. But, as I tiptoe around the village, I'm not entirely sure I want to escape it. Despite the pain, it has brought us somewhere more profound than we were when it all began. As I walk through the village, I smile at the sight of sleeping bodies strewn around every fire and across the shore. Bodies that stayed up way too late drinking way too much berry wine last night, now sleeping contently in the most uncomfortable, awkward positions. The memories of last night. The entire tribe reunited. Talking and laughing and sharing together. Months of being apart, reminding us how much we enjoy being together. Months of resenting each other, reminding us how much we truly love each other. Months of trying to be enemies, reminding us how tightly woven the fabric of this family.

I pick my steps carefully, trying not to disturb any sleeping bodies, searching for one in particular: Mehan. It was impossible to pull him aside last night. His family wouldn't let him out of their sight. The hung on his every word. They stared at him in disbelief, as though he were a dead man who had clawed his way back to life and come to sit by their fire. They held him, hugged him, rested their hands on him, as though he might vanish forever if they let go even for a moment.

I don't see Mehan's face among the strewn bodies. I don't see him when I peek into his hut. I don't see him sitting around any of the fires with any of the other early risers. I don't see him by the shore. I walk to the only other place I can imagine he could be. The place where he stood every day for the last twelve months. As I trace the outskirts of the village, I find him standing in that exact place. In the exact pose. Only no spear in hand anymore. A perfect view of Degi's mound. Mehan stares at it intently. Sensing me drawing near, he severs his gaze and relaxes his posture, as though awakening from a standing slumber.

"Did you sleep?" I ask.

"No."

"Were you standing here all night?"

"No."

The thickness of the morning air. The rolling of the waves. They fill the space and the silence between us. I look out over the sea, slowly letting my eyes follow the contour of the island lifting into the air, rising up the grassy plain to the ridge where Degi's mound catches the sunrise. "I thought I'd never see you again," I say. "That morning that you walked me up to Degi's mound. As you ran down the hill, I thought that would be my last memory of you. I thought, for sure, they were going to kill you. But here you are. What happened?"

Mehan bounces his eyes from me to the hill to Degi's mound. "I thought so, too." He inhales deeply, letting out a sigh as he exhales. "You know the scary thing, Uri? I was hoping they would kill me. Then it would all be done. I wouldn't have to live with the guilt. Or the nightmares that kept me awake. I wouldn't have to live with the fear of myself and the depravity that I'm capable of. Justice would have been served. My life for Degi's life. But justice doesn't always look the way you expect it to look, I guess."

Mehan accentuates the point with a prolonged silence before continuing, "I was ready to die, Uri. I truly was. And the looks on the faces of the watchers when they saw me coming down that hill told me that they were ready for me to die, too. They rushed me, grabbed me, and threw me to the ground. They beat me, kicked me, spat on me, shouted the most horrible things at me. But I felt a peace through it all because I knew that death was coming soon. I was just waiting for one of them to thrust their spear into me and end it all.

"But the spear never came. Instead, they dragged me into the village to Abis' hut. I assumed that since he was Degi's father they wanted to give him the satisfaction of killing the person who killed his son. As soon as Abis laid eyes on me he sent the watchers away. Then he grabbed his spear and came at me. I could tell he was distraught by the sight of me. The way he breathed. The way his voice wavered. The way he paced. He was angry. But he also sounded afraid. And stricken with grief. He kept yelling at me. Things like, 'Why are you here?', 'What are you doing?', 'How could you?' I wanted to explain everything to him. To tell him it was an accident. To apologize to him. To offer my life to him as justice for what I had done. But I was struggling just to breathe. All I could squeeze out was a feeble, 'Your son.'

"And that's when I heard crying. No, not crying. Bawling. Hysterical wailing. I rolled my head to the side and saw Degi's mother, Soka, in the corner of the room. That moment, Uri–" Mehan stops himself short and raises his fist to his mouth to collect himself. "At that moment, I realized what I had done. I hadn't just killed a person. It was hard enough to deal with the thought that I had killed another person. But at that moment, I realized I had also killed a woman's child. I realized I had killed their only son. The hole I left in that family, Uri. And realizing that they would never be able to fill it, it all came crashing onto me in that moment. So I said it again, but this time I placed my hand over my chest, 'Your son.'"

"What does that mean? Were you offering to take Degi's place?"

"I have no clue. I wasn't thinking straight. I don't know what I was saying or how I expected them to respond. But if you could have seen that woman's face for yourself, Uri. The tears. The hopelessness. I can hardly hold it together just remembering it."

"But why did it even cross your mind to offer to take the place of the person you killed?"

Mehan defends himself, "I don't know. The plan was that I would go over to the village and they would kill me. But that all fell apart on me, didn't it? I can't tell you why that felt like the right thing to say. I didn't understand it then and I don't understand it now. It's just what came out. In the midst of all of the pain and sobbing and anguish, that's what came out."

"How did they respond?"

"They didn't, really. Soka just kept crying. Abis walked over to her and gently led her out of the hut. They left me there. But they didn't kill me. Nor did they kill me the next day. Nor the day after that. Abis never returned to the hut. After a couple of days, someone slipped a basket of berries into the hut, but no one came to me. No one spoke to me. A few days later, I felt my strength returning to me, but I was hungry. Hungry like I've never been before. The basket of berries was just enough to keep me alive; not enough to quiet the constant and strained rumbling. And with the basket of berries empty, I became desperate. Desperation drove me to boldness. I left Abis' hut in search of food.

"I wasn't sure what to expect the first time I stepped outside of that hut. Was there an ambush waiting for my emergence? Would they, upon seeing me roaming freely, beat me and drag me back into the hut and guard me from leaving again? But something told me that if they had wanted to kill me they would have killed me already. If they wanted to hold me captive, they would have restrained me from the start. So I didn't feel too afraid to step outside. But I wasn't prepared for how people reacted to me."

"Were they harsh?" I ask.

"No. And that's what shocked me. They weren't harsh. They weren't spiteful. They weren't intimidating. They just ignored me. No one looked at me. No one spoke to me. No one bothered me or asked me what I was doing. It was like I wasn't there at all. I sort of wanted someone to acknowledge me. Yell at me. Sneer at me. Divert their activity when they saw me coming. Anything just to let me know that I was there. But nothing.

"So I just started doing odd jobs around the village. Mending things, tending to fires, cleaning fish. I just kept to myself and worked wherever I saw work that needed to be done. That's how I noticed something that changed my perspective completely. I had thought that the small basket of berries they gave me was a sort of punishment. But when I saw their berry reserves, I discovered that it was actually quite generous compared to what they had for themselves. At first, I assumed that it was because they were sending all of the berries they could gather over to you guys. But then I could see, in plain view from their village, perfectly good clusters of berries ripe for picking! They were just a little hard to get to. I realized that they simply weren't good berry pickers. Not like you and I were. They pick their berries too early; they pick them small. No one bothered to try for the ones that were hard to reach.

"So I grabbed the biggest basket I could find one morning and set out to gather. I spent the entire day gathering, just like you and I used to do. I climbed, I crawled, I stretched. I filled the basket with those big, sweet, juicy berries that were just begging to be picked. That night I set the basket by one of the fires like the other baskets were set by other fires. And I watched as people grabbed a handful. Just grabbing a handful, people didn't notice anything different. But as soon as they tossed one of them into their mouths…Uri, I wish you could have seen the looks on their faces. The best way I can describe it is the way the mountains change with the dawn, going from grey and colorless to illuminated and vibrant. One by one, I watched people do this, until a crowd had gathered around my basket and all they could talk about was how amazing the berries were…which seemed like an incredibly silly thing to go on and on about, but it was the most conversation I had heard since I arrived at the village, so I assumed it was a good thing.

"Anyway, as the basket grew emptier, the crowd grew larger. People were eating the berries one at a time. Closing their eyes and savoring the taste of each individual berry. Smiling every time. People watched each other enjoy the berries, as though seeing other people enjoy the berries helped them to enjoy the berries more themselves. It was the strangest thing. I've never seen anything like it before. But I guess that's what life had become for them: a joyless burden. Even the act of eating had become an act of survival, never fulfilling or satisfying. Then a basket of the choicest berries on the entire island appeared out of nowhere and it gave them some small thing to enjoy. They could escape the burden for just a moment and be satisfied.

"As I was sitting there watching this, I felt a giant hand on my shoulder. Having not been touched or spoken to or acknowledged for several days, it frightened me. I was afraid that someone might have finally noticed my absence from Abis' hut and had come to deal with me. I looked up to the face behind me. Abis. Emotionless, but not angry. He didn't say anything. He didn't look at me. He was focused on the commotion around the basket. But his hand on my shoulder told me everything I needed to know.

"Soon, people started talking to me. By the end of the month, I started to feel like I was slowly being accepted as part of their village. Abis and Soka allowed me to stay with them. And they were kind to me. They let me into their lives, even while keeping a cautious distance from me. Emotionally, that is. Sometimes when they looked at me, there was pain in their eyes. Other times, they just looked like they were lost in thought, recalling some memory or trying to wrap their minds around everything that happened in the last month. But they were always kind. And they never made me feel threatened. I could tell that they were trying to accept me, as hard as it was for them. Uri, it was the greatest act of kindness I have ever experienced or witnessed in my life. Kindness. Forgiveness. And in some peculiar way, family." Mehan drifts, like he's trying to find the words to explain.

I'm trying to comprehend it all. "Wow," is all that I can say as I fix my eyes on Degi's mound. Eventually I ask, "So, all of that explains why you're alive. But it doesn't really explain why you're here. What happened? Why did Abis' village show up at the legacy talk yesterday?"

"That's still a bit of a mystery even to me,"

he confesses. "Once people started talking to me, it seemed like all they wanted to talk about was the old village. 'How is so-and-so doing?' they would ask. And when I'd answer, they'd get this long look on their face like a mixture of happiness and sadness rolled into one emotion. As the moon kept getting fuller, more and more people would say things like they wish they could see that person one last time before they left the island forever.

"I started to realize how things like love and friendship consume people in much the same way as hunger and thirst consume them. And how being with a loved one is just as satisfying as food and water. They are such different needs, such different longings. And yet they are so similar. I can count the number of fish I need to eat to satisfy my hunger. I can draw the amount of water that will quench my thirst. But I can't measure love. It has less to do with time and more to do with presence. It satisfies the same way that food and water satisfy, and yet it is so much less tangible and so much more mysterious."

Mehan pauses, frustrated that he doesn't have better words to describe his thoughts. Finally, he gives up trying and continues, "Yesterday morning, as people woke up and realized it was the morning of the full moon, someone remarked that the old village would probably be gathered up at one of the oldest trees for their final legacy talk. Then people started talking about how nice it would be to see everyone one last time. Before I knew it, people were gathering, planning to venture up to the top of the Old Grove to find you guys. The entire village gathered. It just sort of happened. And now here we are."

Here we are. I study Mehan in the fullness of morning light. Even in the short time he spent living under the conditions of the other village, he became thinner, slightly older. The morning light accentuating the spaces between his ribs and the gauntness in his cheeks. "So what happens now?" I ask.

Mehan responds with an inquisitive look.

"Are you their son now? What happens in a month when we board the boats and you never see them again?"

"I'm not leaving," Mehan replies as though it were self-evident.

"Not leaving?" The words escape me. "What about your family? Your real family, Mehan?"

"It will be the hardest thing I've ever had to do. Harder, even, than when I went down to the other village with the expectation of dying."

"Your parents won't let you stay."

Mehan looks to me as though I'm trying to convince him that the ocean is red. "Uri, we are men now. If it weren't for all that has happened in the last fourteen months to put our lives on hold, you and I might have families of our own by now. We aren't boys anymore. Our decisions are our own now. We are men."

His words sting. Perhaps because of the way he hurled the word 'boys' squarely at me. Perhaps because he's right. Perhaps because, despite him being right, I still feel more like a boy than a man. The last fourteen months have been a raging storm. So disorienting. So tumultuous. In some aspects, it seems like we've aged an entire generation in that time. In other aspects, it seems like we're still stuck exactly where we were when it all began. Back then, I still felt like a boy. And maybe Mehan would have agreed with me then. But even today I still feel like a boy. I've grown taller and stronger. I've learned so much. I've discovered so much about myself. And, yet, despite all the ways I've grown like a man, when Mehan tells me that he's made the decision to stay on the island, all I can think about is whether or not his parents will let him.

"Besides," Mehan continues, "my family will be less affected by my absence than Degi's is by his. I have two sisters and a brother. Abis and Soka had no other children. I took away their only child, Uri. Their only child and their only son."

"But do you really believe that you can take Degi's place? What do you accomplish by staying?"

"No, I can't take his place. I can't be a son to them in the truest sense. But I hope I can be something *like* a son to them. The same way different men were like fathers to you in the absence of your father. None of them could replace your father, but they could fill little gaps. Hopefully I can fill little gaps. Which reminds me, Uri. I have a favor to ask of you."

"What?" I ask, still appalled by Mehan's decision.

"I want you to watch after Mano after you leave." Mano - Mehan's youngest sibling and only brother. "Of all my family, my absence will probably hurt him the most. I need someone to fill in the little gaps in his life that I will leave when we're apart. Will you?"

Even though Mehan and I are the same age, he is the oldest among his siblings while I am the youngest among mine. And with all of my siblings being sisters, I'm not quite sure what gaps I would be filling. "What does that mean?" I ask.

"I don't know how to explain it really. I mean, he'll still have his mother and father and sisters. But there's something about the big brother…something special. Helping him grow from a boy to a man. Kind of like a father, but different because you get to be right there alongside him while he's doing it. You get to share things with him that you went through yourself not too long ago. You get to help prepare him for what's just ahead because you're going through those things yourself right now. It's like the difference between standing at the top of a mountain and shouting instructions down to someone who's climbing it, versus being right there climbing with them. I guess I'm just asking you to help him grow into a man. Like we are. If I can't be there, I want to know that you are."

I think back on times when Mehan and I have been like brothers to one another, especially recently. Times where he has helped me understand the way the world works when I was oblivious to it; times where I have helped him stay focused on the things that give meaning to that world. How we've climbed together. "I'd be honored."

"Me too. Thank you."

At this point I'm swallowing tears. I nod and turn my attention toward the sunrise. The pinks and yellows have given way to blue sky. We stare at it, adrift in thought, until the stirring in the village calls us back.

• • •

The rest of the month passes so quickly. So much has changed so suddenly, it has never quite had a chance to feel real.

We're one tribe again. One tribe working alongside one another. One tribe building boats together, fishing together, carrying water together, weaving together. One tribe carefully dismantling the village on the far side of the island as its residents relocate back to ours. One tribe chasing each other's children, sharing meals, telling stories.

No more watchers. No more exchange trips. No more hunger. No more vacant stares. No more suspicious speculation about motives and actions.

We're together like we once were. Even stronger now. Filled with fondness and gratitude. And abundantly aware of our impending separation. Our prior separation was born out of anger, bitterness, and conflict. Our impending separation is born out of hope, survival, and preservation of things that matter most to us. Both separations are painful. Both separations cause our hearts to break.

There's a certain sadness that comes with every meal. Because every meal is one meal closer to our final meal. We watch sunsets together, aware that our final sunset is sprinting toward us. The moon fades…fades…fades…until one night it disappears. From tonight onward, the moon will grow, grow, grow, until its fullness will mark the day of our final separation.

New moon nights have a distinct kind of beauty to them. Full moon nights transform the island with a white glow, accentuating things that typically blend in with their surroundings under the light of day. The moonlight gleaming off of unexpected surfaces around the island beckons you to understand the island differently than under daylight. But the darkness on new moon nights draws your eyes skyward to a shore of stars that's more vast and glistening than on any other night. And a faint ribbon of lavender cutting across it all. It's beautiful, and mysterious, and breathtaking. Like full moon nights, new moon nights also beckon you to understand the island differently than usual. With your eyes fixed on the depths of the sky, the island that directs much of the way we live our lives almost feels like an afterthought. A breath fixed for but a moment in the midst of a never-ending expanse.

Brisa picks her steps carefully through the darkness toward the shore. As we break through the canopy of trees and the host of stars captures our wonder, our steps become slower, shorter, more sporadic. Until we stop completely. For a while we just stare. We just breathe.

Breathe.

"Do you think the stars will look different from another shore?" Brisa asks. Her words like a gust of wind.

"Why would they be different?" I ask.

Breathe.

"Like how this island looks different from

different places. From this shore, the island looks different than it does from a mountaintop. Will the stars look different from place-to-place as well?"

"The stars look the same no matter where you are on the island."

"But our island is so small. The sky is so big. When we travel far from here, will it change?"

I suddenly suspect that we might not be talking about stars at all. "I hope not."

Breathe.

"Me too." Brisa says, her voice resolving like the calming of a wind.

Breathe.

"Uri?" Her voice gusts again.

"Yes?"

"When we arrive wherever we arrive, let's begin our lives together right away. No waiting. I'm tired of waiting."

"Why wait until then? Let's just do it now. We'll be gone soon. We don't need to put our lives on hold any longer."

"Not on this island, Uri. Too much has happened here over the last few months. I don't want our life together to begin in the place associated with all of that. I want our life together to begin in a new place. With new memories. New possibilities."

I'm enchanted. Enchanted by the thought of spending the rest of my life with Brisa in love fulfilled. But I'm also discouraged. Discouraged by the notion that my actions have stained her associations with this island. That if I hadn't let my obsession with Prem direct my actions, I wouldn't have wounded Brisa, Degi would still be alive, Mehan would be himself. It didn't seem significant at the time, but it changed everything. "In that case, maybe we should hope the stars look different from a different shore."

She just slowly shakes her head and eases her weight into my side. "No. For you and me, the stars are perfect just the way they are."

And in that moment, they are.

Breathe.

• • •

Our final days on the island are a flurry. When the boats are finished, they are loaded with nets, baskets, fishing equipment, and other supplies for our voyage. Each boat is named after the tree that was cut down to shape its mast. I will be riding on the *Santi*. Since they've assigned boats according to the layout of the village, I will be riding with my family, Mehan's family (minus Mehan), and the other families who share our fire pit. Brisa's family will be riding the *Poshar*.

I stand on the shore the afternoon of the day before our departure surveying the twelve boats. Every boat complete. Every boat adorned with sails. Beautiful and magnificent, even more magnificent than they had looked in my dreams. I'm in awe of Chuan, how he built something out of nothing. How he took a boy's fleeting memory of a dream and made it a reality. He envisioned something that had never existed before; he conceived something that had never been conceived. It required bravery, community, art, wisdom, diligence, and almost every other legacy that our tribe celebrates to pull it off; and he did it. What a rare person Chuan turned out to be. I could have learned so much by his side. And, yet, I might never have found my own legacy if I had spent all this time living in the shadow of his. I might still be living under the impression that a handful of dreams that I had as a child was the sum of my life. Now I see there's so much more and that I've only begun to explore it.

The full moon sits low on the horizon, perfectly framing the twelve boats. The sight is so poignant, so full of meaning. I wish I could capture every detail in my memory and never let go of it. It's the last full moon I'll watch from this island shore. By the next full moon, we hope to be settled on a distant shore. Brisa and I will watch the moon together. Remembering all of the full moons past. Looking forward to all the full moons to come. New place. New life. New hope.

Tonight, instead of the typical Council meeting conducted in the Forum, the entire tribe is gathering together on the shore. One last time.

Several people are busy standing up torches in the sand, squabbling over how big the circle of torches needs to be. I laugh to myself, comforted by the thought that the last argument I will witness on this island is over how wide a ring of torches needs to be in order to include as many people as possible. Not over food. Or trees. Or the possibility of war. This almost seems petty, and that's what I love the most about it. I walk over, pick up a torch, and join them.

As the sun lets out its last whimper of light, the fire pits around the village fill with people. We spend the evening telling stories - the best stories we can think of. Our favorite memories. The greatest pranks. The funniest things that children dared to say. The times people nearly got themselves killed attempting something stupid. Legacy talks we'll never forget. Feats of strength. Flagrant sunrises. Loved ones we've lost. And with each story, I notice a common thread through them all - that the island itself seems like its own character in every story. That it has its own role to play, its own nuance to the way in which each story plays out. People begin their stories with phrases like *I remember one time on the island when…* and *We were walking across the island when...* as though there's any other place where these stories could have occurred. The island is our only setting, our only context. But soon it won't be. Soon, there will be this island and somewhere else. Somewhere new. Our lives and our stories will be divided between two times and places: days before we left and days since we've left, the old place and the new place.

People visit from fire pit to fire pit, inserting themselves into conversations, embellishing on one another's stories. By the time the fires are burning low and the piles of spare wood have been exhausted, our stomachs hurt from laughing, our eyes hurt from crying, our hearts hurt from longing. Longing for each other. Longing for some other resolution to this crisis that doesn't involve three quarters of our tribe leaving the island. Longing for the memories that forever unite us, even as the events that shaped those memories grow more distant with each passing day.

We gradually make our way down to the circle of torches on the beach. The circle is big enough, perhaps even a little too big, as the faces in the middle of the circle are hard to see under the dim light. Abis and Sangra stand beside each other awkwardly, neither acknowledging the other, but both warmly addressing everyone who approaches them. If there's any lingering rift between us, it's between those two, but they do their best to hide it.

When the entire tribe has filled the circle of torches, Sangra motions and the crowd silences. “It doesn’t seem real that this day has arrived,” he begins, “but here we are. Together. United. Celebrating. If our tribe must part ways, this is exactly how I would want our last night together to be. We’ve faced pains and trials that we never thought we would have to face. But we’ve survived. We’ve healed. We’ve learned. Abis, carry these lessons with you as you lead those who will remain on this island with wisdom and courage. Preserve this island and these legacies with which you have been entrusted.”

“We will, Sangra.” Abis quickly and graciously replies. “Your legacy to those of us who remain on the island is as great as the legacy of our ancestors who sailed here forty generations ago. Forty generations from now, the children of this island will remember the legacies of those who sacrificed everything so our tribe could have a future. You will be dearly missed.”

Abis is cutoff by a sudden, astonished gasp radiating through the crowd. Someone shouts, “Look!” All eyes shoot up to the sky.

The moon isn’t full anymore. It’s only half. We watch in silent wonder as it slowly ebbs until it is overtaken and fills with a deep red.

I've heard of the Sanguine Moon before, though I've never seen it myself. I'm not sure anyone on this beach has seen it in their lifetimes. None of the descriptions I've heard of it quite capture its majesty. We exchange looks. Looks of amazement. Looks of uncertainty. Looks of disbelief. Then, just as the darkness slowly encroached on the moon, it slowly recedes. No one says a word the entire time.

People came to this island believing that the Sanguine Moon was filled with the blood of an imminent calamity. It inspired dread and fear. But after the several Sanguine Moons on this island passed without incident, and after several calamities befell us that weren't preceded by a Sanguine Moon, it recaptured its mystique. Now it inspires wonder, curiosity, imagination. And tonight it steals our attention away from everything else - the ceremony, the island, the boats, the impending journey, even ourselves. The mouths of chiefs stilled by the unyielding mystery of the moon. So appropriate for our final night on the island.

I don't understand what just happened. But two things are clear: something has passed, and its passing was inevitable. And somehow, that realization gives me courage to face tomorrow.

Chapter 20

Calling Out

There's nothing especially notable about today. The ocean rolls the way it always does. The sun rises the way it always does. The breeze blows like it always does. Fish and berries by the smoldering fires like they always are. By all measures, it's just like every other day.

Except that it's our last day.

As the tide peaks, we will push the boats out into the bay, board them, and sail toward the very spot from which the sun now rises. Never to return. When Chuan was designing the boats, he insisted that they didn't need to go fast. They didn't need to maneuver tightly. They just needed to catch the wind and go. And that's exactly what we're going to do. The boats are poised at a depth along the shore in such a way that a mild storm could have jostled them loose. Risky, but necessary if we are going to launch all twelve boats in a single high tide.

Breakfast is quiet, a nervous energy and heartache circulating through the air. Our last day. When Mehan and I sat in the Forum on the night the plan was devised, this day felt so far away. Then in the midst of all the madness, it felt like it couldn't come soon enough. Now it's here, and no one's quite sure what to do with it. High tide will occur before midday, so we don't have much time to do anything except eat and say our goodbyes.

Choko takes a seat at the fire across from me. Grabs a handful of berries and tosses them into his mouth. He looks up at me and, while chewing, says, "Yours were better."

I chuckle. "Who's going to gather berries for you when I'm gone?"

Choko pauses and slowly, as though the dilemma is dawning on him for the very first time, says, "I don't know." Then he looks at me and confidently asserts, "In that case, you should stay."

"Stay? Just to spend the rest of my life gathering berries for you?" I exclaim with mock appall. "Maybe you should come with us instead."

Choko smiles, entertained by the banter. His eyes slowly fall to the ground and the smile fades from his face, tempered by the reality that he has no intention of leaving this island. He's a stone cutter. What if there isn't work for stone cutters in the new land? At least that's how he explained it to me. The reasons for people staying here are almost as numerous as the number of people who are staying. Of course, the same goes for the number of people leaving and their reasons for leaving. For me and Brisa, it's an opportunity to begin our lives together fresh. To leave the burdens of the past behind so we can move forward unencumbered. For others, it's an opportunity. For others, duty. For others, respect for the legacies of our ancestors. For others, fear. For others, curiosity about what lies on the other side of the horizon. For others, the distinct honor of being part of a story that will be told forty generations from today and begin with the phrase, "When our brave ancestors left their old island and settled here…"

What began as a desperate attempt to save our island from becoming a barren rock in the sea quickly evolved into something far more complicated. It became about the difference between the Seen and the Unseen - how we apprehend them, how we interpret them, how we allow them to govern our lives. It became about an exploration of something we foolishly believed we already clearly understood. But that belief had never been tested before. Not in this way. Not in the way that forced people to look deeply within themselves and decide: will they orient their lives around the Seen or around the Unseen?

Early on, it seemed as though a decision to stay on the island was a commitment to the Seen, whereas a decision to leave was a commitment to the Unseen. But, as it turns out, it was never that simple. Never that clear. Never that either-or. Even Sangra, who was perhaps more committed to the Unseen than anyone, in his pursuit of the Unseen fell short of his own standard, demonstrating that it's impossible to focus solely on one to the exclusion of the other. Both are real. Both matter. Both demand consideration. But how? I still don't know if I'm exactly sure.

The tribe is awake, preparing for the descent down the shore to the boats as the ocean rises to carry us. Now is the time for goodbyes. For leaving everything behind. No turning back.

I stand and walk across the fire toward Choko. I place my hand on his shoulder; he places his on mine, grips it tightly, and then gently pats it. Our goodbye. The first of many I will make today.

Outside of the fire pit, on my way to Brisa's house, I notice Chranit casually walking away from one of the fire pits toward ours. Our eyes meet. I redirect my steps toward him.

"Are you ready to go?" I ask.

He responds with a confused look. "We aren't leaving," he states as though I should have known this already.

"We?"

"The elders. None of us are leaving."

"You're staying?" I ask, stunned.

"The elders discussed it yesterday and

decided that it was for the best. Over the past month, many people have changed their minds. Some who had initially made the decision to stay on the island now decided they wanted to leave. And while some who had made the decision to leave changed their minds and decided to stay, the numbers didn't balance out. People who now wanted to leave were being told that they must stay simply because there wasn't enough room on the boats to fit them all. It was heartbreaking. So the elders decided to collectively surrender our seats on the boats so anyone who wanted to go could.

"All of us elders will be dead within a generation anyway. Our child-bearing years are well behind us, so we won't be multiplying our numbers into future generations. We'll spend our time cultivating and planting new native trees while passing the traditions and legacies of our tribe on to the next generation. It's for the best, really."

I'm speechless. So instead of searching for words, I simply throw my arms around Chranit and embrace him.

"I see great things in you, Uri," he says, returning my embrace. "You have a restlessness about you. It's your greatest strength; it's your greatest weakness. Strength, because it fuels your pursuit of better things, never content with the way the world is. Some of the most memorable leaders throughout our tribe's history were restless in exactly the same way. Weakness, because you allow it to consume you, haphazardly directing your actions and emotions. And a restless emotion is rarely a sound one upon which to base one's decisions. You must find a way to focus this restlessness, Uri. Don't suppress it. Don't abandon it. Focus it.

"The ocean is a powerful force, capable of both unparalleled beauty and unparalleled destruction. But once you draw a handful of water from it, the water in that handful becomes separated from the forces that gave it power. It becomes stagnant, malleable, useless. Uri, if you separate yourself from this powerful restlessness that runs through you, I fear that you would become like the handful of seawater. Instead, you must find a way to give focus to the restlessness.

"This focus comes from an understanding of what stirs the restlessness within you. Some Unseen thing stirs you. What is it? Is it Justice? Compassion? Hope? You must discover whatever it is for yourself. And then focus your restlessness relentlessly on that thing. When you do, the Seen and the Unseen will find harmony in you. It will become the source of your persistence in days of opposition, a salve on your wounds in days of suffering, a rally cry for the lost in days of trial. It will become legacy."

Chranit tightens his embrace and I tighten mine. Eventually, we tear ourselves away from one another, revealing tear-streaked faces. He looks at me intently, smiles proudly, and nods encouragingly. I nod back at him, trying to conform my mouth to a smile, but too close to tears to do so. Instead, we exchange another tight embrace before parting ways.

Another goodbye.

I've never thought about how many different kinds of goodbyes there are. Probably because, on our island, there are really only two kinds of goodbyes: *see you tomorrow* and death. This is a new kind of goodbye - neither death nor *see you tomorrow*. We've never had to give this kind of goodbye, so people aren't exactly sure how to give it. Some people, grasping the finality of this kind of goodbye, offer it as though the recipient were breathing their final breath; others, grasping the optimism of this kind of goodbye, offer it casually. Surveying the village on my way to meet Brisa, I see those expressions and everything in between. Weeping, hugging, kissing, heads buried in hands. But also smiles, laughter, leisurely chit-chat. Then there are people who simply don't know what to do - arms crossed, silent, emotionless. There are intense conversations. There are simple, caring gestures. There are groups of people quietly watching the sunrise together one last time.

For me and Brisa, it's still a different kind of goodbye. There's love. Unsatisfied love. Longing love. Love looking forward to fullness when we meet again upon the shores of a distant land. Who knows how long we will be apart: a few days, a few moon cycles, even longer? What if there isn't any land at all beyond the horizon and we're forever trapped upon twelve island-boats forever adrift? Chuan tells me that isn't possible because of the way the stars and the sun and the moon and the winds and the currents move. Eventually, we'll hit something, even if it's just the other side of our own island. I can't even begin to comprehend that, but he sounds confident when he says it; and I'm confident in his confidence. Still, that doesn't give me any timeframe for how long it will be until I can hold Brisa in my arms again and never let go of her. This time, I will never let go. I will love her. I will fight for her. I will be a safe place for her. All of the things I have struggled to be and to do up to this point.

So on the shore of the island on the morning of our goodbye, I stand with Brisa and hold her. I hold her tightly, feeling all of her against all of me. No words. Just an embrace. And the promise of the rest of our lives just beyond the horizon. We hold each other until the tide rolls in. Until Chuan starts yelling at people to get on the boats or be left behind. We tear ourselves from one another. Kiss one another. Look into one another's eyes. Smile. Try to be strong. But my knees are shaking, my heart is racing, and my throat is filled with tears. The wind blows her hair across her face just so. She pulls a lock of it behind her ear. The perfect image for me to hold onto until we meet again.

Along the shore, a hundred other rushed goodbyes. One last hug. One last look. One last whatever. Tears. Laughter. And then a dash toward the boats. As the boats fill, the people who are staying on the island use long poles to push them free from the last little bit of ocean floor holding them in place.

Our boat, *Santi,* is one of the first to be freed. From its stern, we look back upon the faces of those we will never see again. I notice Mano standing a few feet away from me, gripping the back of the boat, eyes fixed on Mehan. The look on Mano's face. The look on Mehan's face. Seeing them in this moment, I'm beginning understand what Mehan was trying to describe about the relationship between brothers. It's no consolation to Mano that his mother, father, and sisters are on this very boat with him. His big brother isn't here. And his heart is breaking. In this exchange, I recall Mehan's charge to me to fill his place in Mano's life in whatever small way I can. I walk over to Mano. At a loss for what to say, at a loss for what to do, I stand close by his side. He lets me. We quietly miss Mehan together.

Everyone on the boat silently watches the island pull farther and farther away. And as the gap between our boat and the island widens, we feel a similar renting in our hearts. A people, divided. A tribe, torn in two. A family, broken.

The faces on the shore become undiscernible, their bodies blending in with the sparse trees that buffer our village and the shore. Our eyes are drawn upward to the towering trees that adorn the towering mountains. Thousands of voices in unison. Calling out. For us to remember. For us to carry their memory with us. Across the ocean of this world. Across the ocean of time.

The panorama of the island comes into full view. From one end of the island, I follow the sharp climb out of the sea to the narrow peak, gradually curving downhill through the Old Grove, across the ridge of the grassy plain, past Degi's mound (which looks so much smaller from here than it did from our village), gradually uphill through the New Grove, across the bowl of the mountain, then descending sharply into the sea once again.

I try to imagine what it looked like to our ancestors forty generations ago, with dense trees in the middle of the island where the grassy plain now sways in the wind and bald hillsides that are now thick with trees. A forest in the space that our village now occupies. An empty bay where fishing boats now rest. We changed the island. And the island changed us. In our forty generations on this island, we became a people obsessed with the notion of legacy – this notion that there are things in life that are bigger than life, that there are things in this world that the world can't explain on its own.

A memory flashes across my mind, recalling boyhood days building mountains in the sand as the tide rolled in. The tide overcoming them and receding, leaving no trace that mountains ever stood. It was as though they had never existed at all. And I can't help but wonder if our time on this island will follow that same pattern upon the shores of our hearts. What once felt so established now feels so fragile as I watch the island shrink into the horizon. Can it endure? A generation from now, if one of our boats sailed back to this island, would its passengers recognize the people who would greet them from that shore? Or would they be strangers? Strange customs, strange beliefs, strange ideals.

A legacy of sand? Will we hold fast, or will we be undone with every passing tide?

We watch in silence as the island gradually drifts away. Toward the horizon. Until it's gone. And there's nothing but ocean and sky in every direction. And a wind to carry us.

• • •

Days pass slowly from the bow of the boat. But the days are quick compared to the nights. I lay awake, trying to fall asleep. It's something about sleeping in such tight quarters on such a hard surface. The frequent, unsettling sound of creaking. A constant tinge of hunger in my belly. When sleep finally comes, it's brief. I wake up frequently, each time expecting it to be morning, but the darkness shows no sign of lifting any time soon. Falling back asleep becomes even more difficult with each subsequent awakening. If it happens at all.

We spend our days talking, looking out to the horizon for the slightest speck of land, and doing any tasks that the head sailor of our boat requests of us. We eat distinct meals and we eat them together. Apart from sunrise and sunset, meals together are the only thing that give a sense of rhythm and order to our days. Meals of raw fish and dried berries that never quite satisfy.

Otherwise, our days are spent waiting. Waiting. Waiting. Longing for the past. Dreaming toward the future. Anxious. Restless. Wavering between doubt and expectation.

Twelve boats. Twelve little islands. Separated by ocean, united by hope. I crane my neck to see Brisa's boat, the *Poshar*. I can't make out any faces on the boat. But I know she's aboard. And knowing she's there is one of the few things that sustains me through long days and longer nights.

Chapter 21

Passing

A sudden collision of sounds and I'm jolted awake. Thunder, wind, rain, creaking, shouting.

Blackness. Lightning. Blackness. Lightning.

I feel the boat lift and drop, pull and rock, strain and pop. The fury of the storm vying to overcome us. We scramble, trying to do anything to keep the boat together. But it's only scrambling. It's clear that the fate of our boat ultimately belongs to the storm.

"Uri!" Mehan's father calls out to me. "Help me drop the sail."

I brace myself against the rail and pull my way toward the mast. Lightning illuminating my steps. Rain pelting my face. Stinging my eyes. Loosening my grip. Thunder roaring off of every cloud and wave and surface of the boat. It vibrates in my chest, sending shocks of fear through my body.

When I reach the mast, Mehan's father hands me a rope. I've never dropped a sail. Not on a fishing boat, and certainly not on one of these boats. But with the sailors on the boat all scurrying around doing other things, the responsibility has fallen on me. I watch

Mehan's father between flashes of lighting, following his moves, trying to ignore the terror that would otherwise send me cowering into a ball. With my hands pulling against the rope and nothing dry left to wipe my eyes, the rain begins to fill them like tears. Stinging tears. And at this point, for all I know, maybe they are tears.

Is this the end? Is this the culmination of the last fifteen months – all the labor, all the hardship, all the strife? Launching an entire tribe out to sea, only to pummel it to the ocean floor? I want to hold out confidence, but I feel so small and helpless under the storm's commanding anger.

When the rope won't pull anymore, Mehan's dad rushes over, grabs me, and braces us both against the deck. We don't move until the boat stops swaying, the rain stops stinging, and the thunder is only a distant echo.

And then, blackness.

The blackness lingers through morning. A still, calm blackness saturated with dread and ambiguity. I've always found the darkness peaceful. Until now. Until this storm. Until this malevolent silence that fills the moments between the storm and the sunrise with anxious uncertainty.

Sunrise brings little relief. As the light provides enough of a contrast against the sky and the sea, I count the boats. *One-two-three-*

four-five-six-seven. Seven. I should be able to count eleven. Something is wrong if I can only count seven. Mehan's dad stands next to me and conducts the same count. Counts a second time. Looks at me with alarm. *What does this mean?* he gestures toward me so as not to spread his alarm to the others on the boat who are still huddled or sleeping. *I don't know,* I gesture back.

Which boats are missing? I can't tell. But in my deepest place, somehow I know. It's the same dread that I felt last night in the darkness.

The *Poshar*. Brisa. Gone.

• • •

The morning is filled with nervous chatter. Chatter about the storm. Chatter about the relief of being alive. Chatter about the missing boats.

Did they sink?

Are they lost?

How will they find their way back?

Should we try to find them?

People hold out hope that we be reunited. As I listen to them speak, I try to smile and nod at the right moments. But my mind is chaos. As though last night's storm never departed me. I'm doubting our decision to leave the island. I'm questioning whether some flaw in the boat design could have caused the loss of those boats. I'm wrestling with the yearning to be by Brisa's side on the *Poshar* right now. We'd be lost. But we'd be lost together. I should have fought for us to be on the same boat together. Our entire lives, I always should have fought for her.

Around midday, we hear the faint sound of raucous cheering from the next boat. People leap to their feet to see why. A small speck on the horizon. One of our lost boats! A roaring cheer rises from the deck of our boat. Not from me. I'm straining my eyes to see if that boat is the *Poshar*.

The little speck slowly draws nearer to our group of boats, lifting and carrying our hopes on its bow. If one boat can find its way back, surely the other three can as well. We watch it intently. When it becomes clear that the boat isn't the *Poshar*, the tightness in my stomach sinks to disappointment. And then the guilt of feeling disappointed at something that ought to feel so joyous. The storm that refuses to leave me.

Toward the end of the day, we hear another round of cheering from the boat next to us. We spring to our feet. Another speck on the horizon emerging from the same spot as the last. We watch it intensely as it draws nearer. I'm straining my eyes once again, until it becomes clear that it isn't the *Poshar*. And then the storm returns.

Two boats have found their way back, giving me this small, glimmering optimism that the other two will be able to do the same. Until the sun begins to sink low in the horizon behind us. The lost boats can use the stars to chart their course, but without daylight to reveal our boats, how will they ever know if they are getting close to us?

The sunset is crushing. As the band of light shrinks to a sliver of light, my optimism slips away. Night falls. Not a cloud in the sky. Such a contrast to last night's storm. And yet just as dreadful. Tonight, the stars and the half-moon fail to inspire awe. There's only dread. Waning moon; waning hope.

As the sunlight completely vanishes, a light appears from the decks of one of the boats. Somehow, someone figured out a way to light a torch and is holding it up as a beacon so the lost boats can find us through the darkness. Chuan must be furious. He was emphatic in his insistence that absolutely no fires be built on the boats. It's why we eat our fish raw. Or perhaps he's okay with it; after all, he has friends, family, neighbors on those lost boats too.

I stay awake. Watching. Hoping. Yearning. Focusing on the beacon to quell the storm in my head. At some point I must doze off, because the next thing I know, it's morning. My head is pounding. My neck is aching. I straighten to my feet. *One-two-three-four-five-six-seven-eight-nine.*

Nine. I scan the horizon for specks. Nothing. I fall back down to the deck.

Brisa. The name gusts through my mind like the wind just before a storm. Where are you, Brisa? I close my eyes, holding my last image of her in my mind. Standing on the shore. The wind blowing her hair just so. And in my mind, I call out to that image of her. Perhaps she'll hear me, sensing the reach of my heart out to hers. Perhaps she'll call out to me. Perhaps she'll find her way home.

Brisa!

I sit alone, eyes closed with her image behind the veil of my eyes. Dancing hair. Brown eyes. That look on her face; that look she would get when we would talk about the rest of our lives. Wistful. Content.

Why did we wait?

If we had wrapped our lives around one another while we were on the island, we would have been on the same boat together, like my sister is on another boat with her young family. Maybe we'd be lost, but we'd be lost together. Maybe we'd be at the bottom of the sea, but we'd be there together. Instead, we waited. And now we're separated. Maybe forever.

Brisa!

I spend the rest of the day pacing from the side of the boat, where I look for Brisa, to the deck of the boat, where I call out to her in my mind. Night comes. No torch tonight.

Nonetheless, I continue my pattern of pacing between the side of the boat and the deck of the boat, staring into the night and calling out to Brisa in my mind.

The sun rising to mark another day finds me slumped over the side of the boat. Exhausted from a night of barely sleeping, of straining my eyes against the darkness, of straining my mind against the expanse that separates me from Brisa.

I'm startled by a hand on my shoulder. My mom's hand.

"Uri," she says softly as her hand on my shoulder becomes her arm around me. I lean into her. And cry. And cry. And cry. She doesn't say anything. She doesn't have to. "Sweet Brisa," she says. "I know that wherever she is, she is longing for you too." She looks into my eyes with a graveness that I rarely see in her. "I know what it is to love. And I know what it is to lose that love out of time and out of place. It's okay to grieve. And you should grieve. But don't cling to your grief. Don't get lost in it. Don't let it become who you are. Let it run its course. And after it has run its course, move on. Like laughter. When something makes you laugh, laugh hard and loud. But let laughter run its course and move on. Laughter that's clung to ceases to be true laughter, just as grief that is clung to ceases to be true grief. They become something different. Some form of madness. And that's no way to live. Trust me, I almost allowed my grief to consume me after your father died. And if I had, you and your sisters would have worn the scars of that forever."

I've never heard my mom speak this way before, especially to me. Speaking to me not as though I'm her child, not as though I'm a boy; but speaking to me as though I'm a man. I'm taken aback hearing her speak this way with me; but I also find myself indignant, defensive. "It's only been three days," I snap at her. "She could appear over that horizon any moment now. Why are you acting as though there's no hope?"

She exhales a deep sigh with concern on her face. "There's hope. But know the difference between hope and denial."

Denial? I pull myself away from my mom, rise to my feet, and stomp away. I spend the rest of the day avoiding everyone, focusing for specks on the horizon. But Brisa doesn't appear for the rest of the day. Or the next. Or the next.

By the seventh day, I've given up on searching the horizon for specks. It hurts my eyes, breaks my heart, and draws out time so that a morning feels like an entire day. Instead of searching, I hang over the rail staring down its side into the churning water below, asking myself what would happen if I jumped. End this torment. Between the restless nights, the lack of eating, and my all-consuming obsession with the *Poshar*, I'm becoming too weak to hold myself up. Days blur into nights, nights into days. Nothing but darkness; nine boats; and the persuasive, nagging thought that there isn't anything left for me on either this boat or the other side of the horizon. And I'm starting to grow skeptical that we will ever even find a new land.

As the sun sets on the seventh day since Brisa was taken from me, I resolve that the eighth day will be my last. The evening darkness sets in. And trembling. I close my eyes.

When I open them again, it's daylight. I pull myself to my feet and count the boats. *One-two-three-four-five-six-seven-eight-nine-ten-eleven.*

Eleven?

One-two-three-four-five-six-seven-eight-nine-ten-eleven.

Eleven!

I scream out, "They're here! The two missing boats. They found their way back!" I turn around, expecting to rouse the others from their slumber into a roaring cheer. Only the boat is empty. Not a single person on the deck. Perplexed, I return my attention to the eleven boats. Something curious. Their masts have changed. No longer masts with sails, they've transformed back into the trees they once were, rooted proudly and mightily upon steady hulls.

The ocean surface as still as water in a basket, calmer than I've ever seen it before. The air draped in a wistful, entrancing mist. Everything seems to slow down, to the point that I can't even perceive the passing of time. I look back to the deck of my boat. Vacant. Except. I double-take to a figure standing softly in the center of the deck. Could it be?

Brisa.

Standing there. Looking just like my last memory of her on the island. A slight breeze rising to meet her. Tendril of brown hair dancing across her face. Those lips, curled into a smile, squinting her deep brown eyes, taking my breath away.

I want to run to her. I want to grab her and pull her into me and never let go again. Tell her how I thought I had lost her. How much I've missed her. How I couldn't go on without her.

But I'm stuck in place. My feet don't move.

The breeze grows stronger and begins gusting. I notice small flakes, like grains of sand, blowing off of her. Something is wrong. But she doesn't lose her smile. The breeze grows stronger, the gusts gustier, the flakes more numerous. And I notice that she's slowly fading away, becoming more like the mist in the air. Flake by flake, she fades, fades, fades. Stop! Flake by flake. "Brisa!" I cry to her. Her smile, her stance, her gaze, unchanged. Flake by flake. I want to cover her from the wind, to protect her. But my feet refuse to move.

Flake by flake.

Flake by flake.

Flake by flake.

Until she's gone. And the wind ceases. And I'm alone again on an empty deck. "Brisa!" I call out into the mist, only to hear the response of my own echoes. No other sound. Not the ocean, not the wind, not the creaking boat. Just silence and the echoes of my own helplessness. Emptiness. Loneliness. Despair.

I look to the rail of the boat. This is the moment to end it all. To send myself to the bottom of the sea. But my feet are still stuck. Too stuck for love. Too stuck for death.

I scream in frustration, only to be screamed back at by echoes and silence.

And then the breeze picks up once again. The same kind of breeze that makes Brisa's hair go just so. Clearing out the mist. Rays of sunshine busting through crevasses in the clouds and haze, stoking the motion of time, returning life and depth to the world.

Something graces my shoulder more gently than breath. I look down at it, surprised to find a tiny white petal. I pick it off of me and place it in the cupped palm of my hand. Another petal falls onto my palm next to it. A few more petals flutter past my eyes. Then ten petals. I look up. The mast of my boat, returned to the glory of Santi's tree. A deluge of petals falling from her branches. Obscuring my vision, so I no longer see the horizon, or the sea, or the boat, or the place on the deck where Brisa was standing. There is only petals. Catching the wind. Catching the sunlight. Catching my despair.

The breeze gusts and grows stronger. Lifting and swirling the petals around me. Like a dance. My feet are suddenly free once again, unstuck from the force that withheld me from Brisa and from the churning waters. And with their freedom, they slowly turn me among the swirling petals. Closed eyes. Outstretched arms. The petals of Santi's peace raining down on me. An indescribable welling up in my chest and my throat, like something inside of me is lifting out of me. I feel as though I could jump and never touch the ground again.

And then.

I'm awake.

Morning. The eighth day. I roll over to see a deck strewn with sleeping bodies. I jump to my feet. *One-two-three-four-five-six-seven-eight-nine*. Nine. A dream. Even in the midst of it, I had suspected it was nothing more than a dream. But hope…or denial…kept me believing that maybe it was real.

And, yet, in some strange way, it was real. Brisa wasn't real. Nor the return of the *Poshar*. The ocean never stilled, nor the world silenced, nor the crew vanished. The boats' masts never actually changed back into the trees they once were. But the peace. The peace came from some place outside of the dream and has somehow carried with me into my wakefulness.

I had clung to Brisa. In her presence. And even more so in her absence. I can see that now. I clung to her beauty, her touch, the way I felt whenever she was near. Seen things. Passing things. And when they inevitably passed, I was left clinging to air. Grasping for things that weren't real anymore. Passing things pass. Chranit's first great truth. But there were also unseen things that filled the spaces between us, drawing us closer to one another while shaping us. Love. Honor. Sacrifice. Kindness. Enduring things. Chranit's second great truth.

I had confused Seen things for Unseen things, desperately trying to make passing things endure. But doing so only obscured my view of the things that are truly enduring. And in this confusion, I felt like I had lost all things. That the Unseen things had lost their meaning apart from the Seen things that I longed for. I lost sight of the reality that it isn't the Seen which gives meaning to the Unseen, but the Unseen which gives meaning to the Seen. It's a mystery to me: how these two weave together. The Seen reveals the Unseen; the Unseen gives meaning to the Seen. I couldn't have discovered Love apart from experiencing it with Brisa; however, the experiences wouldn't have been so sweet or powerful apart from Love. That's the mystery of the trees. The Unseen made Seen so that we might reach out for the Unseen as we navigate the Seen. And by tracing the fingerprints of the Unseen upon the face of the Seen, we discover the purpose and meaning behind all Seen things. It's what Sophe longed to apprehend. This dance. This balance. This struggle. It's what tore our tribe apart; and, ultimately, it's what brought us reconciliation. It's a constant, ongoing, eternal pursuit.

Living too focused on the Seen is to miss the purpose behind all things; meanwhile, living too focused on the Unseen is to live detached from the world, neglecting or exploiting it in pursuit of an ideal. The former was my error, the latter was Sangra's. And in seeing how easily I fell into my error, I gain a sense of empathy toward Sangra for falling into his. The pull of the Seen is so persistent, it can be easy to ignore the Unseen; meanwhile, the struggle to be mindful of the Unseen can become just as consuming. But we must learn how to understand them as they are: woven together, not isolated or in opposition to one another. All along, the trees were calling out to us with this truth. Only now am I beginning to comprehend it.

My head is pulsing with the rush of realization. I rub my eyes and turn back around toward the deck, startled to find Mano within an arm's length of me, examining me. "You don't seem sad anymore," he observes.

"I'm still sad," I assure him, "but now I think I will be okay."

"What's wrong?"

"I lost my friend."

"Mehan?"

I nearly correct him. Tell him about Brisa, about love, about regret, about the tragedy of lost love. But he doesn't care about all of that. Mehan was his world; a significant part of mine, too. And I promised Mehan that I would fill a little piece of the space that he once filled in Mano's world. "I guess we've lost a lot of our friends, haven't we?" I ask empathetically.

Mano nods.

"You know what I'll always remember, Mano?" I ask as he looks at me expectantly. "Gathering berries with Mehan. When I would gather with him, we would always go to the hardest to reach berries. We'd walk all the way to the other side of the island where very few other people went. We'd climb rocks and trees to get to the biggest, juiciest berries we could find. The berries I gathered with him were always the best berries. And I learned from him that some of life's sweetest treasures can only be found by going to places that others don't. For the rest of my life, every time I see a berry vine, I will think of Mehan. And every time I think of Mehan, I will remember to go to the places where others are too afraid, or lazy, or unwilling to go. Do you understand this?"

He nods his head slightly, blankly. I'm not sure he does. But he will. Someday. Even if I have to tell it to him a hundred times.

A wind catches me from behind, across the boat's bow. I turn and acknowledge it, as though it might have come from a person standing directly behind me.

Brisa.

Where have you gone, Brisa? Toward a distant shore? To the bottom of the sea? To find me? I hope you find me.

The wind gusts again, pressing the smell of the ocean through my nose, the salty air against my skin, the sound of the waves into my ears. This will be her legacy. A gentle breeze brushing my face on a warm day. Giving levity to my senses. An unexpected gust that slips away as quickly as it sneaks upon me. Calling out to me to wake up from a world that would otherwise have me complacently waiting. A wind through the leaves of the forest like a thousand clapping hands. Carrying aromas from distant places, sounds from hidden happenings, coolness from faraway mountaintops. Across the sea and back again. Searching, playing, soothing.

Never resting. Never lingering. Never dwelling on things past.

I close my eyes.

And breathe.